Lily
Hills

Lily Hills

PATTI MOBILE

Printed in the United States of America
Published in Hellertown, PA
Cover design by Patti Mobile
Library of Congress Control Number 2025918769
ISBN 979-8-89420-063-7

For more information or to place bulk orders, contact the author or the publisher at Jennifer@BrightCommunications.net.

I began this book more than ten years ago. When I retired from my full-time job at the end of 2022, I set a goal to finish the story. My cousin, Debra Smith, was interested in the story when I started writing it again in 2023. I sent it to her chapter by chapter, until it was finished. She loved the story and kept encouraging me to publish so that other people could enjoy it, too. So here it is, the story of two families in Oregon, growing up after World War II.

Contents

Neighbors Meet

Kamika Satsuma quietly slipped down from the breakfast nook and went to her bedroom. She pulled off her pajamas and stuffed them under her pillow. She got out battered jeans, her favorite blue turtleneck sweater, pink socks with yellow ducks on them, and tennis shoes. She struggled with the turtleneck sweater, getting her head stuck in the armhole at first. But after a few minutes, she was completely dressed. She pulled over the "time out" stool from the corner in order to reach her raincoat on its hook above the bedpost. Then she silently walked out the front door to follow her brother, Kenji, down the road toward the bus stop.

The rain was coming down in heavy sheets. Kamika could barely see Kenji off in the distance, way down the road, just coming to the top of a small rise. She ran after him and promptly slipped in the mud, sliding on her belly down the path toward the bottom of the hill. She turned over and sat up, inching away from the puddle she landed in. Her clothes were wet and dirty; she had scraped her left hand, but it wasn't bleeding.

Kamika stood, then walked east, making her way down to the rutted road. There was no bus and no sign of her brother. But there were large tire tracks in the mud. She decided to follow them and was delighted when they turned off the road between two hills. One hill was marked with big white stones, making letters on the hillside. *Letters! This must be the way to the school.* She happily trudged up the muddy road, thinking about how surprised her brother would be when she found him.

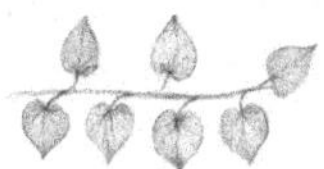

The day before, the local news in Oregon had predicted heavy rains. In preparation, Coral Russell and her handyman, Amos Matthews, hauled twelve half-barrels of oak off the flat-bed truck they borrowed from Suzy Jenkins, another farmer who lived nearby, and put them in the equipment shed above the north side of the house. Then Coral filled the barrels with sand to receive the yearling lily bulbs planted in late February after the last frost. Rain helps the bulbs to root, but not this much rain. The ground was already saturated, and it would likely cause the new bulbs to rot.

Today, Coral raked the bulbs into a pile on a burlap sack before they washed down the hill. Her arms and left ankle already ached, and her back muscles burned with fatigue. She pushed back the hood of her rain slicker while rain soaked her curly black hair. She wiped the rain from her eyes and looked around for Amos. He was using the new John Deere cultivator to scoop up the bulbs south from where she stood. But the hill was washing away fast.

"Amos! Move down this hill and wait for me at the bottom," Coral cried as loudly as she could. She dragged the burlap sack covered with the bulbs from the hillside to the bottom of the hill. "Take these bulbs to the shed and start putting them in the sand barrels."

Amos grabbed the sack and hauled it up into the cab behind him. "You need to get outta this rain, Coral. You'll make yerself sick."

"It's gotta be done. You can come back for me when you're finished. Besides, I'm tough. I'll be alright." Coral put the rake in the cab and waved Amos off.

Coral started up the rise. When she was almost to the top of the hill, a noise made her turn and look back toward the house. *Lord, what now? That sounded like a puppy.* The downpour of the past half hour was letting up slightly. Now she could clearly see the way to the house. Near the bottom of the hill, the churning water with dirt and rocks was making its way down toward the road. But the sound had been close enough for her to hear it through the rain. She walked halfway around the hill, stopping to listen again, but heard only the steady patter of raindrops.

Coral saw that Amos was nearing the oak trees along the side of the hill. Then a flash of yellow against the dark brown of the tree trunk about ten yards west drew her like a magnet. Huddled in a mud-covered raincoat was a small child with wide, frightened, brown eyes. Dark hair was plastered against the face of a small Oriental girl..

"Amos! Stop!" Coral screamed into the wind. "You'll run over her!"

Amos geared down as fast as he could. Stopping the cultivator too quickly would cause it to flip over on the wet hillside. The grinding sound reached Coral's ears as the equipment stopped barely five feet from the child. *Oh dear Lord!* Coral thought. *She might've been killed!*

Coral couldn't imagine how this little girl had gotten there, and she bent down to see if she was hurt. "Hello, young 'un. Are you okay?" Coral asked.

K-k-ken j-j-j-eee." The little girl barely got the sounds out between her chattering teeth.

Oh dear. I don't understand what she's saying. "You poor thing. You must be freezing. We need to get you into the house by the fire so you can warm up. Can you stand?" Coral held out her hand.

The little girl moved her hair away from her eyes, watching Coral steadily. Then she reached up and took Coral's hand. Coral could feel the small girl's body shaking as they walked toward the house. They walked carefully through the mud and rivulets of water. Coral walked to the back of the house, where she could see Amos through the glass in the back door when he reached the shed. She pushed the door open with her shoulder and pulled the little girl in beside her. They stood there dripping puddles onto the kitchen floor. Coral gently brushed the mud from Kamika's face. *She must be from another farm close by. What was it the manager at the market said? A Japanese family moved into the area about six months ago?*

"Amos," Coral called when she finally saw him stand up from behind one of the barrels. "Can you get a couple of big towels and bring them to me in the kitchen?"

"Sure, jest a minute. Who's the little girl?" He asked.

"I don't know, but I'm not likely to find out until her teeth stop chattering. Hurry up!"

Twenty minutes later, the child's wet clothes had been washed out and were drying on the hearth while she sat wrapped in Coral's bathrobe in a large chair by the fire. The little pink socks with yellow ducks brought tears to Coral's eyes. It had been a long time since there had been a child in the house. Coral handed the little girl a cup of warm milk and sat on the ottoman in front of the chair.

"Do you understand what I'm saying?" Coral asked.

The child nodded her head. "What is you name?"

"My name is Coral, and this is my flower farm. What is your name?"

"Kamika. Where is school? Where is Kenji? Why is you face black? Do you have babies? Who is big man?" Kamika babbled happily.

"My goodness! That's a lot of questions all at once, Kamika. First, I need to know where your mama is."

"Don't know. I follow Kenji to school. Where is he?"

"Kamika, this isn't the school," Coral said, shaking her head. "Oh, I see. Kenji must be your sister or brother. Right?"

Kamika nodded. "He my big brother."

She's too young to be in school. Her mother's probably frantic by now. I'd better try to call this girl's mother. Coral picked up the phone and dialed the operator.

"That you, Marsha? This is Coral Russell at Lily Hills. I've got a little Japanese girl named Kamika here that wandered onto my farm. Her family must live nearby. Could you ring their house for me?" She paused, smiling at Kamika. "No, I don't know the last name." She turned aside and asked Kamika.

"What's your last name, Kamika?"

"Satsuma," Kamika answered with pride.

Coral resumed her conversation with the operator. "She says it's Satsuma. Yes, I'll hold on."

After several tries, Marsha said, "There's no answer at the number I have for the Satsuma residence."

"Well, thanks, Marsha. Guess we'll have to try later on."

Coral stood and walked toward the kitchen. "Come with me, Kamika. I'm going to make some sandwiches for lunch. Let's eat and then we'll go find your mama."

Kamika slid out of the big chair and ran over to Coral, nearly tripping on the edge of the bathrobe.

Peanut butter and jelly for her and leftover ham for me and Amos, Coral thought.

Kamika continued babbling questions to Coral as she ate steadily through her sandwich.

When Coral picked up their plates and put them in the sink, Kamika wandered back to the living room and sat on the sofa. Coral cleaned up, peeking around the corner to watch as Kamika slowly nodded off to sleep. The little girl pillowed her hands under her cheek, leaning against the side of the big leather sofa.

Coral pulled out her raincoat and hat and squeezed her feet back into her rain boots. She wrapped two sandwiches in waxed paper, then placed them along with some apple slices and a thermos of coffee in a paper bag, placing the bag in a plastic bucket to take out to the shed for Amos. She knew he would be checking the bulbs for evidence of fungus before placing them in the sand barrels. The procedure to gather infected bulbs into a large plastic tub, allow them to dry out, then treat them with a diluted bleach solution preserved many of the damaged bulbs for future planting.

"Here's some lunch for you." Coral handed Amos the bucket and pulled over a large wooden chair. "Sit down over here and rest while you eat. It's been one hell of a mornin' that's for sure."

Amos took a couple of bites from one of the sandwiches and quickly swallowed them down with a drink of coffee from the thermos. "Where's the little Jap girl?" he asked.

Coral frowned at the racial slur implied in Amos's statement. The war had been hard on the Russell family. Both of Coral's sons had been drafted in 1943 and sent to Germany. After they left, Amos had to shoulder most of the physical work of running the farm. Coral's husband, Jesse, had passed away in 1940. Then telegrams arrived, reporting that both boys had been killed in action in 1944. It was a mighty blow for both Coral and her daughters, Polly and Benita. And Amos took it just as hard as if it had been his own sons who died.

"She's sleeping on the couch. And I don't want to hear you talking that way about our neighbors or their children. This is a different time. She was obviously born here after the war ended. That means she's as American as you are." Coral shook her finger at Amos. "Now you finish your lunch and get back to work. I'm going to try calling her mama again."

This time, a different operator put her call through and told Coral that the line was busy.

That's a good sign. I'd better wake Kamika now, and we can try to get her home.

The child's clothing had dried sufficiently to get her dressed for the return trip home. Coral reached down to shake Kamika's shoulder gently.

"Kamika, time to get up."

Kamika sat up, yawned, and rubbed her eyes. She looked around the living room, adjusting to the fact that she was in a strange place, but didn't appear to be disoriented or afraid. She looked up at

Coral and smiled. "We go to find mama now?" she asked.

"That's right. Let's get your clothes on. Can you dress yourself while I get my raincoat?"

"Yes, I can!" said Kamika, nodding her head.

Coral watched for a few minutes as Kamika pulled on her socks and jeans. Then she went to the shed to collect her raincoat and get the keys to the old Ford pickup truck. *She can't live too far away from here. I'll try the south road first. I already know most of the families that live here on the north road. They've been neighbors for at least ten years. I wonder what her mama is like. Probably a pretty young woman. Kamika is certainly a beautiful little girl with those almond-shaped eyes.*

Coral returned to the living room and pulled an umbrella out of the stand near the door. Kamika was fully dressed, but needed her shoes tied before they could leave. Coral chuckled to herself, remembering when she taught her little girls to tie their shoes. They held hands under the umbrella and headed out to the barn. The rain had let up, but there was no sign that the clouds were moving away. Coral helped Kamika into the passenger seat of the old truck, then went around and climbed in behind the wheel. She mentally crossed her fingers, hoping that the old truck would turn over without having to tinker with the carburetor.

Whrrrrrr. Chug, chug, chug. Whrrrrrr. Chug, chug, chug.

Come on, old girl. You can do it, prayed Coral as she turned the key once again.

Vrrrmmmmm.

Thank goodness. Coral put the truck in first gear with a loud *thunk,* and drove slowly down the driveway toward the road.

When Coral got to the intersection, she looked over at Kamika, hoping the child might be able to point her in the right direction.

"Do you know which way I should turn to get to your house?"

"That way," Kamika said, pointing south without hesitation.

After they had traveled a little way along the road, Kamika pointed to an orange-and-white sign. "That where Kenji get the bus for school."

"Very good, Kamika. I'll bet your house is up this drive on our right," Coral said as she turned the steering wheel onto the muddy road ahead.

Cultures Collide

Hiromi, Kamika's mother, went back up
the path along the stream for the third
time, looking for her errant daughter. Tears
streamed freely down her face. Earlier,
she had completely searched the house,
thinking that Kamika was playing a hiding
game before their trip to the market. When
Hiromi noticed that Kamika's raincoat was
gone; she thought that Kamika had gone
to see if the baby birds might have been
hurt in all the rain. But Kamika was not to
be found anywhere along the stream or in
the trees around the house. Furthermore,
Hiromi could find no sign that she had
traveled that way, although the rain may
have washed away her footprints.

Hiromi had called her husband, Yoshio,
at work to inform him about Kamika's
strange disappearance. He told her to wait
for a little while, then telephone him if
Kamika showed up. They both knew she was
often reckless about her safety, her curiosity
driving her into wooded areas or other
unknown places.

I'll try walking down the driveway toward the road. If I can't find any trace of her, I'll have to call him and let him know.

Hiromi started down the drive when she saw an old, red pickup truck driving toward the house. She waited, hoping against hope that someone had found Kamika and was bringing her back. She was shocked to see a middle-aged, Negro woman behind the wheel of the truck. *Who is she? And why is she here?*

But then Kamika's head popped up from the front seat next to the driver. Hiromi saw her waving and the Negro woman sighing with relief. She quickly ran her hands over her face, then ran them through her hair, composing herself to deal with her little runaway and her deliverer.

As custom demanded, Hiromi went to the driver's side of the truck first and bowed to the driver. "I am Hiromi Satsuma. Welcome to my home. Won't you come in?" She straightened up and gave a warning glance to Kamika, who stayed in her seat, clasping her small hands together.

The driver opened the door of the truck and stepped out.

"I expect this little bundle of mischief belongs to you. My name is Coral Russell," Coral said as she walked around to open the passenger's side door.

Kamika hopped out and grabbed Coral's hand as they walked back toward Hiromi.

A loud burst of thunder announced that it would soon be raining again.

Hiromi guided Kamika toward the front door. "Thank you for bringing my daughter home. Where did you find her?" she said as she motioned for Coral to follow her to the house.

"She wandered onto my flower farm, looking for her brother and the schoolhouse. She was nearly run over by our cultivator when my farmhand, Amos, didn't see her in the rain," Coral answered. "It was only by the grace of God that he was able to stop in time."

At the front door, Kamika turned around to stop Coral from entering. "Wait! We take shoes off. No mud in the house."

"Never mind," Hiromi said quickly. "You don't have to take off your shoes if you don't want to. She turned to Kamika, "However, you take your shoes off, hang up your rain coat, and sit on the time-out stool until I come in for you."

Kamika drooped down like a deflating balloon. She crumpled up on the floor and started to cry. "No, Mama! I not a bad girl!"

The two women stood uncomfortably with Kamika sobbing on the front door entryway between them. Hiromi was ashamed of her daughter's outburst in front of this stranger. Kamika had been saved from an accident that could have caused her to be permanently damaged or die. Now she had an obligation to make amends, called *Ōn* or "life debt" in the Japanese culture, to the older woman.

Coral's face displayed her confusion. Her eyebrows rose, making her forehead a mass of small wrinkles. She reached her hand toward Kamika, then stopped, seeing the look on Hiromi's face, and pulled it back into the pocket of her raincoat.

Hiromi bent down and gathered Kamika into her arms. "Ssshhhhh," she said, rocking the small girl gently. "What am I going to do with you?"

Kamika looked into her mother's eyes. She wiped the tears from her face with chubby hands. Hiromi handed Kamika a handkerchief retrieved from the pocket of her own raincoat.

"Blow your nose. There, that is better. Now, I need to talk to this nice lady. Be a good girl and go into your room. You can use your new crayons and draw a picture for me. The paper is in your brother's desk."

"Okay, Mama," Kamika said as she ran down the hall to the room she shared with Kenji.

"Please forgive my daughter for her outburst. Won't you sit down and have some tea?" Hiromi asked, waving Coral toward the living room.

"I can't stay very long. I've got to get back to the farm. I live just north of you, about a mile up the main road. I'm sorry that we had to meet like this." Coral sat down in a large, straight-backed chair by a window facing the garden.

Hiromi followed Coral into the living room, then sat on the side of the couch nearest to Coral's chair and thought about the complications ensuing from Kamika's actions. *How am I going to explain this to her? It should be Yoshio who negotiates the life debt for Kamika.* Hiromi interlaced her fingers, placing them firmly in her lap. "You...I...," she began, then stuttered to a stop.

"Is there a problem?" Coral asked.

"Our family. We must repay you for saving Kamika," Hiromi whispered.

"Nonsense!" Coral exclaimed. "You would have done the same for me if one of my young 'uns had wandered onto your land."

"This is difficult to explain. It is a matter of honor. My husband should be the one speaking with you to reach an agreement. But you must understand that we are in your debt. This is not something that will go away." Hiromi was pale and appeared shaken, knowing that Coral did not understand her words.

Coral was clearly upset by this pronouncement. She looked down at the floor and shook her head. "You're right. I don't understand!" she said angrily. "This is America, not Japan. We don't ransom our children for simple mistakes. I won't take payment from you—not of any kind. So forget it! What kind of woman do you think I am?" Coral stood, clutching the keys to the truck, and started walking toward the entryway.

"Wait!" Hiromi cried, hurrying after her.

But Coral didn't stop.

Hiromi saw her march through the living room and out the front door to her truck. Coral got in, slammed the door shut, and started the engine.

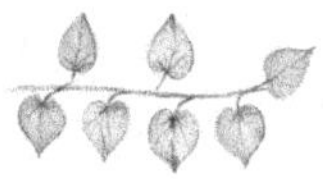

When Coral woke the next day, she felt grumpy. *Why did that sweet little girl have such strict parents? Is it because they are Japanese? Oh well, I don't have time to worry about that today.*

She walked out to the front porch, surveying the twenty-five-acre expanse of the family's flower farm. She still thought of it that way, as the family farm, even though her husband had been dead for twelve years, and her two sons had been killed in World War II. The girls helped out for a little while, but Coral didn't have the heart to hold them back when they turned eighteen and wanted to build lives of their own.

Polly got a scholarship to study marine biology at the university in Santa Cruz. Then Benita enrolled at the college down in

San Francisco to earn a teaching credential. So now it was just Amos, who ran the farm equipment and did the handyman work, his son, James, who helped out when he wasn't in school, and her. *I miss them all every day. It feels so empty here. That little girl, Kamika, just made me realize it. Why am I working so hard to keep this farm going when there is no family left who wants to be here?*

Just then, a new 1952 Chrysler Imperial with large chrome bumpers, white walls, and shiny green paint turned onto the road. Coral watched as the car approached the house. A new car like that, it had to be someone from town. *Better not walk out in the mud. I'll wait here and see who it is.*

Two months earlier, she had slipped and turned her ankle walking down the path to the house. Standing on it most of the day before, trying to save the yearling bulbs, hadn't helped at all.

When the car reached the front porch, Don Jackson from Farmers and Merchants Bank in town, climbed out of the driver's seat. Don reminded Coral of a weasel, a greedy little animal that wanted to be more powerful than all of the other animals. His plump, round cheeks squeezed his eyes until they were mere slits in his face. His expensive suit was too tight, but he always wore it when he came there to collect money.

"Afternoon, Mrs. Russell. How are you doing today?"

"Oh, just fine, Mr. Jackson. Come on in and have some coffee," Coral said, holding open the large oak front door with inset beveled glass windows.

"I'm afraid this isn't a social call, Mrs. Russell," Don said as he entered the spacious living room. The furniture was worn but of good quality. Sunshine filtered through the gauzy inner drapes on the wall facing the west fields. The mornings were still cold, but the fire in the brick hearth made the room warm and inviting. Don sat down in one of the two large armchairs near the fireplace, placing his briefcase on the floor next to it.

Coral went into the kitchen, where she kept a large coffee urn going until the early afternoon during the cool spring days. She placed two cups of coffee, a patterned china sugar bowl and creamer, and two spoons on an oak and ceramic tile serving tray, then carried it into the living room. She set the tray down on the walnut coffee table between the two chairs facing the fireplace.

"Just fix your coffee the way you like it and tell me what's on your mind," Coral said as she picked up her mug.

"You are now thirty days late on the loan payment," Don said, his watery blue eyes peering at Coral intently from behind thick, black-rimmed glasses.

Coral wondered what Don saw when he looked at her. She had a few gray hairs that stood out from the curly black mass she kept pulled neatly into a bun at the nape of her neck. But her skin was firm, and her warm brown eyes sparkled with humor and intelligence. Don probably wondered how one middle-aged, Negro woman with a hired hand and his young son could run such a large farm. Of course, that's why she had taken out the loan in the first place, to buy cultivating and harvesting equipment for her small team to operate more efficiently.

"I know the payment is late, Mr. Jackson. It's not like it slipped my mind or anything. It's just that Benita needed extra money this semester. That college she goes to raised the tuition by $50. She got a part-time job working at Montgomery Ward, but it didn't cover the books, tuition, and her housing. So I had to help out," Coral explained.

Don scowled at this excuse. But Coral knew the bank could give its customers some leeway, for a price. But her cash crop wouldn't be sold until late spring, with the remaining flowers used for weddings and other celebrations. The cash reserve she kept for emergencies was almost gone now, used for oak barrels and sand to save the yearling bulbs.

"When do you think you'll be able to make the payment?" he asked, his voice icy with disdain.

"I need to talk to some people first, Mr. Jackson. Can you wait for one more week?" Coral realized that she would have to negotiate partial payments on her other bills. She might even have to pawn some of her jewelry or other valuable pieces in the house. The farm couldn't continue without the equipment; the loan had to be paid.

"One more week is all that I can give you without a financial penalty," Don said. "You can bring it down to the bank or call me. I'll come by to pick it up if I can." He gulped down the rest of his coffee and stood up. While he reached down for his briefcase, daylight reflected off the growing bald spot at the top of his head. Coral walked with him to the front door and watched as he drove off down the dirt road. Then she picked up the serving tray and returned it to the kitchen. She heaved a great sigh as she entered the hallway leading to the library, where she kept the farm's ledger and the safe that held the cash.

Kenji knew something was wrong the moment he entered the house. It was very quiet. The air was damp from the rain and tasted like salt water to his eight-year-old tongue. He took off his raincoat and left his muddy shoes by the kitchen door. There were no vegetables waiting to be washed for dinner, no rice in a ceramic bowl next to the steamer, and no jasmine tea welcoming him home with its sweet, soothing fragrance. *Where is everyone? Maybe they left a note for me.* He searched the living room, the room he shared with Kamika, and his father's office. But there was no message anywhere. It was not the first time he had been left alone in the house. But this time felt different. Kenji paced from the kitchen to the front door and back many times before he thought, *Mama and Papa would expect me to study and start my home assignments from school.* So he put his books on the kitchen table and started to read.

An hour later, Kenji's mother, father, and sister drove up the road to the house. Kenji put his math homework away and hurried to the kitchen door to greet them. His father opened the door, then held it for his mother and Kamika. There was no talking, no laughing. Their faces were closed. Even Kamika was subdued. *What could have happened?*

"Mama, what is the matter?" Kenji whispered.

"Go into the living room and wait for us there. I'm going to get Kamika into her pajamas," Hiromi said.

Yoshio took Kenji's hand. He put his other hand on Kenji's head, tilting it so that he could look into his eyes. Kenji saw that his father was worried, but calm. Yoshio's hand was firm and slightly calloused from digging up soil samples for his rice research at Carstairs Industries. They walked into the living room together. Yoshio pulled the cord to light the stained glass lamp next to the couch.

"Sit down on the couch and wait for us. I am going to make some tea for your mother. She's had quite a day."

Kenji thought about how his parents were acting. *Why is Kamika being put to bed now? We haven't had dinner yet.* Hiromi came in about ten minutes later with Kamika's picture of Coral in her hand and sat next to Kenji. Yoshio set down the tea tray and walked around the coffee table to sit next to Hiromi. He poured a cup for himself and Hiromi. They each took a sip from their cups, then put them down and hugged each other tightly. They sighed, then looked over at Kenji.

"Your sister tried to follow you to school today," Hiromi began. "She was gone for about an hour before I noticed she was missing. I searched everywhere in and around the house, but I could not find her."

"Kamika got lost and wandered onto our neighbor's property. It was raining very hard, and she took shelter under a tree," Yoshio said. "The farmers there were plowing up some of the hills with a heavy cultivator machine. Kamika was in the way and could have been killed."

Kenji gulped. *Kamika followed me? Into the rain and mud?* His hands started shaking. He gripped his knees and waited for his parents to continue.

"I called your father and we decided to wait a little while to see if Kamika turned up. When I looked out at the road, I saw a red truck driving up to the house with Kamika inside." Hiromi pushed the crayon drawing toward Kenji. "Her name is Coral Russell, and she is the one who rescued Kamika. She doesn't really look like this, but she is a Negro woman, about fifteen years older than I am."

"Your mother tried to explain that we owe her a life debt for Kamika. She became upset and returned to her farm," Yoshio said as he gently pushed Kenji's straight black hair away from his dark, gray eyes. He took another drink from his teacup before he continued. "We both feel that it might be better if *you* intervened for the family. She seems to be a very good woman, and she will not be harsh with you. When you learn more about her, we will find a way to repay her for saving Kamika."

Kenji couldn't believe what he had just heard. He felt so guilty that Kamika had gotten lost because she was trying to follow him. This life debt was really his to pay. Kamika wouldn't understand what her reckless behavior had done to their family.

Kenji followed Hiromi into the kitchen as she got ready to make dinner for them. He opened the refrigerator, looking for vegetables to prepare with the rice and fish. He pulled a large bunch of fresh green beans from the crisper, setting them on the kitchen table.

"Mama, are you going to punish Kamika?"

Hiromi came over and sat down next to Kenji at the table. "Your father and I will decide how to help Kamika make better decisions later. Kamika's spirit is lively and curious. These are good qualities in both of you that we treasure. But she often lets her impulses control her actions. She will learn more if she experiences some of the bad things that can happen as well as the good ones."

Kenji breathed a sigh of relief, but he wondered how he could find a way to convince Coral Russell to accept the payment for saving Kamika's life.

The Farm in Trouble

That night, Coral tossed around the bed for hours. At one o'clock, she woke from a dream where she was sinking into a large puddle of slimy, black mud, unable to free herself no matter what she tried. She found that the sheet had wrapped around her legs and waist, effectively binding her in place. She struggled out of bed and into the bathroom for a drink of water. The night air was cool and moist, a balm to her throbbing head. She doused a washcloth with cold water, applying it to her neck and face.

She returned to bed, but sleep remained elusive. *Oh how I miss Jesse on nights like this! He would lay his head on my stomach, saying, "Tell me about your troubles, Sugar, and I'll tell you about your blessings." Somehow, we'd always find a way to work things out. But I can't see my way out of this one, husband of mine. There's no money for the loan payment, and we just lost about twenty percent of the yearling bulbs.*

Coral knew that repairing the storm damage would be the first priority in the morning. Slowly, Coral's eyes began to droop. Her breathing once again became regular and slow as she spiraled down into a dreamless slumber.

She woke again at dawn, a habit ingrained from years of farm management. The red blush of sunrise fell gently upon the land. Birds warbled their morning songs; the air was heavy and still. Coral headed to the kitchen to start the coffee, knowing Amos would be in shortly. They usually discussed the day's work schedule for the farm over coffee. Coral also started a batch of biscuits, pulling the buttermilk out of the fridge and the canister of flour from the pantry.

They spent the morning roaming through the fields, wading through mud, to view storm damage. Rather than inspecting the plants, they checked the run-off areas to make sure they were clear of debris. Sure enough, leaves, mud, and rocks had dammed up several of the lower channels. When the water backed up, it washed the topsoil away, taking vital nutrients from the flowers. Amos wielded the shovel while Coral used a heavy rake to pull the rocks out of the channel. By midday, her back and shoulders were aching, and her ankle had swollen to fill her rain boot. She called a halt to the work, and they returned to the house to wash and make supper. James would be home from school soon, and they would need a hearty meal to fill their bellies and relax for the evening.

James left his school books in the small house they had all built together for Amos and his family shortly before the war. He was tall for a twelve-year-old, with strong muscles and calloused hands and feet from farm work and running barefoot around the farm. His skin was the color of milk chocolate, like his father's. He kept his brown hair short so he wouldn't be distracted by it when he was working or at school. His mother and Coral taught him to cook and help out in the kitchen from the time he was a small boy. When he came into the kitchen, he went immediately to Coral and enveloped her in his strong arms.

"Your hugs are just about the best thing on God's green Earth after a long, hard day of work," Coral told him.

"I'm so hungry I could eat a whole cow!" James said, dazzling Coral with his big, bright smile.

"Now, Jimmy. You know what to do. Set the table and then you can make dessert. How about using them peaches we got at the Farmer's Market on Saturday? They'd taste mighty good in a crisp." Amos stroked his short brown beard, now streaked with gray, and winked at James.

"I guess we all deserve a treat after that rainstorm. I'll get right on it!" James pulled the dishes out of the cupboard, then went to the sideboard to get the napkins and silverware.

While the greens were cooking, Coral wandered out to the front porch to sit in her favorite rocking chair. She spied a small boy with dark, straight hair walking up the rutted drive toward the house. *Who could that be?* He walked toward her with quick, deliberate steps. *He looks a little bit like Kamika. Her brother? Why is he here?*

Kenji approached the porch with slow, measured steps, careful to avoid slipping in the mud. He climbed the steps to stand before Coral and bowed gracefully from the waist.

"My name is Kenji Satsuma. I have come seeking your help and advice."

What's this? Coral thought. "My name is Coral Russell. I met your mother yesterday when I brought your sister home. What do you think I can help you to do?"

Kenji lowered his eyes, then cleared his throat. "Kamika told me that you have a flower farm. My teacher at school assigned the class to study how one of the local crops are grown. We must write a paper and create a demonstration showing part of what we have learned. I would like to learn about your farm. Is it possible to do this?"

"Well, I don't know. I'd like to help you, but we're making supper right now," Coral replied.

"Please," begged Kenji. "I promise not to take much of your time. Maybe I can even help a little bit while you are showing me how to grow flowers. After I finish my chores on Saturday, could I come here to learn from you?"

Coral was puzzled by this turn of events. After what Hiromi had said, she was expecting a conciliatory gesture from the family, perhaps an invitation to dinner. "You'd better come inside while I think about it," she said, rising from the rocker.

"Thank you," Kenji said, following her into the house. He looked around the living room, his eyes roaming from the furniture to the lamps, and then to the pictures encased in polished wood frames resting on the fireplace mantel. He went over and picked up the largest picture, the one of the whole family taken before the war.

Coral's heart gave a painful squeeze, remembering that joyful time. "I'd best go check on supper. I'll be right back," Coral said as she pulled her handkerchief from her apron pocket to dab the wetness from her eyes.

When she returned, Kenji asked, "This must be your family. Where are they now?"

Coral hesitated before answering. "I'm sorry, but maybe we can talk about them later. Supper is ready, and I'm sure your parents don't want you to walk home in the darkness."

"I always wished I had brothers," Kenji sighed. "Kamika is fun most of the time, but she always wants me to play with her when I am doing my homework." He took a breath, then looked up from the picture. "Thank you for inviting me into your home. Would it be alright if I come tomorrow?"

Coral found herself nodding yes. "You come by after lunch, and I'll show you around the farm." She took the picture back from Kenji's small hands and placed it lovingly back on the mantle. Then she walked Kenji to the door, waving goodbye as he went down the steps.

Later that evening, after Coral had finished washing the dishes and putting them away, she sat down in the soft leather chair by the fire. Her thoughts returned to the loan payment deadline that was drawing ever closer. *There's nothing for it. I'll have to sell my pearl necklace. I'll never forget when Jesse gave it to me on our tenth anniversary. But the farm equipment is more important.* She walked over to the family picture to gaze at his face, smiling with happiness. When she picked it up, she felt something on the back of the picture.

Coral turned over the picture, discovering an envelope slipped between the backing and the frame. Coral was shocked to find $150 in it. *Kenji must have slipped the envelope in here when I wasn't looking. I should return it. If only I didn't need the money so badly.*

Something Bad Happened

Saturday morning dawn was fair, with golden sunlight streaming down through the trees. Coral had spent another night tossing around her bed. This morning, the left side of her head felt like the cultivator was pressing down, trying to make grooves in her brain. She stumbled into the kitchen to get the coffee percolating. *I'd better take some aspirin if I'm going to make it through with this headache.*

The night before, she had decided to sell her pearls to Hal Buskin, an honest and fair man and the only jeweler in town. She planned to return the $150 to the Satsuma family on her way back. And she would call Don Jackson to let him know that he could pick up the money for the loan payment on Monday morning. With her morning schedule planned, Coral returned to the bedroom to get ready.

After her shower, her fingers fumbled with the buttons on her blouse. She felt sluggish, like she was moving through honey.

She shrugged it off, attributing her slowness to the lack of sleep. Coral opened the top drawer of her dresser and removed the black velvet case that held her pearl necklace. Lifting the lid, she gazed at the luminescent, glossy pearls. Each one was a perfect round, the creamy white color touched with a hint of pink. She felt a tear trickle down her cheek to the deep groove between her nose and mouth. She licked at the tear; salty, like the sea from which the pearls had come.

She found Amos in the shed, mixing liquid fertilizer. "I'm going into town for a little while this morning. I should be back by lunchtime. The little girl's brother, Kenji, will be coming by this afternoon. I promised to show him around the farm. If you see him, let me know."

"What'd you do that fer, Coral? We don't need a know nuthin' Jap boy getting' underfoot around here." Coral scowled at Amos, but he continued. "You feelin' okay? You look plum tuckered out."

"I could do with a good night's sleep. I can't seem to settle down and relax. Might be my age is finally catching up with me. But you keep a civil tongue in your head when the boy comes around. You hear me?" Coral said.

"I will, Coral. If'n the weather holds fair a while, try to take it easy fer a few days. You know Jimmy and I can handle the fertilizing."

"I know, Amos," Coral sighed. "There's always so much to do."

Coral climbed into the cab of the truck, hoping that there wouldn't be any problems with the engine today. It turned over slowly, but started up without dying. Driving past the growing fields on her way to town, she thought about how strange it was that two small children should enter her life at this time—and Japanese children at that. Life was certainly full of surprises.

Buskin's Jewelry Shop was located on Main Street, just down the road from the post office. It was small, rural families not needing much in the way of jewelry, other than wedding rings and an occasional anniversary present. She parked the truck outside the shop and entered the shadowed interior. Jewelry sparkled from inside glass cases as display lights shone on the precious gems. Hal Buskin sat behind the counter with the delicate inner workings of a watch carefully placed on a polishing cloth before him. He was around the same age as Coral, in his fifties, with corn-colored hair, thinning on top. He looked up as she entered and smiled.

"Mrs. Russell! I haven't seen you in here since you bought those graduation presents for Miss Polly and Miss Benita. What brings you in today?" Hal asked in his gruff but kind voice.

Coral opened her purse and was about to reach into it for the pearls when a loud humming sound caused her to stop. The sound seemed to be coming from inside her head. She shook her head, trying to make it go away. When it didn't, she tried to speak, but no words would come. Her vision began to blur, and she became so dizzy, she couldn't remain standing. The last thing she remembered before she blacked out was Hal's concerned face as he came out from behind the counter to reach her.

Amos washed the fertilizer mix off his hands in the large copper sink at the back of the shed. After he wiped his hands on the rough cotton towel hanging next to the basin, he went up to the house. Coral was late coming back from town, so he thought he'd watch for the little Japanese boy from there. The phone started ringing as he reached into the refrigerator for some lemonade. *That's prob'ly Coral now, tellin' me why she's late,* he thought while closing the heavy metal door. His long legs brought him to the telephone on the side table in the living room in a few seconds.

"Hello," said a deep, male voice. "This is Doc McGuire at Good Samaritan Hospital. That you, Amos?"

"Yeah, Doc. Miz Russell's not here right now. Anythin' I can do for you?"

"Well, that's just it. The ambulance brought her in about an hour ago. Hal Buskin was with her. She was in his shop when she lost consciousness."

"Whoa, Doc! What's wrong with her? Is she gonna be alright?" Amos asked as he sank down on the couch. *Oh no! Not Coral.*

"I can't tell you much right now, Amos. We took blood, and it's still being reviewed. Her heartbeat is strong and regular; she's breathing on her own. Those are good signs, but she's still unconscious. I've got to keep her here."

Doc McGuire was trying to sound reassuring, but Amos could hear the worry in his voice. His mind started whirling with concerns, and his heart pounding with fear. Coral, his rock, was down for the count. Someone needed to inform her daughters. He had to keep taking care of the farm, but he needed to get to the hospital. Amos felt like the bottom had dropped out of his world. "I'll be there as soon as I can. What should I tell Miss Benita and Miss Polly?"

"You can tell them what I told you. She's in good hands with us here at the hospital. I'll know more when the blood work comes back from the lab. There's no use working yourself and the girls up about this. You need to stay there and take care of James. Give us some time to help Coral."

"I'm just...I don't think...," Amos stuttered into the receiver. Coral was the strong one, the one who held everything together.

"Now you listen to me." Doc's voice was calm but firm. "You're a good man, Amos. Mrs. Russell could always depend on you, so don't let her down now. After you call her children, why don't you walk around the farm with James? That will help you settle down. We'll get through this one step at a time."

"Okay, Doc. Thanks for the advice. I'm gettin' my feet back under me. You'll call here if'n she wakes up, won't ya?"

"We will, Amos. You can count on that," Doc said, then hung up.

Amos put the receiver back in the phone cradle. The house was strangely quiet and empty feeling. He walked to the study, looking in Coral's desk for the book with her daughters' phone numbers. He found it in the right-hand drawer, neatly tucked between her bank passbook and a box of blue pens. A sharp rapping sound from the front door reminded Amos that a visitor was expected.

It's that little Jap kid, he thought, putting the book with the telephone numbers into his shirt pocket. *I'll just send him home. I gotta call the girls. That's more important.* Amos approached the door with hesitant steps, trying to keep his worry under control. Kenji stood patiently as Amos drew back the heavy door.

"Hello. Is Mrs. Russell here? She was going to show me around the flower farm today," Kenji said with a hopeful expression on his face.

Suddenly, Amos felt the stress of the years since Coral's sons were killed in the war boiling up inside of him. The work had piled up after the family was gone, leaving him and Coral, and his little boy to carry the load. The weather conspired to destroy the crops, which were the basis of money for the farm. He had to call and tell the girls their mother was in the hospital. And now, a little Japanese kid was demanding a tour of the place! It was just too much.

"Look here, boy. You better get on home. Miz Russell ain't here, and she won't be back fer while." Amos tried to keep his temper in check, but the feelings of loss and frustration leaked into his voice. "I ain't got time to show you the farm; I've got work to do. And don't bother coming back later. What we needs is peace and quiet around here!" Amos screamed at the boy, watching the color drain from his face.

Kenji backed away from the door and down the porch steps. When he got to the bottom, he turned and ran down the path toward the road.

Amos watched his short, thin legs churning as he ran away. *Good riddance*, he thought as he closed the door. He reached into his pocket for Benita's phone number. He would call her first. *Benita's not too far away. She can call Polly and tell her about Coral bein' in the hospital. Benita can get here on the bus. But first, I better find Jimmy and tell him we'll do the firtilizin' later.* Amos shook his head and pulled on his gray-and-brown streaked beard, wondering if they would ever recover from this disastrous winter.

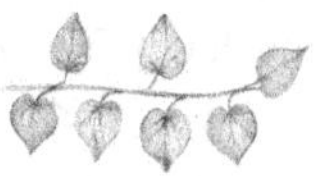

Kenji never did remember that trip home from Coral's farm. He knew that he had never ran faster, tears streaming down his face the entire time. He couldn't see the road, the trees, or the house. He just wanted his mother's arms to hold him and say that everything would be all right. He stumbled through the kitchen door, so short of breath he could hardly speak.

Hiromi was at the kitchen sink drying the dishes from lunch. She turned toward Kenji as he grabbed her legs, sobbing and wheezing.

"Kenji! My son, what on Earth is the matter?" She held him tightly, then picked him up and drew him into her lap on the nearest chair.

Kenji worked hard to control his emotions. He couldn't speak while he was crying. Something terrible had happened, and his mother needed to know.

Kamika was drawn to the kitchen by Kenji's sobs. She crept up quietly beside her mother, placing her small hand on the leg Kenji had wrapped around Hiromi's waist.

Finally, after several minutes of deep breaths, Kenji was able to talk. "I went to Coral's farm, and a big man answered the door. He started screaming at me to go away. I got really scared and ran home as fast as I could. Why was he so mean to me?" Kenji asked.

Hiromi rocked Kenji back and forth in the chair, making soothing noises into his hair. "I do not know, Kenji. Calm down and try to tell us what happened."

Kamika kept patting Kenji on the leg, but she looked into his eyes with a puzzled expression on her face.

Kenji waited until he was no longer shaking, then reached down to his leg and took her hand. "I'm okay, Little Flower. Don't worry."

"I'm glad you okay, Kenji. What did the big man say?" Kamika asked.

"He said that Mrs. Russell wasn't there, that he had to work." He paused, trying to remember what was said. "Oh, and that they 'needed peace and quiet there.' Why would he say that, Mama?"

Hiromi brushed the hair away from Kenji's eyes. "I don't know. Were you being noisy?"

"No, Mama. I was very polite, just the way you taught me."

Kamika put her hands on her hips and shook her head. "No, no, no!" she said. "Something bad happened."

Kenji realized that he felt the same way. His stomach was strangely hollow. Something Amos had said triggered the bad feeling. What was it? He couldn't remember past the shock of the verbal assault. "Kamika is right, Mama. But I can't remember exactly what he said." Kenji felt himself getting upset again.

Hiromi stood up, taking both of the children with her into their bedroom. "We have had quite enough excitement for this afternoon. I want both of you to lie down for a little while. Kenji, if you are not tired, you can read a book, but Kamika needs to sleep."

Kenji went into the bathroom to wash his face, then returned to lie down on his bed. He sighed, looking around the room at the little work table and their flannel bathrobes hanging by the door. A warm feeling of comfort and safety wrapped around Kenji like a blanket. He turned onto his side. He saw that Kamika was already sleeping. He closed his eyes, drifting into a restless dream where Coral kept calling his name.

Benita Takes Charge

The hospital room was eerily quiet. Benita could barely hear her mother breathing under the starched white sheets of the tilted bed. It had been two weeks since Coral's stroke. Precious weeks of schooling had been lost, weeks of preparation she needed to begin her teaching career. And now Benita was dealing with problems at the farm, with that nasty man from the bank, Amos and Polly's fears, and her own sense of inadequacy.

She spent her days listening to Doc McGuire tell her the results of blood tests, range-of-motion exercises, and brain wave detection, but nothing that said when her mother would get better.

Benita felt even more uncomfortable at the farm than she did at the hospital. When she arrived on that first day, she found $150 and her mother's pearls in Coral's sturdy leather handbag. Amos didn't know where the money had come from or what Coral intended to do with it. When Don Jackson had called, Benita informed him that her mother was not available. He began demanding payment for the farm equipment loan that was overdue. Benita gave him the $150 to shut him up and get him out of her hair. It wasn't actually enough for the payment. But when Don arrived to pick it up, he said he would take it as a "good faith" effort and that he expected another payment in a few weeks.

Benita had discussed leaving the farm with Coral before deciding to attend college. She wanted her mother to know that she wanted a teaching career. Now she had been trying to help run the farm, but she felt like a complete failure. Benita didn't know what to tell Amos when he pestered her about buying supplies they needed. She knew that he was worried about her mother and needed her guidance to run the farm. Benita's thoughts scattered around like a hive of angry bees.

Into the silence of the lonely hospital room, a faint noise reached through Benita's confusion. Coral sighed and opened her eyes. Benita ran to her side, grabbing her limp right hand that rested against the covers.

"Hi, Mama. It's me, Benita," she said in her soft, husky voice.

"Mmmm. Bbbbb. Gaaaa." Moaning noises issued from Coral's lopsided mouth.

Doc McGuire had prepared Benita for the possibility that Coral might not be able to speak, but that didn't prevent the tears that started immediately from her eyes. She forced a smile and bent over to kiss her mother's wrinkled cheek. She thought, *Oh, Mama! What am I going to do?*

"You just rest easy now, Mama. Doc McGuire says you had a stroke and that it might be hard for you to talk, so don't try right now. Do you understand what I'm saying? Just nod or squeeze my hand if you do."

At first, there was no response. Coral's work-roughened hand lay passive in Benita's soft, moist palm. Benita looked deeply into her mother's eyes, so like her own, brown and flecked with golden dust. Coral's intelligence and good humor sparkled through. A heartfelt sigh escaped from Benita's chest as she collapsed into the chair by the bed.

"We were so worried about you. Amos is taking good care of the farm. He comes to see you almost every day. I'm going to go find Doc McGuire to let him know you're awake. But I promise I'll be right back." Benita reached up to wipe the tears off her cheek before giving her mother's hand a squeeze. She walked quietly out of the room into the waiting area.

She leaned against the wall, allowing the long-suppressed emotion to shake her from shoulders to knees. After a few minutes, she realized that this was just the first step in a long recovery process. Weeks of physical therapy would be needed; maybe cognitive exercises and speech therapy would be required as well. *I need more information. Maybe Polly can come back to help out for a while. We might be able to switch off taking care of Mom, but what will happen to this year's flower sales?* She walked to the nurses' station and asked for Doc McGuire, informing the nurse of her mother's consciousness. After a quick look around the lobby, Benita ran to the pay phone to call her sister.

Hiromi was at the Sunday Farmers Market when she heard the news about Coral. Yoshio was in Ohio on business with several other men from Carstairs Industries. They were studying a new strain of rye grass that had survived well through the wet winter and strong winds. Hiromi looked over the spring green pea pods, yellow hook squash, and bulb fennel that had just come in from neighboring farms. While Hiromi was examining the fennel at Mrs. Jenkins's produce stand, she asked, "Have you heard anything about Mrs. Russell? You know, the older woman who owns the flower farm?"

"Oh my, yes," Mrs. Jenkins said. "She's been in the hospital in town, Good

Samaritan, for a couple of weeks now. She just collapsed while she was in Hal Buskin's jewelry shop. Some folks said it was a heart attack. But I said 'Naw. That woman's as strong as an ox.' May've been a stroke. Negro folks is known to have high blood pressure and such."

Hiromi wasn't really surprised at the news. Her children had convinced her that something was wrong. And now their feelings had been confirmed. "I hope that she'll be all right. Does she have any family nearby to help her?"

"Well, her husband's been dead these past ten years or so," Mrs. Jenkins explained. "The boys was killed in the big war, and the girls are off at college. But Amos will take care of her when she comes home, if'n he has to."

"Thank you for telling me. I'd better get home now," Hiromi said. She paid for the vegetables, packed up her groceries, and headed to the station wagon. During the drive home, she thought about the life debt that her family owed to the spirited, older woman. Coral was a woman of deep feelings, proud and self-sufficient. She had certainly made an admirer out of Kamika. Kenji too had responded to her as he would to a wise elder.

But the debt was still there. And whether Coral recovered or not, it would still be owed to the Russell family. Who would she negotiate with now? Her mind quickly seized on the fact that if Coral lived, she might be a long time recuperating from this illness. There were too many questions and no answers. Hiromi decided to take the children with her and go to the hospital in town later that day.

Around 2:00, Kenji had finished with his house chores, and Kamika was just waking up from her nap. Hiromi spread peanut butter on crackers, then cut up some apples, wrapping them all in tin foil. She called the children to the kitchen to get them ready. "I found out today that Mrs. Russell is in Good Samaritan Hospital."

"She's sick!" cried Kamika. "Can we go to her?"

Kenji nodded. "Please, Mama. We promise to be good. Won't we, Kamika?"

Kamika placed her hand over her heart. "I promise."

"Good," said Hiromi. "I thought you might feel that way. I will talk with her doctor to see if there's anything we can do to help her. Go get your jackets, then put on your socks and shoes. I will pack up the snacks, and we can take them to the hospital. We'll go as soon as you're ready."

Ten minutes later, they were in the station wagon, heading down the rutted drive toward the main road. Kamika was unusually silent during the trip to town. Kenji kept asking questions that Hiromi could not answer. She didn't want to discourage his natural curiosity, but she realized that hearsay from Mrs. Jenkins at the Farmer's Market was not fact. The Satsuma family had not been to the hospital in town since Kenji contracted the measles when he was five years old. His extremely high fever was not to be taken lightly. Yoshio had told her that the fever could cause damage to Kenji's sight or hearing, and he needed a doctor's help right away. Hiromi had stayed home to keep one-year-old Kamika away from her highly contagious brother.

Yoshio had been the one who dealt with the doctors, staying with his son until the danger had passed. Kenji had not talked about his experience there, and Hiromi wondered if this visit to the hospital would be traumatic for him. She stole a quick glance at him sitting quietly with his hands folded in his lap, his face neutral but for a small crease on his brow. The hospital building, gray and white with a large red cross on the side, was shadowed by tall, evergreen trees lining the parking lot. Hiromi pulled the car into a space close to the building, helping the children with their coats as they got out.

They entered the lobby, Hiromi holding each child by the hand and steering them toward a soft leather couch at the side of the room. "I'm going to talk with the nurse at the counter over there. I want you to sit here and wait for me. You can eat your peanut butter crackers and apple slices or look through the magazines on the table," Hiromi said, handing Kenji the foil-wrapped packets.

Kenji gave Kamika a children's storybook from the table behind the couch and watched her carefully to make sure she was not going to get up and start walking through the hospital. He opened one of the snack packets and placed it next to her. "Are you hungry, Little Flower?" he asked.

Kamika was absorbed with the pictures in the book, but reached over to get a peanut butter cracker, so Kenji didn't wait for her to answer. He was reaching for a magazine when he noticed a flash of red. A young Negro woman in a red sweater and cream-colored pants walked quickly to the pay telephone and inserted some coins. He thought he recognized her round face and wavy hair from the picture on the mantle in Coral's living room.

"Pssst, Kamika," Kenji whispered to get his sister's attention. "I think that is one of Mrs. Russell's daughters." Kenji pointed secretively toward the wall where a young woman was standing at the telephone. "I recognize her from a picture that was at Mrs. Russell's house."

Kamika's eyes grew round with wonder. "Oh. She a grown-up lady."

"When she gets off the phone, I'm going to talk to her."

Kenji waited patiently, watching Kamika, who had stood up on the couch to see what was happening. The woman had a soft voice, and Kenji couldn't hear what she was saying. After what seemed like hours, the young woman placed the receiver back on the hook but stood there, clinging to it with her head down. Kenji walked over quietly to stand beside her.

"Excuse me," Kenji bowed slightly from the waist as Benita looked up from the floor. "My name is Kenji Satsuma. Are you Mrs. Russell's daughter?"

Benita hesitated, then a slight smile creased the corners of her mouth. "I...yes. I'm Benita. How do you know who I am? Is there something I can do for you?" she asked.

"I visited your mother at the flower farm one afternoon a few weeks ago. We are neighbors, and she helped my sister, Kamika, when she got lost in the rain. I saw your family photo on the fireplace mantel. We have been so worried about your mama. The man who works with her told me that she needed peace and quiet. My papa told me to wait until she invited us back. She...I don't know how to explain this, but she became special to us." Kenji felt that there were no words to tell this young woman why

Coral was so important to their family. He watched Benita's face as her eyebrows rose.

"Well, this is certainly a surprise to me, young man. Kenji, is it?" Benita asked as he nodded. "My mother regained consciousness a little while ago, but she is still far from well. Do you understand what I'm saying?"

"I think I understand. She is awake, yes?" Kenji asked.

Benita smiled. "That's right. But I don't know if it would be good for her to have many visitors. I need to talk to her doctor; only the family and Amos are allowed into her room."

Kenji tried not to show his disappointment. But his heart sank, becoming a lead weight in his stomach. He looked over to the couch, expecting to see Kamika turning the pages of the picture book he had given her, but she was nowhere in the lobby area. When he turned around to look at the nurses' station, his mother was gone as well.

"Where are your parents?" Benita asked.

Kenji's heart started hammering in his chest. *Where have they gone? Mama will never forgive me if Kamika is lost again! Maybe they went to the bathroom.*

"My mother went to talk with the nurse, and my sister was sitting over there when I came over to talk with you," Kenji indicated the couch by the window. "She promised to be good," he whispered to himself. "I need to go look for my sister. She is not very good at sitting still."

Benita squatted down beside Kenji and took his hand. "I see that you are worried because they are not where you expected them to be. Let's go over to the nurses' station first and see what we can find out. Maybe your mom is talking with Doc McGuire."

The nurse said that Doc McGuire had asked Mrs. Satsuma to come to his office. She hadn't noticed the little girl leaving the lobby area.

"Kenji, your mother would be frantic if she came back from talking with Doc McGuire and both of her children were not in the lobby. Please stay here until she is finished talking with him. I'm going back to my mother's room now. I don't want her to feel that she is alone," Benita said.

Kenji felt that it was his responsibility to look for Kamika, but he agreed to wait for his mother. While he was waiting, he had a sudden inspiration. He walked back to the nurse at the lobby counter.

"Does the hospital have a garden?" Kenji asked.

"Yes, it does," she replied. "Why?"

"My sister loves trees, flowers, birds... anything outside. I think she might be there. Where is the garden?"

The nurse looked at him for a moment before responding. "I can tell you where it is, but you must promise to wait for your mother before you go looking for your sister."

Kenji was certain that Kamika had gone outside. But he didn't want his mother to return to the lobby to find both her children gone. He nodded to the nurse. "I'll wait on the couch over there," he said.

A few moments later, Hiromi returned to the nurse's counter, wiping her eyes with a delicate lace handkerchief. Kenji ran to her and threw his arms around her legs.

"Mama, I'm so sorry! I saw one of Mrs. Russell's daughters and went to talk to her. When we finished our conversation, Kamika was not in the lobby anymore."

Hiromi bent down and held tightly to her son. "I should have known better than to leave you in charge of her." She took the sting out of her words with a quick smile. "Where do you think she might be?"

"I think she went outside," Kenji said, reaching up for his mother's hand. "There might be a garden where she went to play."

The nurse said, "The garden is at the end of the long hallway on your left. Just follow it to the large double doors. You'll see the flowers and plants as you get near the back of the hospital."

Hiromi bowed slightly to the nurse. "Thank you for helping us. Will you please keep her here if she comes back to the lobby before we find her?"

The nurse nodded. "I will keep her near me at the counter. We can also page you to return to the lobby if she shows up here."

When Benita entered her mother's room, she was shocked to see a little girl with dark hair and a sun-browned body sitting on her mother's bed. She held a small bouquet of pink, yellow, and white flowers in her left hand. Her right hand was firmly grasped around Coral's wrist.

"...like a dimind in the sky. Winkie, winkie, little star. How I wonder what you are," sang Kamika in her sweet child's voice. "Can I sing you more songs?"

Coral smiled with the left side of her face and nodded her head. But before Kamika could start singing, Benita stepped into the room.

"Hello, you must be Kamika." Benita smiled into her dark, almond-shaped eyes and pulled a chair up next to the bed. "My name is Benita."

"You are Mrs. Coral's girl," Kamika said proudly. "Kenji say so."

"Your mother and brother are looking everywhere for you, young lady. Kenji mentioned something about a 'promise to be good.' Did you break your promise?"

Kamika looked down at her hands, then up to Coral's face. "We come to hospital to see Mrs. Coral. Here she is! I finded her. I not make trouble."

Benita stood up and went to her mother's side. "I'd better find Hiromi and let her know Kamika is with you, Mama. Is she bothering you?"

Coral shook her head and reached up with her left hand to touch Kamika's cheek. Benita felt a warm flush begin in her chest and tingle its way to her fingertips. Her mother might not be able to talk, but her heart was just as loving as she remembered. Picturing Kamika with the flowers in her hand, Benita hurried down the hallway, pushing past hospital orderlies and their metal carts filled with pill containers. When she reached the garden, Hiromi and Kenji were looking under the bushes for the wayward child.

"Kamika is in my mother's room, singing lullabies to her," Benita said with a touch of laughter in her rich, low voice.

"Thank goodness," Hiromi said, brushing the dirt off her hands as she rose from the ground. Kenji ran to Benita's side.

"Can we please go see her?" he begged.

"I think we must. It's only fair," Benita said, wiping a smudge of dirt from Kenji's face.

They entered Coral's room quietly, not wanting to disturb Kamika as she finished singing "Happy Birthday to You." Kenji giggled as he pushed a chair for his mother next to the one Benita sat down in.

Before Hiromi sat down, she bowed to both Benita and Coral. She sat gracefully in the chair, reaching forward to pull Kamika into her lap. Coral released Kamika's hand.

"See, Mama," Kamika said. "Mrs. Coral waked up."

"When my children told me that something bad had happened to you, Mrs. Russell, I didn't know what to think. They had no facts, just their feelings. Today I heard from Mrs. Jenkins that you were in the hospital, so I had to verify that information for myself. It seems my children were right," Hiromi said in a soft voice.

Just then the door to Coral's room opened. Amos stood in the doorway, peering into the dimness. He hesitated, first looking at Benita, then at Hiromi and the children. His suntanned face began to redden as he clenched his fists by his side.

"What the hell are they doin' here?" he bellowed.

Cultures Come Together

Kenji gasped and began trembling. Hiromi stood and pushed him behind her. She put Kamika on the floor next to Kenji. Benita walked toward Amos, making pushing motions with her arms. Coral rolled onto her side, looking toward the door where Amos stood.

"Baaa...," she croaked. "Ggoooo."

When Benita reached Amos, she pushed him back into the hallway, thinking, *What's the matter with him? I know he's a stubborn old man. But to start yelling in a hospital?* She stepped with him into the hallway, then closed the door to Coral's room, trying to isolate the occupants from further conflict.

"Amos, what do you think you're doing?" she whispered. "Mama needs to be calm and quiet to get better."

Amos's face got even redder. He looked down at his mud-stained work boots, grumbling. "You don't know them Japanese, Miss Benita. They started this trouble, wandering into Lily Hills without being invited. Coral trying to deal with the rain, the bulbs, the damn bank—and then those two brats. It was too much for her."

Benita shook her head, unable to reconcile her recent experience with the Satsumas and Amos's version of what had happened. "It's easy to blame all of the farm troubles on outsiders, isn't it, Amos? But things have been hard at the farm since my brothers died. You didn't really see what was going on in that room, did you?" she asked him.

Amos squinted and said, "I saw enough."

"No, Amos. You didn't. Mama is very happy to have them there. The little girl, Kamika, was singing to Mama. She picked some flowers and brought them to Mama's room all by herself. 'Brats' don't behave like that."

No matter what Amos thought he saw, Benita knew children from her practical teaching internship as well as her advanced studies. She saw Amos scowl, but she could see that he was backing down. He began to pace the hallway. After about five minutes, he was noticeably calmer. He glanced at Benita's face before approaching to speak with her again.

"I'm sorry I upset you, Miss Benita. That Mr. Jackson from the bank called. He wants another payment of $250 by tomorrow. The next payment of $400 is due a week after that. And what are me and Jimmy supposed to use for money? Groceries ain't free, ya know." Amos explained.

"Does Mama have any savings at the bank?" Benita asked anxiously.

"The truck needed new tires and shocks in February. I think she used the rest of her savings to buy the oak barrels and sand to save the yearling bulbs. Even if there is any money left, we can't get at it. Only Coral can. She's the only one with access to her accounts."

"I just spent my last paycheck on my teaching credential exams and certification filing. Maybe I can get a refund, but it still won't cover the whole amount due." Benita looked at Amos as his shoulders sagged. She thought that Amos looked more haggard than usual. His gray hair stuck out from one side of his head while the other side clung tightly to his scalp. Deep wrinkles carved grooves into his weather-chapped face. His eyes were bloodshot, with dark circles beneath them.

"Damn," Amos whispered. "I don't think your mama would want you to do that anyway."

Hiromi peeked out from behind the door to Coral's room, opening it slightly to step into the hallway. Walking almost silently, she hurried over to speak with them.

"Excuse me," she said, making a slight bow to them both. "My husband would like to speak with you on a matter of some urgency. He will be returning from a business trip tomorrow morning. Would it be possible for you to meet with him in the evening?"

Benita shot a warning glance at Amos, hoping to keep him from another outburst. He acknowledged the glance with a nod, but folded his arms in protest at their negotiations.

"Things are so jumbled up right now," Benita explained. "Is there a telephone number where I can reach you?"

Hiromi nodded, retreating to Coral's room, presumably to get something to write with and on from her purse.

"Amos, go back to the farm. I want you to take the rest of today and tomorrow off. Go somewhere with Jimmy. You could go to the waterfalls near St. Justin's Gap. It's only an hour or so away. Or go fishing." Benita suggested.

Amos opened his mouth to argue with her when he suddenly stopped. He rubbed his cheeks with both hands, then ran them through his hair. "You know, I think that's a good idea. Not for me, but for Jimmy. I've been neglectin' him something shameful. He deserves better than that from me."

"Good," Benita said. "You go on home now and get ready for your outing tomorrow." She watched as Amos strode down the hall with a little more energy in his step. After he entered the lobby area, she went back to her mother's room. Hiromi handed her a slip of paper on which she'd written their family name and phone number.

Kenji was placing an extra pillow behind Coral's neck and shoulders so that she could sit more upright. Kamika was back on the bed, stroking Coral's right cheek.

"You side face is tired. Maybe is time for a nap?" Kamika said.

"You are definitely right about that, young lady," Benita said. "But I think Mama really enjoyed your visit. Thank you for the beautiful flowers and your songs."

Hiromi helped the children put on their jackets. "We will be going home now and leave Coral to her rest. It was very nice to meet you, Benita. Come children, say goodbye," Hiromi said.

Kenji walked to Coral's side and took her hand in his. "I hope you feel better very soon, Mrs. Russell."

Coral smiled her lopsided grin, her eyes glowing with emotion she could not express in words.

Kenji bowed slightly to Benita. "Goodbye," he said in a soft voice. "I hope we will see each other again."

Hiromi led her children from the room. Benita sat down in a chair, wondering how she could find $250 by tomorrow. Coral patted the bed, indicating that Benita should come closer. She stood and leaned over her mother's face. Coral kissed her on the cheek, then slowly closed her eyes. As her breathing became deep and regular, a contented smile remained on her face.

Yoshio's return from his business trip filled Kenji with both excitement and apprehension. In Kenji's eyes, his father embodied everything good and honorable in a man. Yoshio was firm but loving to all members of the family. He constantly reads books to learn new things. He rode a bicycle, ran, stretched, and meditated to achieve balance with mind, body, and spirit. But mostly, Kenji loved his father's deep respect for the land.

When Yoshio came through the front door, Kamika and Kenji ran to the entryway, bowing deeply from the waist as he set his briefcase by the wall. He removed his shoes, then opened his arms to the children. They ran to him, wrapping their arms around him as he bent to kiss their heads.

"It seems as though you have each grown at least five inches since I have been gone. What have you been eating? Giant beans?" he teased them. "Where is your mother?"

"Here I am, my husband." Hiromi's dark eyes sparkled with happiness. Her long black hair stood out sharply against the red satin of her kimono. Kenji knew that his mother was pretty, but at that moment she looked like a young queen.

During lunch, the phone rang. Yoshio glanced at Hiromi and raised his eyebrow. Hiromi nodded. He went to the living room, talking quietly while they finished their meal. Hiromi began clearing the dishes when he returned to the table. "It seems that we have an appointment with our neighbor this evening. Mrs. Russell's daughter Benita asked us to come over to Lily Hills tonight after dinner. Kenji will go with me to represent the family."

Kenji felt his heart begin to beat faster. What would his father say to convince them to accept the debt payment? He noticed Yoshio was looking deeply into Kamika's eyes.

"Well, Little Flower. What are you willing to do to help our neighbor, Mrs. Russell?" Yoshio asked her.

"She need help for her little baby flowers. I pull out bad weeds. I give flowers food to make grow big. I make peanut butter samwich for Mrs. Coral," Kamika explained.

Her face was so serious that Kenji almost laughed. But he knew it would not do to mock her sincere wish to help.

"Good. You are really thinking of what Coral needs and not thinking of yourself.

That is the way we help each other," Yoshio said.

Hiromi shook her head. "This is not a pie crust promise: easily made, easily broken, Kamika. You must be true to your word."

Kamika sat very still, looking small in the oak kitchen chair. One fat tear fell from her eye and trickled slowly down her rosy cheek. Kenji wanted to comfort her, but he did not interfere, knowing this was an important moment for his sister.

"I know, Mama. This is 'portint. She save me from lost and rain. I want to help."

Hiromi smiled at her little girl. "Yes, it is *important*. Now go wash your face. You can play with Kenji for a little while before your nap."

Kenji got up from the table, wondering what would happen at Lily Hills that evening.

Yoshio drove up the dark lane to the meeting with Benita, with Kenji sitting quietly at his side. The cool evening breeze rustled the leaves on the trees lining the drive. As they approached the front door, they heard a heated discussion in progress inside the house. Yoshio shook his head. This was not a good time to call; however, he had accepted Benita's invitation. Honor demanded that he knock to let Benita know they had arrived, as promised. He put his hand on Kenji's head.

"We may be walking into a very difficult situation," Yoshio said, a wry smile turning up the corner of his mouth. "I expect you to observe and learn. Do not interfere or speak unless we ask you a question. Do you understand?"

Kenji looked into his father's eyes. They demanded his cooperation in this. Yoshio grabbed the worn bronze doorknocker, rapping twice on the plate. The conversation inside immediately quieted. Benita opened the heavy door, nodding to Kenji and offering Yoshio a tentative smile.

"You are right on time, Mr. Satsuma. I'm afraid that we have an unexpected visitor as well. But won't you come in?" *At least they can provide a distraction. If Amos can only hold his temper long enough for me to try negotiating.* She gestured to Yoshio, indicating that she would follow him and Kenji into the living room, where oak and cherry wood burned cheerfully in the grate.

Amos stood next to the hearth, tending the fire. Don Jackson stood nearby with his arms crossed at chest level, his face an imperturbable mask. Yoshio acknowledged him with a slight nod, moving across to the couch with Kenji in tow. Kenji sat down, but Yoshio remained standing, waiting to see what Benita would say next. However, Jackson broke the awkward silence first.

"I can't imagine what you're doing here, Mr. Satsuma, but Miss Russell and I have business to discuss that can't wait. I suggest that you and your boy come back another time," Jackson said, barely containing his impatience.

Benita and Amos both started talking before Yoshio could respond to Jackson's "suggestion." Amos stuttered to a stop when Benita held up her hand. "I can handle this, Amos. I invited Mr. Satsuma over this evening. You didn't return my call this afternoon, Mr. Jackson. So I was surprised when you showed up," she explained.

"I thought you called to say that the rest of your overdue payment was ready for me to pick up." Jackson's voice growled at her implied error in his thinking. "You have the money, don't you?" he asked, applying pressure to the already tense situation.

Benita took a breath and stood to face him. "No, I don't have the money, Mr. Jackson. You could have saved yourself time and trouble by returning my phone call." *A good businessman he obviously is not. How can I use that to my advantage?* she wondered.

"That's not how your mother does things. She always calls me when the payment is ready to pick up. Well, now. What should we do?" Jackson asked, now pacing back and forth in the entryway area.

"I'll tell you what you should do," Amos growled. "You should stop bothering us when we are trying to take care of Mrs. Russell and the farm."

Jackson stopped pacing and walked over to Amos until they were standing almost toe to toe, glaring so intently that Benita thought someone would burst into flames. Yoshio edged closer to the two men, placing himself between them and Kenji.

"You just listen to me, Amos," Jackson shouted. "The bank has every right to repossess that farm equipment you bought with *our* money. Those payments are due, and it's my job to collect them. By rights, I should have taken that equipment back three weeks ago. Don't try to intimidate me. I don't scare easily."

The vein going down the middle of Amos's forehead between his eyes was enlarged and throbbing. His face looked like thunder.

Benita gasped at Jackson's temerity in talking back to Amos. Worse, she knew Amos was barely containing a violent outburst. Amos balled up his right fist and took aim at Jackson's protruding chin.

In two quick steps, Yoshio thrust himself between them. He pushed Jackson backward and grabbed Amos's fist, holding it still at shoulder height. Jackson tripped over the threshold down from the entryway and fell back, landing on his butt, and sat there with his mouth open. Kenji moved over next to where Benita was standing and grasped her hand. "Wait," he whispered to her. "Let my father talk to him."

Benita sank down into a chair, still holding Kenji's hand.

Yoshio talked softly to Amos, his voice clear and low. "Think about what you are doing. If you hit this man, he could have you arrested. How would that help Mrs. Russell or her daughter? Why would you want to give this man power over you? He doesn't seem to understand how to use the power that he has. And you are needed here, far more than the farm equipment."

Amos stopped struggling against Yoshio's firm grasp and lowered his arm to his side. Yoshio stood quietly, waiting for Amos to compose himself. After Amos had taken a few deep breaths, Yoshio stepped away from him and said, "You are wise to rethink the situation. We are neighbors and should help each other when we can. My son and daughter count themselves as friends of this family. And now, so do I." He gave Amos a slight bow, then turned to see what had become of the banker.

"I wish you hadn't stepped in like that. He deserves a right hard smack in the face. But yer probly right," said Amos.

Jackson got to his feet, brushing the back of his pants with his hands. He looked at Amos, then at Yoshio. Finally, he turned to Benita. "I'm going to talk to the bank manager about this little incident. I don't know what he'll say or do, but if I were you, I'd make good use of that equipment because you won't have it for long."

Benita stood up, holding her head high, and pointed toward the front door. "Don't even try to threaten me! You can leave now. If you come back, you'd better have legal documents to take possession of the farm equipment from us. Oh, and this is private property. We are within our rights to have you arrested for trespassing if you appear without an invitation. Now go."

Jackson's face got even redder, but he held back any remarks and left, slamming the screen door behind him.

The tension seemed to melt away as the sounds from Jackson's car faded. Amos looked sheepishly at the floor, then came over to where Benita was standing. "Well I'll be darned if you didn't handle him just fine. You sure didn't need any help from me. Your Mama would've been so proud of you. I almost made a fool of myself, me and my darned temper."

"Amos, please go back to planning your outing with James. You need this break to think about what would be best for all of us," Benita said calmly.

Amos went back to tending the fire as Yoshio and Kenji sat together on the couch.

Benita went to the kitchen and returned a few minutes later. She wanted to share the warm fragrance and soothing flavor of tea with their guests. She poured each of them a steaming cup of the herb-scented brew. Yoshio sipped the hot liquid, quietly waiting for Benita to speak.

"It's chamomile. I find it soothing before bed. I've had too many sleepless nights these last few weeks," Benita said. "Now that Mama has regained consciousness, we can all try to put our lives back together again."

"How is your mother doing?" asked Yoshio.

"Doc McGuire said she can come home in a few days. Thank goodness. But it may take weeks or months before she is fully recovered. I'm afraid that I must return to school. I will lose all the credits I earned for this semester if I don't take my final exams."

"May I ask a few questions?" Yoshio asked. Benita nodded. "Have you talked with your mother about what's going on?"

Benita lowered her eyes and clasped her hands together. "No. I didn't want to burden her with anything that might make her condition worse. She may remember that the loan payment is due; she may not. Her speech is sometimes garbled, but Doc says it will improve over time. Amos and James are taking care of the plants. Although I grew up here on the farm, I only helped box up the flowers, tape them closed, and carry them out to the truck. I didn't pay attention to when the harvest began, the preparation of the lily packages, Mama's customers, or even if she markets them locally or ships them. Amos told me that the rains destroyed some of the younger bulbs. What can be done about that?" Benita asked him.

Yoshio sighed and smiled at Benita before speaking. "I meant what I said a little while ago about neighbors helping each other. My family would like to work with you all in any way we can. But it is up to you to tell us if there is any help we can offer that you will accept."

Benita hesitated to respond, thinking, *I don't know what we need right now, except money, of course.* "I think that I need more information before I can address your offer. After Mama gets home, Amos, James, and I will think about how you can help us," she said.

Yoshio sighed. "Then it is time for us to leave. I am sorry we had to meet under these uncomfortable circumstances. But I am very happy that we have become acquainted at last. It was very hard for us all through the war and afterward. There was so much bad feeling: anger toward the Japanese, especially after the Pearl Harbor attack. Then guilt after the devastation of the atom bombs dropped on the island.

We have not been exactly in hiding, but reclusive." He looked down at Kenji, reaching out to put his hand on Kenji's head.

Benita was silent, stunned by the intimate confession from Yoshio. She cleared her throat before speaking. "I never thought about what it must be like for Japanese families trying to make a life for themselves in America. I lost two brothers in the war. We all grieved, slowly healing. But I was young; the war was far away. Mama was the strong one. She saw the possibilities that had opened up for women, and she encouraged me and my sister, Polly, to go to college. Back then, most people were caught up in their own personal grief." She paused, wiping at a tear that slowly leaked from her right eye. "I suppose it will be children like Kenji and Kamika who figure out how to build a future where powerful technology will not destroy us all. I truly hope they can."

Yoshio stood with Kenji and headed toward the front door. Benita followed them. "I will call Hiromi to let you know when Mama is here and can see you. I suppose that I must consult a lawyer about the bank loan," she mumbled under her breath.

Yoshio looked at Benita with new resolve. "I will be going to the bank to deal with some business matters on Tuesday. My company, Carstairs Industries, has a large amount of money invested there. When Mr. Jackson said that the money belonged to the bank, he made a grave error in judgment. The money there belongs to the people and businesses of this community. There would be no bank without us. The bank manager will make time for me if I ask for it. I believe that there are other options that can be explored," Yoshio offered.

"Heavens!" Benita exclaimed. "I never looked at things that way. There are definitely advantages to being in business. Having other options would be helpful, to say the least." She bent down to look into Kenji's eyes. "You have been strangely quiet tonight. I wondered why your father brought you with him. Now I think I understand. I hope you have learned as much as I have from this evening."

Kenji looked up at Yoshio for permission to speak. After Yoshio nodded, Kenji said, "There are many times when I don't understand why people do what they do. But I think that when people take time to listen, we can know one another better."

"I couldn't have said it better myself," Benita said.

Kenji and Yoshio waved goodbye as they got into their car for the short drive home.

Coral Comes Home

I'm home, thought Coral as Amos helped her from the passenger seat of the truck. *Oh how I've missed the smell of growing things! And there's Benita with that worried wrinkle between her eyes.* Coral lifted her left hand to wave at her daughter. Amos kept a firm arm around her waist, just enough to keep her from stumbling. The rains and windy weather had made the rocks lining the pathway up to the porch steps into a jagged mess.

Benita came down the steps to greet her mother with a wide grin and open arms.

"Welcome home, Mama. I'm so happy I could just burst. Let's get you into the house where you'll be more comfortable."

"Please, no," Coral said, clutching the sturdy handrail to maintain her balance. She took careful, controlled steps onto the porch risers. When she reached the top, she turned to look at the hills, now bedecked with the green stems and leaves of emerging lilies. "I wwant to sstand here... and loook."

"Just don't overdo it, okay?" Amos said. "You know how you are. Keep an eye on her, will you, Benita? I'm gonna put the truck back in the barn."

Benita stood by her mother's side, quiet and attentive. But Coral just wanted to drink in the sight of Lily Hills. The rolling hills, the warmth of the sun, her favorite rocking chair on the porch—she almost felt whole again. When she had been in the hospital, fighting to make sense of what happened to her, she felt like half of her life was missing. And here it was. The farm had saved her when she lost Jesse and the boys. She had buried her grief as she planted the new bulbs in the fertile earth. The daily routine of taking care of the farm and the girls provided a framework in which to rebuild her self-image. And now? *And now I have to save the farm.* Coral could feel that things were still not right, but she couldn't put her finger on what was out of place.

"I promised to call Hiromi and Yoshio, Mr. and Mrs. Satsuma, when you got home from the hospital. You remember them, don't you Mama?" Benita asked anxiously.

Coral clearly remembered Kamika, huddling beneath the oak tree in the rain. But when she tried to talk about it, the words got all jumbled up in her mouth and wouldn't come out. Doc McGuire told her not to worry about talking, that it would take time, just like teaching the rest of her body to bend, stretch, and move again. As she stood thinking things out, the phone rang. Coral started and turned toward the door. But Benita held up her hands to stop Coral from going in.

"I'll get it, Mama. Just stay on the porch till I get back." When Benita pulled the screen door open and hurried into the living room, Coral caught a glimpse of the polished wood floor and deep red Persian carpet under the high-backed armchair. The familiar furnishings made her gasp: What was it that she wanted to remember? She was overwhelmed with a sudden sense of dislocation in time. She groped her way to the rocking chair through a wave of dizziness. As she settled into the chair, she heard Benita's voice coming from inside the house. She was arguing with someone. *What could Benita be arguing about? Who was she talking to?*

About ten minutes later, Benita came out to the porch. Coral studied her face. It was clear she was worried, tired, and... conflicted. When Coral closed her eyes, the image of Benita being pulled apart caused her to wince. Benita sat down next to Coral, reaching out to pat her hand resting on the arm of the chair.

"How are you feeling, Mama? Getting tired yet?" Benita asked with a false note of cheeriness in her voice.

Coral pointed to the house. "Wwwhat?" was all she said and rocked, waiting for Benita's answer.

"Can't we talk about it tomorrow?" Benita asked hopefully.

"Nnow." Coral stated firmly.

"You're going to be stubborn about this; I can tell." Benita sighed before continuing. "The bank has given us another thirty days to catch up on the loan payments for the farm equipment. That awful Mr. Jackson wants to come over and talk to you about it. I told him you just got home from the hospital and, under doctor's orders, can't see him for a few days. At first, he wouldn't take no for an answer. I had to remind him, forcefully, that he would be hearing from our lawyer if he came here uninvited."

"Mm. Mm. Mm," Coral huffed, shaking her head. *The loan payment. I didn't want to remember that. Poor Benita. Having to deal with the bank and my illness, too. No wonder Benita looks like she's being torn apart. And Amos, too. He must be worried something awful. There's something else. I wish it would stop buzzing around like an angry bee and settle.*

There was nothing more to say. The bank had given Coral extra time, and well, she would take it. She leaned back in the rocker, feeling the warm afternoon sun fall on her face. Her eyes closed, and in moments, she was asleep.

James and Benita were in the kitchen making breakfast the next day when Coral awoke. The smell of bacon and coffee called her out of a hazy, restless sleep. *Oh my! Bacon! It's been so long. Wish I felt steady enough to make flapjacks. I know Benita loves them.* She slowly made her way down the hallway, hands pushing against the walls to keep her steady. She made it to the table in the kitchen and sat down just as Amos came in with a jug of buttermilk.

"Here's the buttermilk for the flapjacks, Jimmy," Amos said as he brought the jug to the counter where James was measuring flour and baking powder into a large ceramic bowl painted with cheerful yellow daisies. James had straight brown hair with blond highlights courtesy of his French mother, high cheekbones, and amber-colored eyes that shifted to gray or brown depending on his mood. He was tall and strong for a twelve-year-old, with milk chocolate skin and calluses on his hands. James helped outside in the flower fields, and he often did the cooking and the laundry.

"Thanks, Pa. Breakfast will be ready in about ten minutes," James said.

As Amos washed his hands at the kitchen sink, Benita started setting the table. "How was your day off with James? Did you go to the falls or go fishing?" she asked.

"We went down to the Rogue River for some mighty fine fishing," Amos explained with a big smile. "I 'spect we'll have steelhead for dinner tonight if y'all would like some."

Coral nodded, then thought, *How long has it been since I gave him a day off? Seems like we've been working for three years straight. And now I'm only half here. I've got to get better.*

"Come on, James. Let's hear the whole adventure!" Benita requested.

"Well, it's been a while since we went fishing, so once we got to the river, we hurried into our waders, grabbed our poles and creels, and scrambled down the hill." James giggled and looked over at Coral. "Our rushing turned into a slide directly into the water! Good thing we had our waders, on or we'd a been covered in mud!"

Coral laughed. "So mmmuch fffun."

Amos added details to the mishaps of the day. "When we hooked some of them big ones, Jimmy couldn't reel his in fast enough, and our lines got all tangled! I cut mine loose so's Jimmy could haul his in first. It was one of the biggest steelheads I ever seen! After I got my line re-rigged, we spread out a little to keep from gettin' tangled agin'."

"I do love being out by the river," James sighed. "The sound of the rushing water, the glint of sunlight through the trees, sometimes the silvery fish jumped out of the river right in front of my nose!"

Benita started filling plates with flapjacks and bacon. "Here you go, Mama," she said putting a plate down in front of her. "Sounds like you men had a wonderful day of fishing! Amos, you look much better than you did a couple of days ago. I hope you're feeling better, too."

"Miss Benita, you sure know the right medicine fer a man with troubles on his mind. And, Jimmy, we'll go up to them falls in St. Justin's gap real soon."

Coral knew that things would be much too busy for Amos and James to get another day off for a while. Somehow, they would have to find a way to bring in some money before the big lily shipments in May. When Coral finished breakfast, she got up from the table, walking toward James, who was cleaning up the griddle at the stove. She wrapped her arms around him, holding him tightly to her the way she had many years ago after his lost his mother and sister. "Jjjamess," she said through her tears. "Thhhannk you."

After the breakfast dishes were cleaned up and put away, Amos took Coral for a short walk to the shed and the barn. Benita watched them go slowly out the back door when the phone rang in the living room. She hurried to answer it.

"Benita, is that you?" Polly asked after hearing her sister's voice.

"Polly! It's so good to hear from you," Benita replied. "Guess what? Mama is home! She is weak and still stuttering. But she looks so happy."

"Thank goodness you came up to take care of Moms. But, Benny, you can't stay there. You've got to go back and finish your teaching credentials," Polly warned her.

"I know," Benita sighed. "Our neighbors, the Satsumas, have offered to help. Amos, Mama, James, and I will need to discuss what they can do to help us. But they have been very supportive. And Mama is really taken by the little girl, Kamika, and her brother, Kenji."

"We have Japanese neighbors? When did that happen?" Polly exclaimed.

"I don't know exactly, but I don't think they've been there long. I'll call you back when we figure things out." Benita said. "I miss you and the adventures we used to have when we were young."

Polly laughed, then sniffled. "I miss you, too. Give Moms a big kiss for me. Talk to you again soon."

Benita hung up and wondered if the farm would survive the multiple disasters that had hit them during the spring.

How to Fix Lily Hills

Kamika heard the phone ringing and ran to the table in the hallway. "This is Satsuma house. Who is this?"

"This is Benita, Coral's daughter. Do you remember me? We met at the hospital."

"Oh, yes! You are teacher lady." Kamika replied.

"That's right. Can I please talk to your mama?" Benita asked.

Kamika put the phone receiver on the table. "Mama, Benita calls for you."

Hiromi went into the hallway and shooed Kamika into the living room. "Thank you. Your brother is busy with his homework, but you can look at the *National Geographic* magazine that came in yesterday."

Kamika said, "Okay, Mama," and ran to look at the wonderful pictures from all over the world.

"This is Hiromi. How is your mother, Benita?"

"She's home from the hospital now and starting to get accustomed to the farm schedule again. She's talking more every day. I think she would like to see Kamika and Kenji."

"I'm sure the children would love to see her. When would it be convenient for us to come for a visit? I know there is a lot of work on the farm that needs to be done. Is there anything we can do to help you?"

"Thanks to your husband, the bank has given us another thirty days to make a loan payment. Would it be possible for you to visit tomorrow night?"

"I need to confirm with Yoshio, but I think that we are available. When do you have to leave?"

"I can stay through the end of the week, but I must return to college to take my final exams. There are decisions to be made that neither Amos nor I can do without Mama's approval. Doc McGuire said she needs to take on the farm business slowly, so that she will fully recover," Benita explained.

"What a difficult situation for you! That doesn't leave much time to develop a plan. But I'm sure we can do it," Hiromi said.

"I don't know how to thank you," Benita replied. "Mama was always the strong foundation of the family. It's hard to see her this way. But we all get older, and life is never what we expect it to be. Let me know if you can visit tomorrow night."

"I will," Hiromi promised.

Benita's eyes lifted to the picture of the family on the mantle that was taken just before her brothers went off to fight in the war. There was Mama, smiling and holding her children around her. Her hair was just starting to gray, but her back was straight and her eyes sparkled with life. *Where did she find the resolve, the drive to make the farm work? How could she support Polly and me when we wanted to go away to college? And how can these neighbors we barely know help us through this troubled time?* She wished that she had some answers, but there were only questions.

The night was cool and clear, a good sign for warm spring weather to spur growth in the lilies. Amos and James helped Benita clean up after dinner. Coral looked better, regaining some color in her cheeks and sparkle in her eyes. She sat on the porch in her rocking chair, humming a little song and waiting for their guests to arrive.

James surprised Benita by baking chocolate chip cookies for them to have when the Satsumas arrived.

He blushed slightly when he said, "Ma taught me to cook. We had so much fun in the kitchen. Then Mrs. Coral took over and taught me her recipes after Ma died when I was six."

Benita looked at him, realizing this young man had grown up on her family's farm, but she didn't really know him at all.

"James," Benita said shyly. "Will you write to me when I return to California? I know you'll be very busy helping your dad, but I think that you're the best person to tell me how things are going here. You can be very honest with me. Tell me the bad things along with the good ones. That is just how life is. Although I won't be here, I still want to help."

"I'm not a very good writer, Miss Benita. But I sure will try. It's been real nice having you here for a while. I sure do miss you and Miss Polly," James said with a kink in his voice.

"You're a very smart young man, James. I feel like you're my cousin or little brother. Please call me Benita, and the same for Polly. I promise to call and check in. And I think we'll be good friends from now on." She took the platter of cookies into the living room just as a gentle knocking sound started at the front door.

When Benita opened the door, the children were standing in front of Yoshio. They bowed to Benita, and she waved them in. Kenji looked around as the fireplace glowed, gently lighting the room. Kamika ran straight over to Coral and threw her arms around her. Coral sighed as she hugged the little girl. When Kamika drew back from the hug, Coral pinched her cheek and smiled. "Ssit herrre," she said, pointing at an upholstered chest next to the leather chair near the fire.

Kamika scrambled onto the chest, crossed her legs, and gave Coral a bright, happy smile.

Kenji and James sat on a bench that Amos brought in from the kitchen. Yoshio and Hiromi sat on the sofa. Benita stood on the steps leading down to the living room while Amos sat in the wing chair, arms crossed and forehead wrinkled. Benita cleared her throat, and everyone stopped their conversations to hear her.

"Welcome to our home. It is so nice to have neighbors who want to know us and be part of our lives. My mother is recovering well, and I know she is happy to see you all. The doctor told us that it will be good for her to take on small jobs every day to regain her strength and to oversee us as we work to keep the farm going. We are very grateful for your offer to help us. What do you have in mind?" Benita asked.

Yoshio stood up and walked to where Benita stood on the stairs. "Please sit next to Hiromi while I tell you our thoughts." Benita went to the sofa, smiling at Hiromi as she sat beside her.

"We can contribute to your household and the farm in small ways. I would like Kenji to come here after school. He will help with the housework—washing clothes and cleaning the kitchen and other rooms. He can do his schoolwork with James after they finish their chores. Hiromi will come during the day with Kamika. Hiromi will prepare meals and do the shopping as needed. Kamika can help Coral with her small jobs around the farm. Coral, would you be willing to teach Kamika about growing lilies? She is a fast learner, and she loves flowers. In fact, we call her 'Little Flower' at home," Yoshio explained.

Coral looked over at Kamika. "I wwwilll," she said. "Iss that okkay?"

"Papa says I take care of you. We work ev'y day. I help, and you teach." Kamika nodded at her wisely.

Coral laughed and nodded back.

Yoshio nodded at Amos. "We feel that you, Amos, should set up the schedule for planting, harvesting, marketing, and shipping. James will be tasked with maintaining the farm equipment and work areas, like the shed. Both he and Kenji can help with the farm tasks on the weekend. You and I will make a list of what we need to buy to complete these tasks. I will need to look at the records from the previous years to see the costs and the revenue from sales. Benita, you can help me with that before you leave. I think Coral will be able to help me if I have any questions later. Hiromi and I will use some of our savings to sustain the farm and the people here until the flower sales are going smoothly."

Benita had taken Hiromi's hand, and tears were trickling slowly down her cheeks. She was overwhelmed by the generosity of their offer. She took a handkerchief from her pocket and dabbed her eyes. "I don't know what to say. How can you possibly do all of that for us? You have your own garden, work in the city, school for the children. It seems impossible." Benita shook her head.

Hiromi said, "In Japan, there is a saying: Time expands to fill the needs of people who are busy. I think there is truth in that. We become part of your lives; you become part of ours. The time is shared, and so it becomes enough for both. Kenji and Kamika will have two sets of parents nearby; so will James and Benita. We teach our children that nothing is impossible when we work together."

Yoshio looked over at Amos, who was now sitting forward, looking down at the floor, hands folded between his knees. "Amos, you have not said anything since we started our meeting. I want to hear how you feel about it. We have taken over your life and the life of your son. But we won't do this without your consent. You have the right to say 'No,' and we will respect your decision."

Amos looked around the room. His son was smiling, sitting next to Kenji. Coral, holding hands with Kamika, looked calm and content. He looked over at Benita, who was still shocked by what Yoshio had proposed to help Coral. "I can't rightly say how I feel. I think 'humble' is the word. But you'll need to be learnin' the way we do things around here. It's probly different from how y'all do things. Me and the boy, well, this is our home. We'll show you how we do the work. What do you say, Jimmy boy?"

"I have a lot to learn about maintaining the farm equipment. But I think there are books in the library that will help. Maybe Mr. Satsuma can help me find the right ones?" James asked.

"We have lots of manuals for farm equipment where I work. I can borrow them or make copies for you," Yoshio said.

"As long as I can get my schoolwork done, I'll be okay. I can even help with the cooking. And speaking of cooking, how come no one is eating the chocolate chip cookies I made for us? Don't you like cookies?" James teased.

Kamika sprang off the chest and ran over to the platter before anyone could move. She grabbed four cookies and ran back to Coral's side. She put one cookie in her mouth and another in Coral's mouth. Then everyone started to laugh.

Benita said, "Well! I think I'd better get the milk and coffee to go with the cookies. Kenji, can you help me?"

Kenji and Benita returned with the drinks. Kenji poured glasses of milk for himself, James, and Kamika. He walked over to the chest where Kamika was again sitting and handed her a glass. "Be careful, Little Flower. That glass will break if you let it fall."

"Mmmffff. Not drop," Kamika mumbled through a mouthful of cookie.

As everyone discussed the plans for helping at the farm, the snacks were soon gone. Kenji and James returned the glasses and cups to the kitchen. A short time later, Hiromi stood up to gather her children for their return ride home. Amos finished his conversation with Yoshio, then walked over and offered his hand to help James off the bench. They walked through the kitchen and out the back door to their little house at the top of the next hill. Benita stood on the porch with Coral and waved goodbye to the Satsuma family. She turned to her mama and asked, "Did I dream the whole thing? I feel like it can't be true."

Coral turned to her and said, "Tis true— and I amm sso gratefull."

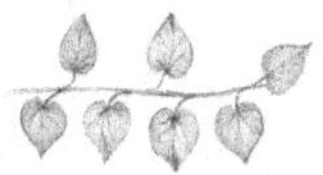

Even with everyone working together, it took several weeks to get the farm schedule right. After Benita returned to college, she called every day to check in with Coral. Her mother was determined to get stronger; she did the exercises that Doc McGuire gave her to regain her balance. She walked slowly around the house, then out to the shed to check the flower packaging inventory. Talking about the tasks with the children helped Coral to speak more clearly, although her sentences remained short. Kenji was like a little whirlwind when he started helping around the house. Coral showed him how to wash and dry the clothes and linens, helping him fold them up and put them away.

To Coral, Hiromi and Kamika were like rays of sunshine on the rainy March mornings. Hiromi introduced her to Japanese food. Ramen noodles, with broth and vegetables from the Satsuma's garden, was her new favorite meal. Coral and James started cooking dinner for everyone at night. Conversations about the farm continued until everyone was sure of the next steps.

The biggest problem was still the shortage of money. The thirty-day extension from the bank was ticking down. Coral felt the strain, racking her brain to come up with anything to bring in cash for the loan payment.

"Do you think...we can sell some small lilies...at the Farmers' Market?" Coral asked Hiromi.

"You can share our rented space with me when I go in on Saturday. The men will be working to ensure the bigger lilies are doing well for the Easter shipments. How much would you charge for the smaller flowers?" Hiromi asked.

"A small bundle...with some ferns. Maybe five or...six bucks," Coral said. "And churches need flowers...for Sunday services. Maybe sell some there?"

"Are you up to doing that much work right now? How about talking with the doctor first? You are recovering well, and we don't want any stress to get in the way of that," Hiromi stated.

Coral knew Hiromi was right. If she pushed herself too hard too fast, she could have another stroke. "Talk to Doc McGuire... see what's what."

The doctor approved the Farmers' Market idea, but limited Coral to one day per week for the next four weeks to visit churches for possible orders. He knew that she would need a few days to recover from a day of talking and selling.

Kamika was excited to help with this project. Coral taught her how to cut ferns for the flower bouquets and how to arrange the greenery and flowers, then tie them with colorful ribbons and wrap them. Coral and Kamika worked together, Kamika singing songs to Coral and handling the flowers like baby bird eggs.

Coral knew Hiromi was nervous about taking her to the market, where there were many vendors selling and many people coming and going all day. Coral told her that she would "be a good girl" and take a rest at lunchtime. Yoshio offered to go with them, but Coral was not having it.

"Amos and James need you. Kamika can watch me. She is pretty...attract people to flowers," Coral explained.

Kamika was quick to approve that idea. "Papa, I take care of Mrs. Coral. She tell me what to say. I sell flowers gooder than anyone."

"The word is 'better,' not 'gooder,' What would you say to get me to buy some flowers?" Yoshio asked.

Kamika looked at the flowers and then at Coral. "I say, 'These flowers are for special people. You have special people, don't you? They will love to get flowers from you!'"

Hiromi laughed and said, "She has you there! That was quite a sales pitch."

Coral was delighted with Kamika's insightful wit and how quickly she got to the heart of the matter. She was right. Flowers were tokens of love.

On the morning of the next Farmers' Market, they loaded up Hiromi's station wagon with Hiromi's vegetables and Coral's flower bundles. James made them sandwiches to eat and packed a thermos of hot cocoa as a special treat. After Coral, Hiromi, and Kamika had gone, James and Kenji cleaned up the kitchen and went out to the barn to work on the equipment.

Questions Answered

Kenji asked James where the tools and lubricants were kept. On Saturdays, equipment maintenance came first. Today, they would clean the loader and the tractor and look for loose parts to tighten down. They worked steadily for about an hour, then Kenji asked, "James, are you going to stay on the farm after you finish school?"

"I haven't really thought about it. I s'pose I could get lots of different jobs now that I can fix machinery. I can operate the tractor and the loader, so I could work on a bigger farm for money. I can cook, so I could work at a restaurant in town. But, I don't know if I could leave Pa alone here. I'm the only family he has left," James told him.

Kenji was glad that James had opened up to him. They didn't have much time together, and when they did, they always talked about school or the farm. "Where is your mother?"

James bowed his head and swallowed before he could answer. "About seven years ago, my ma and little sister were visiting a neighbor's farm where they grew wheat. It was the middle of the summer and very hot. A spark from a passing car started a fire in the field. The men were working on the other side of the hill and didn't see the smoke until the fire had burned most of the way into the house. I don't remember all of the details, but they died in the fire."

Kenji was horrified that he had stirred up such a painful memory for his new friend. "I am so sorry, James. I feel terrible for making you remember that. It must have been very hard for you afterward."

James nodded. "A grass fire is no joke around here. They spread quicker 'n lightning. We have all been trained to fight fires. If you and your dad don't know how, we can teach you."

Kenji noticed how quickly James changed topics to the dangers of fire. The pain of that day was there in James's voice. "What happened after your mother and sister passed away?" Kenji asked.

"That was when Mrs. Coral took us in. She made us feel like we weren't alone. We could come to her and her children if we needed help. I cried in Mrs. Coral's arms off and on for about three weeks. At first, Pa wouldn't talk about it. He just clammed up and found extra work to do."

It's been seven years. I wonder if he's noticed how things have changed since we started working together, Kenji thought. "Does it feel different to you now? Your dad seems to be happy, and he likes working with us to help Mrs. Russell. We all look forward to coming here. I will talk to my father about firefighting. We should know how to do that so we can be safe and help our neighbors. You have already taught me so much about machinery! But I always seem to get too much grease on my clothes," Kenji said.

James laughed, "That's the only way to learn! You're doing a fine job helping in the house, too. And thanks for working with me on my homework. Benita used to help me before she left for college. She will be a very good teacher, I think."

Kenji inspected the tractor motor and thought he spotted a problem. "Look, James. The belt is breaking apart on this edge. Do we need to replace it?" Kenji asked.

"I think you can handle it. I am going to check in with Pa to see if he needs me to do anything for him. I'll see you in the kitchen later." James waved goodbye and walked north toward the planted hills.

The Farmer's Market brigade returned to the farm at 5:00, when the sun's rays flamed golden and orange across the horizon and the sky turned a deeper blue.

Hiromi called Kenji to take Kamika inside to wash up, while she and Coral unloaded the station wagon. Coral walked into the kitchen and sat at the table. James poured her a glass of iced tea and started to prepare dinner.

"How did the sales go at the Farmers' Market?" James asked.

"Really good. We sold out...all the bundles!...$85. Kamika worked hard. I talked to Suzy Jenkins...mostly," Coral summed up the day.

"Well! That's good news. What a great idea you had," he told her.

"Thank you, James. What's for dinner?" Coral beamed at him as he washed the potatoes.

"Looks like we're gonna have a fish fry with all the trimmings. Mr. Satsuma brought over two big fish called 'Mahi Mahi.' I'm gonna make fried potatoes and onions. And Mr. Satsuma said his wife is making a big salad."

"Mmmm Mmmm! I think I can make dessert. Pineapple..." Coral flipped her hands over, "cake?"

"You know that's Pa's favorite. Are you sure you can handle it? I don't want you to wear yourself out."

"Now, now. I feel... fine. Kamika can help."

Soon the smells of food cooking wafted through the house. Amos and Yoshio came in from the farm. Kenji set the table. Kamika put the pineapple and cherries on the bottom of the pan, then Coral poured in the cake batter. Hiromi made a light batter for the beautiful white fish, with a creamy sauce to go with it. Everyone was eager to dig in, but Coral stood up at the head of the table before the meal began.

"You all are...so dear to me. I feel...my family is so big. The empty places...in my heart...are full now." Coral noticed Hiromi blush and a small tear roll down Kenji's cheek. "We owe you...so much. I know you must return home...to your work...your children. You are always...welcome here. Now, let's eat!" Coral said with a joyful smile.

The table was quiet for a few moments, then Kamika said, "We love you, Mrs. Coral. You like Gramama to me."

Yoshio nodded. Hiromi bent over and ruffled Kamika's shiny black hair.

"Please pass...salad, Little Flower," Coral said. Then everyone began to fill their plates and talk about the day. The lilies were growing well and would produce a good cash crop in another four weeks, just in time for Easter and spring celebrations. But money for the loan payment was due, and the supplies for the shipments were also running low.

Early one morning, a week later, Hiromi and Kamika showed up at Lily Hills. "I have so much to do today," Hiromi said to Coral. "Would it be alright if I left Kamika with you? She is learning to fold laundry and sweep. If you could encourage her in these activities, she will learn faster."

"Sure thing," Coral replied. "We have lots to do here. I have letters to write to Polly and Benita."

"Thank you so much. Your speech is getting better every day. You must be practicing with James." Hiromi nodded to Coral. Then she looked over at Kamika and said, "Remember your promise. I will be back around lunchtime."

"Yes, Mama. I take good care of Mrs. Coral. I help her, and she help me." Kamika smiled at Coral and waved goodbye as Hiromi returned to the station wagon.

"Do you know how to write a letter, Kamika?" Coral asked. "It is a way we talk to each other, 'specially when we are far apart. Let's go to the study. I can write my letters at the desk." She took Kamika's hand and sat her by the end table where she could write or color.

"Kenji taught me to write my name. Can I show you?" Kamika asked proudly.

"The word is 'taught,' not 'teached.'
I will get some paper and a pen for you.
Come over here and sit in the big chair with
me."

Kamika climbed up next to Coral and
looked at the large, wood rolltop desk. Coral
pushed up the cover, revealing all of the
little compartments. Kamika clapped her
hands with delight. "Wow! It's like a big box
of little presents."

Coral reached into a large compartment
on the left side of the desk and took out a
few sheets of paper for them to use. She
gave Kamika a pen, and she began to write
her name. She wrote the letters carefully,
so that they were straight and even on the
page.

"Kenji did a good job when he taught you
to write your name. It is so straight...and
easy to read," Coral complimented Kamika.

"What is in that little space?" Kamika
pointed to one of the cubicles that had a
small booklet in it. "Is it a storybook? I like
stories."

Coral reached into the opening for the
small booklet, then laid it on the desk.
She switched on the desk lamp so that she
could see it better. It was a bank account
passbook. She remembered that Jesse
had taken all of the children to the bank
when they were about Kenji's age and
opened savings accounts for each of them.
Each child earned money by helping out

neighbors with chores on their farms. They put the money into their savings accounts and used it later to buy birthday and Christmas presents for family and friends. *Maybe this passbook was one of the boy's?* she wondered.

Coral opened the passbook and examined it more carefully. She was stunned by what she saw. Kamika looked worried when Coral stopped talking. "Are you okay? What is wrong? Should I get Amos?"

Coral blinked her eyes a few times and smiled down at Kamika. "Do you know what this is?"

Kamika shook her head. "It not a storybook."

Coral took a deep breath, and her eyes widened as she flipped through the little booklet, finally landing on the last page with writing. "This is a bank book. I had completely forgotten about this. My Jesse opened a savings account for us at the bank...when we got married. He never mentioned it again, so I never paid it any mind."

Kamika smiled at Coral and said, "This is you money that you need for the farm. Yes?"

"You're right about that, Little Flower. Do you see these lines of numbers? This is Jesse's writing. It looks like he was adding money to this account practically every month for twenty years! This little book shows that there was $57,486 in this account when Jesse died. And then because this is a *savings* account, the bank adds money to it. They call that 'interest.' That means this account has even *more* than fifty-seven thousand dollars in it because it's been earning interest for the twelve years since Jesse passed away."

Coral sat quietly and thought about how the bank staff had been treating her like she wasn't as important or as valuable to them as her husband. And now she had evidence that the bank was holding their money. How could they not have mentioned this account when Jesse died, or at least when she applied for the loan to buy the farm equipment? "I guess we need to go to the bank and look into this. Are you willing to go with me?" Coral asked.

"Oh yes! Much better than do sweep or folding," Kamika replied.

Hidden Treasure

Robert Browning considered himself to be
a man of the people. At 5' 11" tall, slim with
warm brown eyes and a friendly smile, he
inspired confidence in the people he worked
with at the First National Bank of Portland,
the oldest bank in Oregon. There, he was
inspired by the founders' determination
to create a financial institution that would
support the citizens and businesses in
the growing city of Portland. When Robert
moved to Salem with his family, he applied
for a position with Farmers and Merchants
Bank. He learned a great deal there. Salem,
in the heart of the central valley, was home
to the largest agricultural businesses on the
West Coast. They grew wheat, rye, barley,
oats, grass, and many other crops that were
sold throughout the country.

Robert was surprised when Coral Russell
came into the bank with a little Japanese
girl in tow. His office assistant informed him
that Mrs. Russell had asked for a meeting
with him today on a matter of great
importance. Don Jackson had told him that
she was behind in her farm equipment loan

payment. *That's probably why she's here today,* Robert predicted. He knew that she was recovering from a stroke and that he should take extra care with her concerns. He told his assistant to bring Mrs. Russell to his office in ten minutes.

Kamika had never been in a bank before and had many questions for Coral. "This is big building. What do people do here?"

"The people who work here help us to manage our businesses by keeping our money safe," Coral told her.

"Is money not safe in you house?" Kamika asked.

Coral thought about how to explain this to her. "If I kept the money in my house, there could be a fire that would burn the house, barn, and the shed. That happened to our neighbor about eight years ago. They had their money in the house, and it burned up. This bank loaned them some money to rebuild their house. Do you understand?"

"Yes. Money not burn up in big building of stone. Poor neighbors have to start over again. I feel bad for them."

At that moment, Robert's assistant came over to escort them to his office. Robert stood, running one hand through his hair, welcoming them with a big smile. He helped Coral into a comfortable chair and brought over a smaller chair next to her for Kamika to sit on.

"Would you like some water or coffee?" he asked.

"No, thank you, Mr. Browning. I just need to talk with you about my husband, Jesse's, savings account."

Robert wrinkled his brow, looking confused and startled. "I didn't know Jesse had a savings account with us. I worked with him on the business operating account for several years. But I think Don Jackson took over handling that account before your husband passed away."

Coral handed him the bank passbook that she had found in the desk that morning. "Could you please look up this account? The last deposit was in September 1940. There is quite a bit of money there that has never been withdrawn. That would sure come in handy for three months of loan payments for our farm equipment."

Robert sat down carefully at his desk. He knew that Jesse Russell had been dead for more than ten years, and so the amount in the account would have grown substantially since the date of the last entry in the passbook. "Let me check into this. I'm sorry that I didn't work with your husband more closely. He was a good man, and you have done a wonderful job with Lily Hills."

Coral looked down at Kamika, sitting quietly in her chair and listening to them talking. "I would like to keep the bank book. If you could write down the information you need to research the account, I will wait."

"Of course," Robert said, then he wrote down the account number, date range for the deposits, and the final balance showing on the last date of entry.

Coral stood up and took Kamika's hand. Robert returned the bank book to her and shook her hand warmly. "Thank you for coming to see me. I hope to have news for you very soon."

Kamika was strangely silent on the way back to the Satsuma home with Coral. Coral looked over at her often, wondering what she was thinking about. When they reached the Satsuma home, Coral asked, "Are you alright, honey? You haven't said a word since we left the bank."

"I'm okay, Mrs. Coral. I have money, but not in bank," Kamika said.

Just then, Hiromi emerged from the side door of the house carrying a basket of vegetables. She opened the passenger's side door of the truck and urged Kamika to get out. Hiromi put the basket on the floor of Coral's truck and said, "Here are some fresh vegetables for you to keep your strength up. We will be over later to talk. Thank you for watching Kamika for me today."

"Thanks for the vegetables. I will make a pot of soup for me and the boys this afternoon. If I make some biscuits to go with it, we'll have a great meal. Kenji does love my biscuits!" With a wave to Kamika,

Coral pulled the truck around and drove back toward her farm.

After Hiromi and Kamika went into their house, they sat in the kitchen. Bright yellow sunlight poured onto the tabletop from the open window. The sound of birds chattering seemed to penetrate Kamika's consciousness. She smiled up at her mother, who asked, "What have you been doing this morning, Little Flower?"

Kamika briefly narrated how she had shown Coral that she could write her name and the discovery of the bank book. "We drove to the city and went to the bank. It is so big! She tell me about why banks are here. She say to keep money for ev'ybody safe." Here she paused and tried to think of how to ask the questions she had.

Hiromi said, "Do you have any questions for me? It looks like there is a lot on your mind."

"Yes, Mama. Is you money safe in bank? Is Papa's money safe in bank? Mrs. Coral say all her children have bank books. I not have bank book. Why?"

"Now that is a very good question. You learned a lot about banks today. Do you have any money to put in the bank?" Hiromi asked.

"Yes, Mama. I have five pennies and two nikses that I finded on the road."

"The word is 'found,' not 'finded.' And a nickel is the same amount as five pennies.

I think we need to teach you about money and start paying you for the chores you do for us and Mrs. Russell. We will do the same for Kenji. When both of you have saved enough, we will go to the bank to keep your money safe. But I must talk to your father about this first."

Kamika's eyes opened wide as she thought about going to the bank again. "I learn about numbers now. Kenji will teach me. And I will write more and better soon and read all the books."

"Well! You have a lot of interesting things ahead of you. But let's make some ramen for lunch first. What would you like in it today?" Hiromi asked.

Kamika ran outside to gather vegetables, and soon the soup was ready. After lunch, Kamika went to the living room to look at some of the magazines her father had left on the tea table. Hiromi found her asleep on the floor, with her face lying on a *Time* magazine. She picked up Kamika and carried her to the bedroom. "Don't grow up too fast, Little Flower. I do so love the child that you are today." She leaned over and kissed her forehead before quietly closing the door.

As Coral became more active, working around the farm and in the house, she felt more secure and hopeful that she could put the stroke behind her. One afternoon in early April, Kenji showed up at the farm promptly after the school bus dropped him off on the road. He shouldered his backpack and ran up the drive to the house. Now that the flower harvest was getting closer, dirt was constantly tracked in by Amos, James, and Coral. His first task would be sweeping and disposing of the dirt, especially in the kitchen. But it was present all through the house. He started sweeping the kitchen, humming one of his favorite songs.

Coral was talking to herself in the study and didn't notice Kenji's arrival. When he was almost finished, she came into the kitchen to check the pot of stew simmering on the stove.

"I didn't hear you come in, Kenji. How was school today?" Coral asked as she stirred and sampled the stew.

"School is always very interesting," Kenji said as he deposited the dirt and dust in the garbage bin "But we learned about something today that I don't understand. The teacher said I should understand it because of what happened to Japanese people in America during World War II. She called it 'prejudice.' It sounds very bad. Do you know how it happens?"

"Benita mentioned that your father told her that both he and your mom were placed in internment camps in California. They didn't do anything wrong. But the government was worried about Japanese people in the United States after the attack on Pearl Harbor. The government was afraid that the Japanese people living here would be loyal to Japan, and not America," Coral said. "Maybe we should sit down at the kitchen table." She sat down with him and asked, "Do you understand what I am saying?"

"What are internment camps?" Kenji asked.

"They are places where people have to live who have been forced out of their homes. The places are not very nice. And the people who forced them to move didn't know anything about them, only that they were Japanese. They were not allowed to leave the camps until the war was over."

Coral held up her hand and continued. "The same prejudice happened to Negroes in America and Native tribes. They were moved to places where they could be contained, and they were not considered equal to White men and women. This is an important idea for you to understand. If you saw a person sitting on a bus bench that was Negro, what would you think about that person?"

"I would think that the person wanted to catch a bus to go somewhere," Kenji replied.

"Prejudice is judging what a person is like without knowing anything about them. If you saw that person on the bench hitting a child sitting next to him, what would you think then?"

Kenji looked puzzled and said, "I'm not sure. Maybe the child was bad. Or maybe the person was mean. It would depend on what they were saying, the looks on their faces, and what was happening around them."

Coral smiled at him. "Yes, you would look for more information. I wish everyone did that. People make decisions about what they see very quickly. They don't really think about it. It's because their thoughts have been influenced by others—their parents, their religion, and their community. Some people are afraid of anything different from them. That fear makes them say bad things or act to drive the different people away."

Kenji said, "We learned about slavery in school. Negroes were brought to America as slaves to landowners. And President Lincoln wanted them to have the same rights as other people. And they fought the Civil War, and Negroes were freed from slavery."

Coral caressed Kenji's cheek and looked sad. "Ahhh. That is a very small part of the story. Even when Negroes were freed from slavery, in many Southern States that used slaves, they were still considered property.

They were not given the same rights as White people. Many families were broken apart. The men travelled to the northern states to find jobs so they could free their wives and children from ownership by White people. Negroes could not vote for people in government who would stand up for their rights. And so, White people continued to influence laws that would keep Negroes from going to school, owning businesses or land, and worshipping God the way they wanted to. The legislators made all of these decisions without knowing much about the people the laws were affecting. That is what prejudice means."

Kenji gritted his teeth. "That is so very wrong! How could people here let that happen?"

Coral said, "Just like you, they are not taught the whole story. The history books were written by White people who wanted to make themselves look better than they really were. White people did the same things to Native tribes who lived on all the lands in America. In history books and movies and magazines, Native tribes are often shown as vicious, violent people, when in fact, they were fighting to hold onto their land. Most of them wanted to live in peace with the White people. But the White people wanted their land for themselves, and so made the tribes look bad to justify taking what did not belong to them. Do you understand this better now? Or do you have more questions?"

Kenji's face was starting to turn red, and tears began falling from his eyes. He put his head down on his arms and cried. Coral pulled him into her lap and put her arms around him. "You have a good heart, Kenji. Trust it when you feel that something is bad," Coral told him.

"Oh, Mrs. Russell. How can people be so mean to each other? It isn't right!" Kenji said, wiping the tears from his face.

Coral took a handkerchief from her sleeve, handed it to Kenji, and told him to blow his nose. She held his head up to look into his eyes. "Look at me now. There are many, many good people all around us. Many White people tried to help the Native tribes and the Negroes who were trying to live in freedom. But they are not talked about in history books. Look at what your family has done for me and my family. It is up to good people to stand up for those who are misjudged by others. To treat each other fairly, we must take the time to get to know one another. We must share love and teach this to our children. School books leave too much information in the shadows."

The Lily Harvest

Yoshio stopped at the flower farm on his
way home from work to talk with Amos.
It would soon be "all hands on deck"
to prepare the lilies for shipment. They
had orders from California, Oregon, and
Washington, plus some coming in from
Idaho recently. Yoshio needed to review the
supplies on hand and determine what would
be needed to fill the orders. Yoshio found
Amos in the supply shed. "Hello, Amos.
How are you feeling? Not too overworked
yet, I hope."

"Thanks for asking, Mr. Satsuma. The
boys have been a big help. Jimmy marked
all of the boxes here with the total number
of shipping containers and packing
material. We can go over the supply list
tonight if you have a few minutes. Coral
and your wife are going to take care of the
orders in town. They will be put in vases
with florist wet padding for delivery. I still
don't know where the money will come from
to buy all of these things, but Coral seems

to have a plan. She hasn't talked to me about it much. She made stew and biscuits for dinner. Let's go in and have some before we start to work."

"Sounds good to me. And you know, you are supposed to call me Yoshio. We are friends now."

"Thank you. I just can't help but remember how you stopped me from deckin' that snooty Don Jackson. You saved my hide, and no joke, I'm grateful to you."

"Thank you, Amos. I only did what was needed at the time. Time to go in. I am hungry!"

That evening, when Yoshio returned home, he took off his shoes and left his briefcase in the hall on the table. Hiromi was waiting for him in the living room with moonflower tea, one of their favorites. She heard him and motioned for him to be quiet and come sit next to her. She served their tea and began to relate the story about Coral's trip to the bank.

"I am concerned about the bank book that Coral found. Kamika said it was Jesse's bank book, and Coral didn't know about it. If that is true, there may be some money to help Coral through this time. Could you go to the bank with her? She may need some support to fight for Jesse's money, especially if it was not mentioned in his will," Hiromi said.

"I will need to research the property laws in Oregon concerning family members. She should be entitled to ownership of his property after he passes away. I hope that the farm property is now in her name. She may need a lawyer to help her with the legal paperwork, but we can research the laws at the college library."

The next morning, Kenji was sitting at the kitchen table when his father walked in for his morning tea. "Papa, I ask pardon for listening to your conversation with Mama last night. I wanted to talk to you, but you were talking to Mama about other things. I am sorry."

Yoshio took a sip of tea and sat down. "I forgive you, my son. Thank you for being honest with me. You need to realize *when* it is the right time to talk to someone. If that person is talking to someone else, you need to come back another time. Is there something else?"

"Yes, Papa. I want to help more than doing simple chores. I heard you say that Mrs. Russell needs to know what the property laws are in our state. I can read about them and ask my teacher questions. I can take good notes and give them to you."

"That is a very generous offer. But I have a more important job for you. I want you to teach Kamika about money. First, you can both learn about coin and paper currency. We will test you to make sure you understand. The *value* of money is harder to teach. Your mama will have some helpful suggestions for you there. Second, we have set a goal for you of $10 each to open an account at the bank. We will establish some rules for you both on how to use the money."

Kenji sighed, and Yoshio saw the disappointment in his face. "Kenji, the laws Coral will have to deal with are hard to understand because of the way they are written. There are a lot of terms and language you will not understand until you are older and have had some experience reading legal documents. I will bring home a business contract for us to study. Can you be patient?"

"Yes, Papa. Sometimes it seems like there is so much to know, I will never have enough time to learn it all."

Just then, Hiromi walked into the kitchen to make breakfast. "Such a serious discussion for so early in the morning! I will have to make pancakes to cheer everyone up."

Yoshio laughed, and Kenji ran into the bedroom to wake Kamika. Hiromi's pancakes were a treat never to be missed.

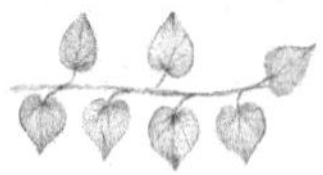

Five days later, Yoshio and Coral journeyed into town to meet with Robert Browning at the bank. They had discussed the Oregon state laws regarding property rights after a spouse has passed away. Under Jesse's will, Coral and their children had jointly inherited the farm property. Under Oregon inheritance law, Coral inherited all other property belonging to Jesse, including the newly discovered savings account. The question remained in Coral's mind: *Why was this information not shared with me?*

When Yoshio and Coral entered Robert's office, Coral politely asked, "Could Don Jackson participate in this meeting?"

"I don't see why not. Hold on while I ask him to join us," Robert said.

Don entered the office, looked over at Coral, and grimaced. Then he noticed Yoshio. He gasped and immediately addressed him. "Mr. Satsuma, why are you here? Is anything the matter with your accounts?"

Robert asked Don to sit down, saying, "This meeting is about Mrs. Russell's accounts, which I believe you manage for her. Is that so?"

"That is true. She is almost in default on the loan we gave her for the farm equipment purchase. I guess she will have to return the equipment to us."

Robert was very quiet after this statement from Don. Yoshio squeezed Coral's hand, and she stood up to address Don. "I recently found out that Jesse had a savings account with the bank. The account had $57,486 in it when he died. Why didn't you mention that when I came to the bank to request a loan to purchase new equipment for the farm?"

Don jumped out of his seat and took a step toward her. "That money belonged to him! If Jesse wanted you to have it, he would have given you the bank book before he died. Obviously, he didn't think you deserved to have it. Besides, what would you have done with that money? Spent it on yourself, that's what! No woman understands what it takes to run a business."

Coral crossed her arms over her chest and glared at him. "I'm within my rights to sue you and the bank for withholding money that is legally mine under Oregon inheritance laws. I've hired a lawyer, and he will be serving you with documents demanding records of the account and all of the interest that has built up since my husband's death."

Robert stood up and walked out from behind his desk. "Don, how dare you speak to Mrs. Russell that way? She is right and you know it!"

Don yelled at Robert, "I'm just treating her the way she ought to be treated is all. And Mr. Satsuma, too. He thinks he's so important because his company keeps its money here."

"Coral Russell has kept the Lily Hills farm business going without Jesse. She buried two sons who died fighting for this country, and she sent her two daughters to college," Robert said. "And she did all of that *without* Jesse's money."

Robert turned to Coral and Yoshio and said quietly, "I am deeply sorry for the way Mr. Jackson has treated both of you. He doesn't know it yet, but his time here has come to an end. Mrs. Russell, you now have over $100,000 in the account that Jesse opened with us. That money is yours to use as you wish. I have the current balance and would be happy to update your bank book with the information. The account will be transferred into your name today."

Robert took a few steps away from his desk and motioned for Don to follow him to a corner of his office. "I'd like to fire you in front of every employee in this bank right now, but I am a better businessman than that. Pack up your office and go home. Your final paycheck will be sent to you in the mail."

Don's mouth gaped open. His face turned bright red as his hands balled into fists at his side. He grabbed the handle of the office door, walking quickly away from Robert and the customers in his office. Robert watched as Don left the office to ensure that he didn't disrupt other customers on the bank floor. Coral clasped her hands in her lap, peering down at her worn-out, laced-up, black boots. She shook her head, then looked up at Yoshio.

After Robert returned to the chair behind his desk, Yoshio spoke up. "My family and I have been working with Mrs. Russell and her family since she returned from the hospital. None of us can succeed without help when unfortunate medical or other situations arise. What surprised me the most was how much Mrs. Russell helped me and my family to grow during our time with her, Amos, and his son, James. We have been taught to fight fires. We are now deeply tied to the land and have become better neighbors. Mrs. Russell and her kin have shared their home, their traditions and taken care of our children. No one else has reached out to us the way they have. I know Mrs. Russell does not want to sue the bank. She just wants to be treated fairly and with respect. We all deserve that."

Robert stood up and walked over to them. "You are absolutely right, Mr. Satsuma. Looks like I need to attend more staff meetings." He looked embarrassed by the scene in his office. "This bank owes you a lot, Mrs. Russell. What can I do to help you?"

"How would you feel about helping to deliver flower shipments in town on the weekends?" Coral asked.

"I would be honored. Can I help you withdraw $10,000 from your account today to buy supplies to prepare those shipments? You can pay back the missed loan payments after your customers start paying for the flowers. I'll show up at 8:00 on Saturday morning to help with flower shipments or delivering supplies. Come in or call when you have time to talk. I'd like to know how things are going."

When Coral and Yoshio got back to Coral's farm, Kenji, Kamika, and James were preparing arrangements using the supplies in the shed. Coral asked everyone to stop what they were doing so they could discuss changes to the shipment responsibilities. Then she got on the phone to order more supplies. Yoshio told Amos that Robert Browning had volunteered to use his truck to deliver the prepared flowers or pick up supplies in town on the weekends. Kenji and James kept working under Hiromi's supervision, but Kamika crept away to find Coral.

"What happened at the bank?" Kamika asked.

"It turns out that Jesse's bank account had a lot more money in it than we thought. And we found out that Mr. Jackson knew about the account, but didn't tell me. He could have made a lot of trouble for the bank, so Mr. Browning fired him. You and

I will now be in charge of preparing the flowers. I can't wait for the new ribbons and vases to get here!"

"Really? I can do it. I am best at getting the flowers and ribbons together." Kamika paused and looked closely at Coral. "Are you happy now?"

Coral reached down to hug her. "Well, I am feeling much better. I need to call Benita and Polly and tell them about the money so that they will stop worrying. Why don't you see if James is making some sandwiches for lunch? You could help him with that ." Coral watched Kamika run out of the study, yelling for James. She shook her head, thinking, *She sure is a little whirlwind when there's work to be done.*

During the next week, school was closed for Easter break. Kenji and James worked at the farm from dawn until dusk, helping to unload supplies and load shipments for delivery. Robert Browning showed up on Saturday morning wearing jeans, a plaid shirt, and work boots. He was skeptical about Kamika doing the floral arranging. So she walked him out to the shed where the packaging supplies were laid out on a large wooden table.

Kamika handed him an apron and said, "You wear this to keep you clothes clean. And I show you how to do it." She laid out the greenery, including Snow Berry and Sweet Woodruff leafy branches. Then she cut several lengths of yellow ribbon using a ruler for exact lengths.

Robert was amazed at how Kamika expertly weaved the yellow ribbon around the greenery and lily flower stems and buds, then tied them into neat, beautiful arrangements for shipping. When the truck was loaded, Robert bought one of the larger arrangements from Coral after they bargained like old fishwives over the price. After he finished offloading the truck with Yoshio, he brought the beautiful arrangement into the bank, setting it in an area where everyone could see it. On Monday morning, the bank staff "oohed" and "aahed" and asked about placing orders with Coral for their families.

The week flew by. Every day after lunch, Coral sat in the study with Amos and Yoshio, who was on vacation that week, to coordinate incoming and outgoing shipments. On Thursday morning, the farm's old red truck finally broke down after they had fully loaded the bed with shipping containers.

Coral called Robert to explain and ask, "Could I borrow or rent a truck in town?"

"I'll take the morning off and bring you mine to use," Robert said graciously. His truck was painted a deep blue, with large chrome bumpers and black mud flaps. The bed was larger than Coral's truck, and there was more room in the cab as well.

Amos, James, Kenji, and Robert transferred the shipping containers from one truck to the other. By the time they were finished, Robert was sweating. "Whew! I haven't worked that hard in many years. But thanks to you all, the truck is ready to go."

Yoshio drove the truck around the farm for a little while to get the feel of it before he went into town. Meanwhile, Robert walked around the house to the kitchen entrance in the back. He grabbed a towel and washed his face and hands at the sink. Then he sat down to lunch with the entire work crew. Coral introduced him to Amos and James, Hiromi and Kenji.

"How is everything going?" Robert asked. "Easter is just three days away!"

Coral beamed at him. "Couldn't be better. Except for the truck breaking down, we would be ahead of schedule. We only have one more load to ship out tomorrow morning, and then you can deliver the church arrangements to town on Saturday."

After lunch, Kenji and James excused themselves to check out what was wrong with Coral's old truck. James tried to get the engine to start, but it was evident that the power was not being transferred to turn the motor over. James thought that the alternator would need to be replaced. But Amos or Yoshio would have to go into town to buy the part. When Yoshio returned to the farm, the boys told him what they had found when they examined the truck motor. After helping Hiromi dry the dishes from lunch, Robert came out of the house. He listened to Yoshio talking with the boys about fixing the old truck. The battered, red truck had served the Russell family for almost twenty years.

Robert walked back into the house to discuss an idea with Coral. He found her in the study talking with Amos. "Thank you for lunch, Mrs. Russell. I was wondering if you would be interested in buying my truck. My family doesn't use it very much. It's only five years old, with low mileage, and I make sure it is tuned up every year. I would sell it to you for a very good price. Will you at least think about it?"

Amos's mouth dropped open. Coral watched Amos's face as his reaction to Robert's offer became apparent. Before Amos could say something offensive, she took a deep breath and answered his question. "I certainly will think about it, Mr. Browning. I'll just have to go over the finances after the money from the flower shipments comes in. Now, I'm sure you need to get back to the bank. But we really appreciate the loan of your truck this morning."

"Why don't you keep it until Saturday? I'll be here first thing Saturday morning to make deliveries. Maybe Hiromi can drive me back into town now? Then we can meet at the bank next week to discuss whether you would like to buy the truck or return it."

There was no doubt that the truck was needed for the next few days, but Coral felt bad about using it without giving Robert something in return. "How about this? I'll pay you six dollars a day for the use of your truck until Monday."

"Make it four dollars a day, and you have a deal. Remember, you still have to put gas in the truck."

They shook hands, and Robert went to find Hiromi to ask her to drive him back to the bank. Amos was shaking his head when Yoshio came in to talk with Coral. "Would you believe this? Mr. Browning is renting his truck to us until next Monday. Coral worked out the whole deal with him. And I just sat there with my head spinning!" Amos told Yoshio.

"Mrs. Russell is quite the negotiator. I have seen her at work. This is good news. After talking with the boys and checking the engine, it would probably cost more than the rental cost to get it running, not to mention the hours needed to work on it." Yoshio looked over at Coral. "I knew Mr. Browning was a good man after he talked with us at the bank. He is like a shepherd looking after his flock."

Coral nodded. "He offered to sell me his truck, and I am seriously considering it. But now we need to get back to work if we are going to get all the shipments out on time."

The shipments were delivered with no further delays. Coral knew that she had enough money to negotiate with Robert for his truck, even without the income from the recent shipments. She called Benita to talk with her about it.

"Mom, you know what is needed at the farm. Dad's old truck is on its last legs. And you need reliable transportation. How much do you think he will charge you for it?"

"James is doing some research to see what a good price would be for that model year. He said that they originally sold for fifteen hundred dollars. The mileage is very low for a five-year-old truck. I'm thinking that twelve hundred fifty dollars would be a fair price," Coral told her.

"That seems like a lot of money, Mom. Can you afford it?"

"I wouldn't even consider buying it if I couldn't. Now don't you worry. Robert and I will figure it out. You'll be coming home for Christmas, won't you? I can't wait to see you and Polly. I miss you girls so much."

"We miss you, too, Mama. Please tell James how much I appreciate his letters. It feels like I am there with you when I read them. Let's talk next week. Love you."

Benita hung up, and Coral sighed. Children grow up so fast.

Special Times

A month later, southern Oregon was basking in June's radiant sunshine. The trees had leafed out to shade the front porch, and Coral decided to sit in her rocking chair to enjoy the late spring afternoon. She emptied her mind to let the sounds and smells of her farm wrap her in comfortable memories. On days like this, she and Jesse would walk the hills, designating where the new bulbs would be planted, looking for birds' nests in the trees, and eating ripe peaches from the Farmers' Market. She was surprised to see Kenji walking up the road to the house. The Satsumas often came by to visit, but they were not spending as much time with her as they had right after her stroke. Coral missed the sense of extended family she had when they were with her.

Kenji walked up to the porch and smiled at Coral. He climbed the steps and handed her an envelope with a pink ribbon tied around it. "Open it," he said.

It was a card from Kamika, inviting Coral to her fifth birthday party. Kenji explained, "Kamika wrote and decorated the invitation herself. She was so proud of how good it turned out. And she especially wants you to come. You don't have to bring anything but yourself. You will come, won't you?"

Coral felt tears start in her eyes. These children had become part of her family, and she had always felt that birthdays were special celebrations. "I wouldn't miss it for anything!" Coral told him. "I have some gifts for her that I know she will love. Don't tell her, though. I want it to be a surprise."

"Of course, Mrs. Russell," Kenji replied.

"Would you like to come in for some cookies and milk? James made them fresh this morning," Coral asked.

"I wish I could, but I promised Papa I would teach Kamika about money. She is getting very good at counting. Maybe she will be a teacher like Miss Benita when she grows up." Kenji waved goodbye and headed back toward his home.

The day of Kamika's party dawned clear and bright. Coral packed her gifts in a basket tied with red, yellow, and green ribbons. James had created a balloon bouquet for Kamika. And Amos had found an old wagon for her that he sanded and repainted. They loaded everything up and headed over to the Satsumas' house right after lunch. When they drove up in the blue truck, Yoshio came out to greet them.

"Welcome to our home. So, you decided to buy Mr. Browning's truck after all," he said to Coral. "I think that was a wise decision. Please come in. Can I help you with anything?" he asked.

"Hello, Yoshio. We were so happy you invited us. I think we can handle everything," Coral replied.

Hiromi came out to greet them and said, "Kenji is having trouble keeping Kamika from running out here to greet you! Please come in. I'll take you around the back way so that you can hide her birthday gifts in the pantry."

When they entered the living room, Robert Browning was sitting on the floor with Kamika playing with her origami animals. Kamika jumped up and ran to Coral. "You came! Where is James and Amos?" she asked.

"They are here, child. What are you doing on the floor?"

"I show to Mr. Robert how to make origami. It is tradition in Japan. Mama showed me how when I was only a little girl." Kamika took Coral's hand and led her to a large, comfortable chair. "Here is a pelican bird. And this is a camel."

Coral examined the tiny pieces of brightly colored, folded paper. She could

see that this skill was perfect for small
hands and for developing concentration.

Hiromi said, "Now that everyone is here,
we can start the celebration."

James walked in with his balloon
bouquet for Kamika. He stood before her
and said, "I remember my fifth birthday. My
ma made a balloon bouquet for me, and it
was the best present I ever got. I hope you
like it."

Kamika was speechless. She stared
in wonder at the colorful balloons, some
with shiny sparkles, others with "Happy
Birthday" written on them. They floated in
the air and were tied together with ribbons.
"It is a wonder!" she finally managed to say.
"Thank you, James. I love them."

Hiromi took the balloons and tied them
to a railing in the hallway, where they
bobbed merrily.

Amos was next. He pulled in the newly
refurbished wagon and parked it in front
of Kamika. "This is a wagon, and it can be
many things. For me, it was a ride down the
hill in summer. It was a cart for carrying
wood for the fire in winter. But I 'spect that
you will use it for gardening, like Coral
does." Amos blushed as he gave Kamika the
handle.

Kamika clapped her hands. "So fun, this
wagon! I show you." She ran off to her room
and came out with several stuffed animals:
a black-and-white panda bear, a yellow

rabbit with a fluffy white cotton tail, and a wolf or large dog with one missing eye. She put them all in the wagon and pulled them around the living room. Robert, James, and Kenji could not hold the laughter in.

Yoshio stopped Kamika from running and said, "You will need to give them rides in the wagon outside the house. But it is a very nice wagon."

Hiromi pulled the wagon through the kitchen onto the back porch. When she returned, Coral had retrieved the basket for Kamika from the kitchen. They walked back to the living room together.

"Kamika, come sit in the big chair with me, and I will give you my gift," Coral said. Kamika's eyes grew large as she looked at the basket. Coral removed the towel covering the top, folded it, and laid it aside. Inside were gardening gloves, a trowel, a digging spike, a large floppy hat, a long-handled forked instrument for raking the ground, two small buckets, and a pair of cutters. The buckets and the cutters had Kamika's name on them. "These are for you, Little Flower. I am hoping that you will come to the farm when you are not in school and help me plant the flower bulbs that we rescued from the rain when I found you huddled under the big oak tree."

Kamika picked up each of the items, touching them gently, and replacing them in the basket. When she put on the hat, Robert asked, "Will you let me take a picture of you and Mrs. Russell?" Kamika nodded, and Coral's face lit up with a big smile.

Kenji marveled at Robert's camera and asked if he could look at it. Robert showed him how to load the film. Then they adjusted the aperture and viewfinder. After the picture was within the frame, Kenji adjusted the knob to make everything in the frame clear and sharp.

Robert said, "Just press the button on the top to take a picture. Then we'll take one of the whole group, so that Kamika can keep it." They all arranged themselves on the steps down to the living room from the entryway. The balloon bouquet was just visible in the background. Kenji took several pictures, but Kamika and Coral were always in the center.

Two months later, as fall was beginning to blow cool, fresh breezes across the land, Kamika entered school for the first time. She was eager to explore everything, including her new classmates. Kamika's teacher quickly evaluated all the new students for their familiarity with numbers, letters, words, colors, animals, and a variety of other topics to determine where to start with them. Kamika did well in all subjects except for words. She lacked a lot of linking words, which is typical for a child growing up in a bilingual household. Other children in her class spoke Spanish, as well as English and Japanese. During the first week, they all began learning to speak full sentences in English.

Kenji's 4th grade teacher excelled in the sciences and began teaching the children to use microscopes to look at very small objects. Hiromi and Yoshio had their hands full as the children came home from school each day, bursting with their new experiences. Kenji walked Kamika to Coral's farm from the bus stop after school. He walked home to do his homework, then returned to pick her up before dinner. Kamika and Coral were planting the bulbs saved from the spring rains. Amos plowed rows for the bulbs before Kamika arrived. Coral showed Kamika how to select bulbs for planting from the warm sand barrels. As they worked together along the hillside, Coral shared her knowledge of flowers and herbs.

Kamika asked if she could take a small area near the house to plant some of her own flowers. She wanted to make bouquets with more flowers than just lilies, but she knew she had a lot to learn. Coral took her to the library to get some books on flowers. They read the books together, Kamika learning many new words and about which flowers would grow well in the southern Oregon climate.

In November, Kenji's teacher moved on to astronomy. The class was learning about constellations, comets, meteors, galaxies, and other astronomical objects. Once a week, the children came to the school at night for two hours to use the telescope housed there. Kenji and a girl named Johanna were the most enthusiastic students and always arrived early to use the telescope. They began to share books from the library to learn more about distant stars. The planets were also favorites for everyone in the class. The rings of Saturn and the great red spot on Jupiter provoked questions for days on end.

As the daylight hours dwindled, the class could start using the telescope much earlier for stargazing. The teacher warned the students that they would be moving on to world history and geography after the winter holidays. The children groaned at this, but the teacher assured them that there were lots of exciting things to learn. Trips to visit caves and the mountains were planned for early spring, depending on the amount of snow they received.

Coral had an idea that she wanted to share with the Satsuma family. She called Hiromi and asked her to come over on the Saturday morning after Thanksgiving to discuss it. When Hiromi arrived, she couldn't help but notice the twinkle in Coral's eyes.

"Good morning. I brought some tea and little Japanese sweet cakes for us."

"How lovely!" said Coral. "Thank you. I'll just add a few logs to the fire, and we can be warm and cozy in the living room."

They settled down next to the fire, sipping their tea and talking about what had been happening with their families. Coral started with her children. "Polly has been offered a position with the Oceanographic Institute in San Diego, where she has been doing some advanced studies. She was thrilled and nervous, but it was an opportunity she could not pass up. Benita will finish her teaching credentials in March and will apply for teaching positions in California, Oregon, and Utah. She wants to teach the middle grade levels. She says they are the most challenging because teachers must deal with the many changes the students are experiencing as well as the more complex educational material."

Hiromi said, "I was so hoping to meet Polly and to spend some time with Benita again before she went off to her teaching career. She really impressed us when she was here during your recovery."

"Well, that's what I wanted to talk to you about. I'd like to have your family over for Christmas Eve and Christmas Day to celebrate. Both Polly and Benita will be here then, and it will probably be the last time I see them for quite a while. I have some special gifts for Kamika and Kenji that I would like to give them with you in attendance. I realize that Christmas might not be a religious holiday for your family, but could you just think of this as a special winter party for us? What do you think?"

"I love that idea, but I will need to discuss it with Yoshio. Will you tell me about how you celebrate Christmas with your family?" Hiromi asked.

"When the children were little, we would decorate the house with lights and greenery. On Christmas Eve, we would go to church and make a big dinner together. On Christmas Day, there would be presents for everyone." Coral became quiet, and a tear trickled down from her eye. "Things changed after Jesse died and the boys went off to the war. The family was broken apart, and it seemed only to bring sadness when we tried to decorate during Christmas." She took a breath and wiped the tear away.

"This year feels different. I would really like to celebrate with family and friends."

"The children will especially be happy to celebrate with all of you here. In Japan, there are many winter celebrations. My favorite one was at the beginning of December. It is called the Chichibu Night Festival," Hiromi said.

Coral was quiet for a moment. "Could you please tell me more about why this celebration is special in Japan? I know so little about Japanese culture."

"This festival is to honor and express gratitude to the gods represented in the Chichibu Jinja Shrine. Myoken, a female deity and the dragon spirit of Mount Buko, are in love. They meet secretly at the Night Festival. There are fireworks and floats with lanterns and tapestries on them. The night is filled with drum and flute music. It was there that I had my first taste of *amazake*, a sweet rice wine that is heated for the cold winter night." Hiromi sighed at the happy memories.

How wonderful!" Coral exclaimed. "There is so much to learn. The way you and your family stepped in to help me when I needed it, I guess I should have asked about your Japanese culture earlier. I hope that you and Yoshio will share some of your traditions with us during the rest of the year."

Hiromi stood up and gathered the teapot, cups, and plates that were left empty once the cakes were eaten. She promised to call Coral soon after she talked with Yoshio, then she left to return home.

Coral went to talk with Amos about getting the Christmas decorations out of the basement and asking James to string the lights on the house and the shed.

Hiromi was taking no chances that her children would overhear her conversation with Yoshio about the celebration at Coral's farm. That night, after their baths, she played the wooden flute, and Kenji and Kamika were soundly asleep after fifteen minutes.

Still Hiromi spoke with Yoshio in Japanese. Kenji and Kamika knew many Japanese words about daily activities, but American holidays were rarely discussed. Hiromi explained Coral's request to join their winter celebration.

"Are they celebrating Christmas, the birth of the Christ child?" Yoshio asked.

"Coral said that for them the holiday was not so much about Christianity as it was about the family being together and exchanging gifts. But she was very sad when she told me that after her husband and sons had died, Christmas reminded them of all they had lost. She wants us to join them this year because of all we have done for her and the way she feels about us." Hiromi watched Yoshio's face, remembering how he felt when his parents had died. After that, the winter holidays were still celebrated, but they were touched with sadness.

Yoshio asked, "If this is to be a gift exchange celebration, what do you think we should give them? I know Coral, Amos, and

James much better now, and Benita some. But we don't know Polly at all."

Hiromi smiled at him. "We should ask Kenji and Kamika what they would like to give. They know the family better than we do. And I will ask Coral about Polly. She told me what Polly was like as a little girl—adventurous, always out exploring beyond the next hill, just like Kamika. I imagine that the vast oceans of the world are the ultimate adventure for her."

"Hmmm," Yoshio said. "I have some ideas that might work for Polly. How about a carved dolphin or whale? I used to be quite good at carving when I was young."

"Do you have enough time to do it before December twenty-fourth?" Hiromi asked.

"That is a good point. I will partner with Kenji. He always has good suggestions for me about gifts," Yoshio mused.

When Kenji and Kamika had each saved more than $10, Yoshio took them to the bank to open their own accounts. Yoshio told both his children that they could spend half of the money they saved to buy or make presents for the winter celebration. Kenji had saved thirty dollars. He bought a cookbook for James and a small china doll for Kamika. Yoshio bought a new jacket for Amos and matching sweaters for Benita and Polly. Kenji spent weeks making a picture of the planets, the sun, the asteroid belt between Mars and Jupiter, and small dots of white for the many moons in the solar system for his mother and father.

Kenji was stumped regarding a gift for Coral. He went to his mother for help and suggestions. "Mama, you know Mrs. Russell better than anyone. What do you think she would like for the winter celebration?"

Hiromi smiled at her son. "I have an idea about that. I think that she would love to get a picture of our family in a nice frame to put on the fireplace mantel next to her own family."

"You are a genius, Mama! That is the perfect gift. Can we ask Mr. Browning to take a picture of us?"

"We can do even better than that. You and James can *make* a picture frame. I bought your father a camera for his winter gift. In order to have the photograph in time for Mrs. Russell at the winter celebration, I will ask Mr. Browning to take a picture of us and get it developed in town. How does that sound?"

"I will go over and ask James if he can help me. They have so many tools there that we will need. What size should the frame be?"

Hiromi thought for a moment. "I think that eight inches high by ten inches wide is the standard size for family pictures. So you can make the frame nine by eleven, then Kamika can make a border for the picture in the frame. She can even decorate it with origami figures for Coral. I'll call over and see if James is available to help you."

Kenji found Kamika outside the house. "What are you doing, Little Flower?"

Kamika took several steps down the path toward the stream. "I was looking for the ducks or the squirrels. Even the little birds are gone. Where did they all go?"

Kenji walked with her toward the big oak tree. "Look up there," he said, pointing to the large branches farther up the tree. "The squirrels hide nuts and other food up in the tree so they won't be hungry during winter. But they stay in their dens most of the time. The ducks and other birds fly south to California, where it is warmer. They will be back in the spring."

"Oh," Kamika said. "I have been so busy with school and helping Mrs. Russell plant the lily bulbs. I didn't notice that they were gone." She looked sad; Kenji thought it was because she hadn't even said goodbye to them.

Kenji knew that the family picture for Coral would cheer her up. "I talked to Mama about what we should give to Mrs. Russell for the winter celebration. She said that we will take a family picture and give it to her. I will work with James to make a frame for the picture. And Mama said that you could make a pretty border to go around it in the frame."

Kamika clapped her hands. "We learned how to make pretty designs with colored paper and scissors last week in school. I can make snowflakes to go around the picture. It will remind her of winter, when we were together."

"That is a great idea. Let's go in and let Mama know about it."

They walked toward the house as the sun was setting. Kenji looked to the east, where the stars were appearing as the sky darkened. "Look, Kamika. There's Orion, just coming up over the horizon. This is the best time of year to see it. Orion is called 'The Hunter' because it looks like he is holding a bow for shooting arrows."

Kamika looked at the stars. "To me, they will always be twinkling like diamonds in the sky. I love that song."

When Coral woke early to decorate the house on Christmas Eve morning, it was cold, with a gentle mist of rain falling. "Polly, Benita, time to get ready for the party!" she eagerly called for her daughters. "Amos should be in at any minute with the evergreen runners to hang along the tops of the windows and doors."

Benita tied ribbons to the runners to brighten up the room. Polly placed candles on all of the side tables and along the windowsills. When Coral took out her collection of bells, Polly said, "I always rang my bell at the wrong time and screwed up the melody, but everyone just kept on singing." Coral smiled with her eyes shining at the thought while Benita and Polly broke into gales of laughter.

James came in to say good morning to the family while they were decorating. He tied an apron around his waist and went into the kitchen to make breakfast. Coral came in while the coffee was percolating on the stove. "Can I do anything to help?" she asked James.

"Yes, please. Could you set the table? I'm making some steamed milk with sugar, nutmeg, and cinnamon to go in the oatmeal."

"A perfect breakfast for a rainy morning." Coral paused. "How do you feel about the Satsumas joining us tonight?"

James hid a smile. The frame he made with Kenji was of curly maple, a rare and beautiful wood. They stained it with a light tint to highlight the swirls in the wood. Coral would be so surprised. "It will certainly be more lively than the last few Christmases we've had. Getting to know and work with Kenji and Kamika makes me feel like I have little cousins nearby," James replied.

Coral looked at James with interest. He certainly had grown into a fine young man. She no longer thought of him as Amos's little boy. James was a unique person—his lively curiosity, diligence in caring for the farm equipment, and support of his father and the Satsuma children had deepened his character. *Yes, it would be a wonderful gathering.*

At the Satsuma household, Kamika was strangely quiet. Yoshio noticed it first and asked her to sit with him near the fireplace. "Is something wrong, Kamika? You are so quiet today."

Kamika looked into his deep black eyes. She wanted so much to ask him if what she wanted to do was right, but she was afraid that he would tell her she was too little to do it. Mama would think the same way. Only Coral would understand, so she had to wait.

"It's okay, Papa. I am just excited to see everyone. Did you get a special gift for Kenji?"

"School has really improved your English. You don't sound like a baby anymore." Kamika smiled at that. "Coral, your mama and I bought a gift that we know Kenji will really like. It will be a big surprise,

so you will have to wait until tonight to
see it."

Kamika knew that she had to earn his
trust, and Mama's too, after she had broken
so many promises. She would prove to
them that she wasn't a baby anymore.

After dinner, Hiromi and Yoshio loaded
up the station wagon as the children
dressed in their warm winter finery. The
rain had stopped earlier in the afternoon,
but the roads were still muddy. Yoshio drove
slowly over to Coral's farm. The children
squirmed in their seats. He knew they
wanted to get out and run or to beg him
to drive faster, but Hiromi had talked to
them about being respectful and not selfish
this evening, so they sighed and held each
other's hands, looking out the windows to
the brightly lit house on the hill.

Candles glowed through the windows.
Benita met the family at the door and
helped them inside. Muddy shoes were left
on the porch, but she provided them with
warm socks to wear. Polly brought their
gifts over to a table set up in the corner.

Hiromi brought the children over to the
table to introduce them. "You must be Polly.
We have heard so much about you. I am
Hiromi, and these are my children, Kenji
and Kamika," she bowed as she introduced
them. "My husband is Yoshio. He went into
the kitchen to help James, as he did so
often during the flower harvest."

Polly looked more like Benita than her mother. Her black hair was tied back with a red ribbon, but some curls escaped at the sides of her heart-shaped face. She had a warm smile for them all and said, "Welcome to our home and winter celebration. I've been looking forward to meeting you. Come sit down and have some hot chocolate or apple cider." Polly paused and looked down, then took a breath. "Benita and James have written to me during the last year with details about how you have cared for Moms and helped here on the farm. I don't know how to thank you." She stuttered to a stop.

Hiromi pushed the children toward the mugs of hot chocolate and put her hand on Polly's arm. "I am told that my little Kamika is much like you were as a child—always running toward the next adventure." Polly nodded. "Coral rescued her during one spring morning when she wandered after Kenji, trying to follow him to school. It was raining hard, and Kamika got lost and took refuge under a tree. Coral found her just before the equipment Amos was driving was about to run over her."

Polly gasped. "Well, I didn't hear that part of the story! So that's how you all met. The little scamp! I feel for you. I 'bout drove Moms crazy. It was Dad who civilized me."

Hiromi shook her head. "It's more than that. In Japanese tradition, our family owed your mother a life debt. This concept is central to Japanese social structure. It emphasizes the reciprocal nature of relationships and the importance of repaying obligations."

Hiromi continued, "We tried to explain that to your mother, but she was having none of it. To her, Kamika was just a child who needed help, and she was there to give it. The children became attached to her very quickly. I think her loving spirit drew them in. And so, when she needed help, we were happy to be there for her. And now we are more than friends, and the life debt is paid."

At that point, Coral came into the room. She chatted happily with Kenji and Kamika, who were sitting on a bench near the fire drinking their hot chocolate. She smiled at their chocolate mustaches and offered them napkins.

"How's about we open some of these gifts?" Amos asked. He started handing the wrapped packages to the recipients. Ooohs and aaahs floated around the room as the gifts were opened. James hugged Kenji to thank him for the cookbook, and Kenji was just as happy with the carving tools that James gave him wrapped in a leather pouch.

Coral opened the box from the Satsuma family to see their smiling faces looking up at her. She was quiet as she gently touched the beautiful wood frame. She looked at

Kamika and asked, "Did you make the snowflakes around the picture? They remind me of your origami animals."

Kamika climbed up to her lap and hugged her. "I hope you like them. They are specially for you."

"And what would you like as a present from us?" Coral asked her.

Yoshio, Hiromi, Kenji, and Benita leaned closer to hear what Kamika would say. They had all been puzzled about her behavior during the last month. It was so...focused. Not like a five-year-old at all.

Kamika looked up and blushed. Then she took her bank book out of her pocket and handed it to Coral. "I have twenty-seven dollars and fifteen cents in the bank. More than anything else, I want to be a flower farmer like you, Mrs. Coral. If I give you the money, can I be your partner?"

Hiromi and Yoshio were stunned. Benita and Kenji smiled and nodded their heads. It seemed inevitable to them that Coral and Kamika would end up together.

Amos said, "Well, I never!" and abruptly sat down on the leather chair next to the fireplace.

Polly walked over to Coral and said, "Seems like a pretty good offer to me, Moms. What do you say?"

Coral placed her hand against Kamika's cheek. They had been working so hard to get the lily bulbs planted and to research other flowers that they could grow. Kamika had taken excellent care of the tools and wagon she had received for her fifth birthday. "Are you sure that's what you want, Little Flower? Farming is very hard work for a child."

"I have thinked about it very hard since my birthday. It is really what I want. It makes me happy to be with you, to grow flowers, and make pretty bunches to sell."

"You *thought* about it," Yoshio said. "This is Mrs. Russell's decision. If she agrees, you must keep up with your schoolwork first."

"Thank you, Papa." Kamika bowed to her father, then turned to Coral. "I know that I won't really be your partner until I am bigger and more besponsible. When do we start, Mrs. Coral?" Kamika asked.

Everyone laughed and Coral said, "I think you mean responsible. And you are right. If we are going to keep working together, you will have to call me Coral. But if that is not proper for a little girl, you can call me Grammy Coral." Coral chuckled as she imagined the looks they would get at the Saturday market when a little Japanese girl called an older, Negro woman "Grammy"!

When they had settled down and started to eat the little frosted cakes that Hiromi had made for the celebration, Polly said, "There is a gift here that hasn't been opened. It says it's for Kenji. Why don't you come over here and open it?"

Coral watched as a stunned look appeared on Kenji's face. The gift had been placed underneath the table and hidden by the cloth draped over it. Coral held her breath when the other gifts were handed out, hoping he hadn't noticed that one was missing. Kenji walked over to the gift that was taller than he was and wrapped in plain paper with a red-and-green ribbon. Amos and Yoshio moved the table away so that Kenji could unwrap the gift. Coral and Hiromi stood near the table to help him if the wrapping paper got tangled. When the paper and ribbon were removed, a black, shiny, cylindrical object on a metal tripod with a large mirror and focal lens at either end stood there, reaching above Kenji's head.

"It's a telescope," Kenji whispered, not believing what was right there in front of his eyes.

Coral sat down in the nearest chair and told him how she felt. "I know that most times I have my head down and my hands in the dirt. But I was hoping that you could help me look at the stars and see the beauty there through your eyes and this telescope. Your mama and papa and I got this for you because we believe that you will keep looking through it and find something amazing one day."

Growing Pains

Five years seemed to pass in the blink of an eye. When Kamika was ten, she and Coral had to fight off an invasion of cutworms on the flower farm. Amos found them chewing through the stems of the emerging plants in the southwest corner beds. She and Coral didn't want to use chemical pesticides on the flowers. The peonies and tulips they had planted two years before were just beginning to flower that spring, and Kamika had big plans for making new arrangements with the flowers.

That year, James was sixteen, and he started working part-time after his morning classes as an apprentice in Yoshio's agriculture firm. His work focused on treatments for crop diseases and pests. One day, Coral called to ask for his advice on how to rid the farm of the cutworms.

"There are two natural ways to get rid of the cutworms," James told her. "First, you can use soapy water to kill them. This won't hurt the flowers, but be careful not to get it on the emerging leaves. It will burn them."

Overhearing the conversation, Yoshio interrupted. "Tell Coral that if she sprinkles cornmeal around the base of the plants, the cutworms will eat it, but they won't be able to digest it and will die. It is a slower method, but safer for the young flowers."

James relayed that message, explaining that was the other natural way. Then he added, "You can try a combination of both methods for faster results."

"Then that's what we'll do," Coral said. "I've got a pump sprayer in the shed that we can fill with soapy water. We can get started right now."

When Kamika arrived at the farm after school, she called her mother to see if she was also having trouble with cutworms in the garden.

"They haven't bothered us this year because we planted a lot of sage between the rows of vegetables. Cutworms hate sage, and it is a great deterrent for other pests as well." Hiromi said.

"Do you have any pump sprayers we can borrow? James told us that spraying the cutworms with soapy water will kill them quickly. Or we can sprinkle cornmeal around. Papa suggested that method," Kamika told her.

"We have two sprayers. I will clean them out and bring them over this evening."

"You're the best, Mama. Imagine how terrible it would be if Coral had to face another disaster so soon after the floods five years ago! I'll go look for the cornmeal to help Coral get started," Kamika replied.

"You are certainly turning into a good partner. But remember that you have schoolwork to do as well." Hiromi reminded her.

Kenji's fourteenth birthday was coming up in February. He overheard his father talking with Benita in California. Something was mentioned about a visit to the Mount Wilson Observatory as a birthday present for him. He couldn't believe what he was hearing! *What an incredible gift that would be! We might even have to fly to California! My first airplane trip!*

"Wait a minute, Benita," Yoshio said as he handed the phone to Kenji, who had just walked into the room.

"Hello, Miss Benita. We all miss you. How are you doing with your new teaching job?" he asked.

"You know, Kenji, it is harder than I thought it would be. Sometimes I have fun with the students; other times it feels like I'm not reaching them at all." Benita was quiet for a moment. "But let's talk about your birthday. My friend Bianca has a brother who works at the Mount Wilson Observatory. Isn't that amazing? I think he will act as a tour guide for us. I'll call back later today or tomorrow after I talk with her." Benita said.

"It's wonderful for you to do this for us. Thank you very much," Kenji said, then handed the telephone back to his father.

"Goodbye, Benita. We look forward to hearing from you soon," Yoshio said.

Kenji thought about the last time they had been together and wondered if Benita would be surprised at how much he had grown during the five years they had been apart. The letters James shared with him just weren't long enough to include all of the details about what was happening. And long-distance telephone calls were very expensive. Just hearing her voice brought back so many memories of the times they were together.

"Your mama and Kamika will not be able to go on this trip with us, Kenji. Arranging things at the last minute is difficult for them, and we don't want to overload Benita with too many guests. Do you understand?" Yoshio asked.

It's probably too expensive as well, Kenji thought. "I...think so. Thank you for considering it and thinking about the other people involved. I don't want to make it hard for them."

"Good," Yoshio said. "Let's look into flights from Eugene. It might be hard to get tickets quickly."

Benita called Yoshio back to let him know that the observatory visit was all set. They could fly into Los Angeles and stay with her overnight, then go to the observatory the next day. She told him that Bianca wanted Benita to go along with them to meet and introduce her brother, Gerardo. Yoshio did not want to inconvenience Benita by staying at her home, but she told him, "We are family now. We have to stick together. I'll probably talk your ear off all night, so don't fret about it."

Kenji was so excited he felt like he was jumping out of his skin. Hiromi and Kamika had gifts for them to bring to Benita. Kamika made a beautiful bouquet with a hand-painted note from her and Coral. Hiromi boxed up a china teapot and cups she had found at the Saturday market. They had lily flowers on them to remind her of home.

"What should I pack for our trip to California, Papa?" Kenji asked.

"It will be warmer there than it is here; Los Angeles is much farther south. We won't be staying long. Your school clothes and a warm jacket should be fine. Are you excited about your first airplane trip?"

"Yes, but I am also a little afraid. But flying will take me closer to the stars. How could I pass up an opportunity like that? Are you going to bring your camera?" Kenji asked.

"Hmmm. I hadn't thought about it, but it would be a shame if we didn't have pictures of our trip to share with everyone and for us to remember this trip to California."

"I don't think I could ever forget my first trip to an observatory," Kenji replied.

They flew out in the afternoon of the next day, landing in a very short time at the international airport in Los Angeles. Kenji suppressed his fear during the flight. Looking out over the ocean from so high above made him realize how big the Earth and the universe must be. The airport was also much larger and busier than Kenji expected, with so many people travelling from all over! But as they followed the crowds to find their luggage, they spotted Benita, waiting for them by the baggage carousel. Kenji ran to her and proudly presented the bouquet from Kamika and Coral.

"These are for you. Thank you so much for everything you did to make this possible for my birthday." Kenji gave Benita a hug that nearly crushed her.

"My goodness! You have grown at least six inches and are as strong as an ox now! How did that happen?" Benita joked with him.

Yoshio replied, "He built up quite a few muscles carrying his telescope around southern Oregon and loading the flower supplies and shipping boxes into the truck, fixing the farm equipment with James... hard work does make for strong muscles.

Here come our suitcases. Kenji, please get the smaller one."

Benita led Yoshio and Kenji out of the large airport, then they piled into Benita's white, four-door sedan for the ride to Santa Monica. Benita pointed out various landmarks and talked about living in a beach city. "There is so much to see and do here! But first, I'm taking you to my favorite restaurant. I hope you're hungry. I ordered dinner for us. This is a meal we couldn't get at home in Oregon. I think you'll like it."

After parking the car, Benita walked with them into a small storefront with a bright red, white, and green flag painted on the window. The room had round and square tables set with red-and-white checkered cloths. A wine bottle with a candle in it sat in the center of each table. Yoshio and Kenji exchanged puzzled looks. What was that delicious smell? An older gentleman with a gray mustache and twinkling blue eyes walked up to them and said, "Signorina Benita, how good to see you! We have a table for you and your guests right here."

He seated them quickly and winked. "We have prepared a special dinner for you. Shall we start with soup or a salad?" he asked.

"Giovanni, you are so kind. Definitely the minestrone. They will love it."

A young man with dark hair wearing a black apron over his clothing brought over a tray and set it down on a folding platform.

He served them bowls of soup, glasses of water, and a basket of freshly baked bread, with cups of butter on the side.

Yoshio looked at Benita and said, "You will have to help us. How do we eat this meal?"

"Oh...the bread and butter are for everyone at the table whenever they want some. Usually, we just break off a piece of bread and put it on the plate next to your water glass. The butter is passed around, and then, you start on the soup. It is the beginning course for the meal. More is coming. The soup may be very hot, so be careful."

Benita took a piece of the loaf for herself, passing the basket to Yoshio next. Kenji took a piece and spread it with butter. He bit into the crunchy crust, with the soft, chewy bread underneath. The butter melted into each little opening in the bread. His eyes opened wide. "This bread is so good. How do they make the outside crunchy and the inside soft?" he asked Benita.

"It is a family secret for now. Maybe when I get to know Giovanni and his wife better, they will tell me how it is done."

"The soup reminds me of the ones Mama makes for us when we have fresh vegetables from the garden, except it's missing the ramen," Kenji said.

The dark-haired waiter cleared the first course away, placing wine glasses for Benita and Yoshio on the table. Then

Giovanni brought over a large pan with a flat bread and many toppings and sauce on it. "This is the house special pizza for you," he explained to Yoshio and Kenji. "Benita says that you do not have any Italian restaurants or delicatessens where you live. You must each take a slice, wait for it to cool a little, then bite off the point and eat toward the rounded edge. Here are extra napkins for you. Sometimes pizza is a very messy meal!" He laughed and headed off to another table.

Kenji did not wait for an invitation. He reached for a slice, carefully pulling it away and putting it on his plate. He saw strings of cheese stretch between the pizza in the pan and his plate.

Benita said, "That's mozzarella for you! It's the stretchiest cheese in the world." She took a bite of her piece and rolled her eyes. "I love this stuff. Pepperoni and sausage, oregano for spice, more of their great bread, and the sauce! That's another secret. Every Italian family has their own version of tomato sauce." She took another large bite, finishing with a sip of wine.

"Is Kenji old enough to taste wine?" Benita asked Yoshio.

"If we were in Japan, he would taste his first wine at the Chichibu Night Festival. Hiromi told your mother about this tradition before we had the winter celebration at Lily Hills many years ago. I think he can taste it, as long as he understands that wine is for special occasions."

Kenji took the glass his father handed him. His first sip of the dark, red liquid brought tears to his eyes. It burned a little but had a sweet, fruity taste. "It is good. I think I like the smell of it better than the taste. But I don't think I should have anymore," Kenji said.

After they finished their meal, Yoshio insisted on paying for it. Benita agreed, but secretly bought Italian dessert pastries for them before they left. It was a quick drive to Benita's apartment, which had two bedrooms, two baths, a living room, dining area, and kitchen. She showed Kenji and Yoshio where to put their luggage, clothing, and toothbrushes. "I'm going to make some tea. Would you like some, Yoshio?" Benita asked.

"Oh yes. That sounds good. My head is a little fuzzy from the wine at dinner," he replied.

Yoshio brought out the box with the tea set Hiromi had bought for her. "This is a present from my wife. She cannot help herself when she sees something that is the perfect gift for one of her friends."

Benita unwrapped the beautiful china tea set. "Oh look! It is covered with lilies. I love it. I'll just give it a quick wash and then we can have our tea."

Kenji wanted to have tea with them, but he was falling asleep on his feet. In the guest bedroom, he got into his pajamas and returned to the kitchen to wish them goodnight.

"Sleep well, my son. We will have a busy day tomorrow," Yoshio told him.

Kenji hopped into bed, but he heard Yoshio and Benita talking as they drank their tea. The sound of their voices and the smell of the tea reminded him of home. And soon he drifted off to sleep.

"Let's walk a few blocks over to the beach," Benita said when Yoshio and Kenji greeted her in the kitchen the next morning. It was a beautiful day, cool with a slight breeze. The seagulls were flying around, making lots of noise. "Look over there." Benita pointed to a large wooden structure in the distance. "That is Pacific Ocean Park on the pier at Santa Monica," she explained. "It has a rollercoaster and lots of fun games. We've got too much to do to go there today. But I thought you would like to walk along the ocean."

Kenji thought, *I understand how Polly is drawn to study something so huge and powerful. There are so many secrets to explore, just like the stars and planets I see using my telescope.*

Benita hustled them back to her apartment, where they prepared for the journey to the Mount Wilson Observatory. "I've never been there myself, so this will be a new experience for me, too," Benita said. They made sandwiches to take with them for lunch and got underway.

Benita drove north and east toward a range of mountains dotted with trees and rocky areas. In addition to the large, domed building at the top of the mountain, there were several smaller buildings. In Kenji's mind, the most interesting was a long, horizontal structure. Several large towers were visible as they drove upward. Benita parked in a wide, cleared area well below the dome. They followed a winding path that took them up to the observatory at the top.

The building was one of the largest structures Kenji had ever seen. He stood gazing skyward until his eyes rested on the opening where the gigantic telescope rested. His father waited patiently, then motioned for them to follow Benita inside.

When they checked in at the main desk, the receptionist said that they were expected. She made a phone call, then invited them to explore the lobby area while they were waiting for their guide. There were pictures of the observatory being constructed and the telescope being installed. Benita looked up as a tall, dark-haired man entered the lobby, greeting her with a beaming smile.

"Hello! You must be Benita. I am Gerardo Torres. My sister considers you a good friend, and she is *very* picky. And these must be your guests from Oregon. Please introduce me to them."

Benita walked him over to where Kenji and Yoshio were reading about astrophysicist George Ellery Hale and the Carnegie Institute in Washington, the co-founders of the Mount Wilson Observatory.

"Gerardo, this is Yoshio Satsuma and his son, Kenji. This is Bianca's brother, Gerardo Torres, who will be our guide today."

Yoshio and Kenji bowed slightly at the introduction, as Yoshio extended his hand. "We are so pleased to meet you. And thank you for offering to be our guide today. My son will have several thousand questions for you, so please be patient with him." He winked at Kenji, who blushed as he realized he would probably do just that.

"I will be good, Papa, and only ask him five hundred questions today!" he joked back.

They all laughed and headed upstairs. Gerardo explained, "The original telescope was built for studying our sun. The solar flares, sunspots, and magnetic rings are endlessly fascinating to me. One of the observatory's founders, George Ellery Hale, was interested in how solar activity affects the Earth. Do you know much about that, Kenji?"

"The most obvious effect is the Aurora Borealis that can be seen in the northern skies during the winter when the sky is very dark," Kenji replied.

"That's right. It's only recently that we have been studying the deeper reaches of the sky. That work occurs at night, but I can show you some of the pictures from the telescope that we have compiled during the last month or so." Gerardo led them to a small conference room where a projector had been set up to show the pictures.

Kenji gasped as huge images of star clusters filled the screen in front of them. Benita reached over and held his hand; she was just as astonished as he was. Yoshio leaned forward to take it all in. He was a frequent user of Kenji's telescope and was learning about stellar photography. "How are you able to capture so much of the sky in your photographs?" he asked Gerardo.

"We have a digital computer that reduces the photometric data. The computer interprets the information coming in and compresses it into images we can study." Gerardo sighed. "There is so much to learn. And every time we look through the telescope at these star clusters, we are looking millions of years into the past. These stars are so far away, it takes a long time for the light to reach us. When we are able to see the farthest stars, we are discovering how the universe was created." Gerardo winked at Benita, then asked Kenji, "No questions for me?"

Kenji smiled at his father. "You know, I think I will need to find the answers to my questions myself. And I am looking forward to doing it."

Benita said, "I think it's time for lunch. Would you like to join us, Gerardo? We made lots of sandwiches, and we have fruit and Italian pastries for dessert."

"What a feast! How could I turn that down?" Gerardo replied.

They went out the south doors of the observatory to an area with picnic tables and benches and a fine view of the hills and ocean beyond. Lunch was quickly unpacked, with everyone chatting about the amazing pictures they had seen.

Kenji was finding it hard to be patient. "Papa, can I go inside and look around by myself for a while? I promise to be respectful."

Yoshio chuckled softly. "Well, my son. It is your birthday, after all. What do you think, Gerardo? He's not as adventurous as his little sister, who always seems to get into trouble."

Gerardo said, "As long as you stay in the lobby area, you can be on your own."

"Thank you. Papa, may I use the camera? I remember how to change the F-stop settings and the focal length."

Yoshio hesitated, then handed him the camera bag. "Just put the camera in the bag when you are not using it."

The adults lingered a bit longer after lunch, then Gerardo helped Benita clean up the table and dispose of the trash. The rest of the afternoon was spent taking pictures of the telescope and the observatory itself. Just as the sun was going down, Yoshio took a picture of Benita, Kenji, and Gerardo standing next to the observatory with the beautiful sunset behind them.

Gerardo walked with them to Benita's car to say goodbye. He whispered something in Benita's ear that made her laugh, then she said, "I think that can be arranged."

During the return trip to Santa Monica, Benita, Yoshio, and Kenji talked about their favorite parts of the day and the wonders of the observatory.

Kenji asked Benita, "What did Gerardo whisper to you before we left?"

Yoshio said, "Kenji, I believe that was meant to be a private moment, or he would not have whispered. Please be respectful of their privacy," Yoshio admonished him.

Kenji said, "I am so sorry, Miss Benita. He seems like a very nice person. If you give me his address, I will write a thank-you note to him when I get home," Kenji apologized.

Benita smiled. "I'm sure he would really like that, Kenji. Perhaps I will tell you what he whispered one day. But now we are almost home. I don't know about you, but I am going to take a shower and sleep like a baby!"

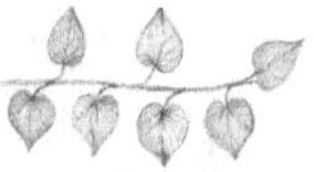

The airplane for the flight from Los Angeles back to Eugene, Oregon, was larger than the plane they had arrived in. Kenji noticed ice forming on the windows as they flew north, then he felt some turbulence. "Did you feel that, Papa? We are flying in a winter storm. The plane feels like it's travelling on a bumpy road."

"Are you feeling afraid?" Yoshio asked. "Let's ask one of the cabin attendants some questions. They do not seem to be bothered by the weather."

Kenji gulped, but he pressed the call button above his head. When an attendant arrived, he asked, "Is the airplane in trouble?"

The attendant, a small woman with dark brown hair and a cheerful smile said, "We are flying through an area where the air pressure varies depending on the temperature and winds. The pilots will let us know if there is any trouble. We have flown through worse storms than this many times! This one is fairly easy to handle," she assured Kenji.

When Kenji and Yoshio arrived at the Eugene airport, gentle snowflakes were falling. They boarded a bus that took them to Cottage Grove, where Hiromi picked them up.

Kamika was waiting at the house and ran to Kenji as he opened the front door. "I missed you! How was California? Did you get to look through the telescope? How was Benita?"

Hiromi put her hand over Kamika's mouth and said, "Patience, Little Flower. You have not greeted your Papa. Where are your manners?" She gave Kamika a light shove toward Yoshio.

Kamika bowed her head. "I am sorry, Papa. I am very glad that you are home. Did you take a lot of pictures?"

Yoshio laughed and looked at his wife. "Teaching manners to these children will be a never-ending task for us. They both tend to forget them when they are excited." Then he turned to Kamika and asked, "Can we save the questions until we get unpacked? I am a little cold and would love some tea."

Kenji was bubbling over as he related details of their trip. The following week, he wrote thank you cards to both Gerardo and Benita, including copies of the picture they took together next to the observatory at sunset. *This is the best birthday I ever had,* he thought.

The Need to Change

Almost a year later, in late January, Coral noticed that Amos was coughing frequently with chest congestion that made him light-headed and weak. "Amos, you look like a wilted flower. Tell me how you are feeling. I won't have you working out in the cold weather and getting sicker. What's going on?" She pushed him down into a chair at the kitchen table and made him drink some hot tea.

"It ain't nothin', Coral. I just got me a little cold is all," he replied. Then he started coughing again and almost fell out of the chair.

"'A little cold', my foot," she snapped back at him. "You are really sick. Get into the bed in the boys' room right now."

He muttered some words under his breath, but did as she commanded. Coral thought, *He better not try to fight me on this, the old coot!* Coral called the hospital and asked for Doc McGuire.

"Hello, Mrs. Russell. Nothing wrong, I hope."

"Hi, Doc. I'm fine. It's Amos. He's coughing and looks terrible. I made him get into bed, but I am worried that he needs more than rest. What do you think I should do?"

"Have you got a thermometer in the house? If you do, take his temperature. If it is over one hundred degrees, bring him in to the hospital. There are a lot of chest colds, flu and bronchitis—not to mention pneumonia, spreading around this time of year. At his age, a bad bout could put him out of commission for months."

"I have a thermometer. I don't think any mother can be without one. I'll bring him in if he's got a fever."

"Good! Don't hesitate to call back if his condition gets worse. In fact, call if he improves, too. I want to know how he is doing."

"Will do, Doc," Coral said. She hung up the phone and went to find the thermometer. Sure enough, Amos's temperature was 102; he needed medical attention. She decided to call Hiromi and ask her to come to the hospital with her.

"Hello, Coral. How are you today?" Hiromi asked.

"Oh, I'm fine. It's Amos that's doing poorly. I talked with Doc McGuire, and he said to bring Amos to the hospital if his temperature was over one hundred. Will you come with me to take him in? I would really appreciate it."

"Of course, I will. I just need to make some phone calls to make sure the children and Yoshio know what's happening. It shouldn't take more than ten or fifteen minutes. Can you wait that long?" Hiromi asked.

"I think that will be okay. I'm going to put a cool towel on his head and give him some aspirin. Call me back if you aren't able to come. I understand that things don't always work out the way we want them to," Coral sighed.

"I will be there as soon as I can." Hiromi hung up, called her husband and the school, then went looking for her coat.

When Hiromi got to the farm, she told Coral it would be better to have Amos lie down in the back of her station wagon to get him to the hospital.

"Good idea," Coral said. "Let's hope he doesn't put up too much of a ruckus."

Amos wailed and complained as they got him out of bed, putting a warm coat around him for the trip into town. He was very disoriented, asking Coral why they were driving around when there was work to do. Coral tried to soothe him, but he was restless and started coughing again.

Coral knew Hiromi was driving as fast as she could, but it wasn't safe on the roads, which were slippery with ice and snow. When they finally got to the hospital, Hiromi drove directly to the emergency entrance. Coral hurried in to ask for Doctor McGuire and a wheelchair for Amos. A male nurse got a wheelchair and met Hiromi outside the station wagon.

"Let me help you get him into the wheelchair. When people are very sick, they're difficult to move because they don't know where they are or what's happening to them," he told her.

"Oh, thank you. I will help as well. He knows me and may remain calmer if I am near him." Hiromi told him.

After they had gotten Amos into the wheelchair, Coral came out with Doctor McGuire. Doc took one look at him and yelled for a gurney. He told the male nurse to order antibiotics and fluids as they wheeled him toward the emergency room. When Amos was on his way to the intensive care unit, Doc McGuire sat down with Coral and Hiromi in the waiting room.

"Thank goodness you brought him in. I'll examine him and see what he needs. Are you going to stay here? It could be quite a while."

Coral nodded. "I'm staying. If I go home, I'll just wear myself out pacing back and forth, worrying about him." She turned to Hiromi. "You can go back home. I'll call you later. Would you please ask Yoshio if James could be excused from his internship duties to keep an eye on the farm? He can pick me up in the truck later."

Hiromi said, "I'll stay with you for a while. I'm going to get some tea from the hospital cafeteria. Would you like some tea or maybe a cup of coffee?"

"Tea would be fine. My stomach is in knots. I hope the tea will calm it down some." Coral took a deep breath. "Thank you for staying with me. I could use a friend."

"It is my duty as your friend to provide comfort and support. And Amos is my friend, too; even if he is a cranky, old man sometimes!" Hiromi replied.

Coral gave her a quick smile, but she was too worried to laugh at Hiromi's joke.

A few hours later, Doc McGuire came out to sit down with the women in the waiting room. "It was a near thing, but we have Amos stabilized for now. Could be bronchitis, but my guess is pneumonia with all the coughing he's been doing. He'll be in the intensive care ward for at least five days. Thank goodness we have penicillin and other therapies available now. The antibiotics will be fully active after three days, and they will keep his fever down and the infection from spreading. Do you have any questions for me?" Doc McGuire asked.

"How long do you think it will be until he is fully recovered?" Coral asked.

"That's hard to say. He has been working hard for a long time. He has a strong will to live, but his body is weak and breaking down. It will probably be at least two months before he can get up and walk around without getting tired. The winter cold is very hard on patients trying to recover from a bout with pneumonia. A full recovery to his previous strength and stamina might not be possible. I think you should consider hiring on some extra help for this season. Amos can supervise, but his days of working the fields and harvesting for you are likely over."

Hiromi saw the look on Coral's face and reached over to hold her hand.

Coral sat silent in shock. *What will I do without Amos? I can't take care of him and the farm, too. Thank goodness we applied for health insurance when the Kerr-Mills Act was passed last year. Between me and Amos getting older, hospital costs could put us out of business!*

Hiromi took a deep breath and spoke quietly to Coral. "We will figure it out, Coral. Now is not the time to make these decisions."

"Can we see Amos now?" Coral asked Doc McGuire.

"Not today. He will be going in and out of consciousness. Give him time to let the medication do its job. I promise I will call you if his condition changes."

Coral bowed her head, a few tears trickling down her cheeks. "I...I just can't take it in. He's like my right hand. What will I do without him?"

Hiromi said, "I'm going to take you home now. And I will stay with you until the children get back from school. I will call Yoshio. If James is there, you can tell him about his father."

"That poor boy. I'm sure it will be as much of a shock to him as it was to me." She looked up at Hiromi. "Thank you."

Doc McGuire put his arm around Coral's shoulders and said, "I'm here for you, and we'll take good care of Amos. But now I have other patients to see." He waved goodbye to Hiromi, then walked away down the corridor.

Hiromi and Coral returned to the farm. The cold, gray day weighed heavily on hearts already laden with worry. After Coral called Yoshio, he left work early and brought James back to the farm. When they walked in, Hiromi and Coral were seated in the living room near the fireplace. Yoshio went and sat next to Hiromi. She turned to him as he held out his arms to comfort her.

James sat next to Coral. "Thank you for taking care of Pa. I knew he was getting sick with the cough and all, but he must have taken a really bad turn during the night. When can I go see him?"

"Doc said not today. I'll call in tomorrow to see how he's doing. But Doc said he would be in the intensive care ward for three days. They are strict about visitors there 'cause the patients are very sick. I think it will be at least two more days before anyone can visit. I'm so sorry, James. This must be very hard for you."

"Mrs. Coral, Pa's in the best place he could be. Doc McGuire will take good care of him, the way he took good care of you." James looked over at Yoshio. "Do you think I can ask my supervisor to take a few weeks off to help Mrs. Coral at the farm?"

Yoshio nodded. "It is more important for you to be here now to help your family. You can work with Coral to develop a schedule for getting the work done. And our family will help as much as we can. You have three months left in your internship. Then you will need to decide what you want to do with your life."

James nodded. "Why does everything happen so fast? What if I can't make up my mind?"

Coral looked at him and took his hand. "You're like one of my sons, James. I want what is best for you. Just like I did when Benita and Polly decided that they needed to go out and explore the world, I would never force you into anything. You can try different jobs in different places to see what suits you best. I'm just glad you're here now. Your pa needs your strength and all of our support to help him get better."

It took a full week of therapy in the intensive care ward before Amos was stable enough to move to a regular hospital room. He needed a week after that to bring the congestion under control. At that point, Doc McGuire released him to Coral's care at the farm, noting that without continued rest and recovery, he could easily relapse. Coral assured him that Amos would not be working. They would share caretaking tasks between Hiromi, James, Kenji, and Yoshio. James, Coral, and Kamika began preparing for the flower season.

About two weeks later, Amos was strong enough to walk around the house. Kamika found him sitting in the porch rocking chair, soaking up the early spring sunshine, when she came over to work with Coral after school. School was much more challenging this year, with world history, algebra, English, and science taking up much of her time. But she had an idea that she wanted to discuss with her partner, and so she greeted Amos and took off her backpack filled with the heavy school books, as she sat on the porch steps.

"Good afternoon, Amos. You're looking much better. What have you been up to today?" she asked him.

"Howdy, Kamika. I am feeling better and love bein' out in the sunshine after weeks in the hospital and in bed. Your ma is taking good care of me. I am lovin' that ramen soup she makes with carrots and greens." He was slightly out of breath after this short conversation, and Kamika thought she should let him rest while he could.

"I need to talk to Grammy Coral. Is she in the house?" Kamika said.

"She's probly in the shed," he replied.

"Thanks." Kamika picked up her backpack and laid it on a chair in the kitchen before going out the back door to the shed. She found Coral sorting through stems of dried freesia and tree ferns for use in the arrangements they planned for the spring.

"Grammy Coral," Kamika called. "Can I talk to you for a little while? I have a lot of homework, but I have a new idea that I want to talk about."

Coral chuckled at her choice of words. "Well, I guess we'd better sit down and have a business conference. Let's go inside where you can get a snack, and I can make sure Amos has some tea and his afternoon medication." *Thank goodness he's getting better,* Coral thought. *That illness he had really opened my eyes. I can't be so careless with his time and health. Soon the way Amos helps at the farm must change.*

Kamika was eating an apple when Coral returned. "What's on your mind, partner?" Coral asked.

Kamika put her apple down and took Coral's hand. The concept and words rushed out of her. "I've saved up a lot of money since we started in business together. I want to invest some of it in expanding the shed. We should keep all of our supplies there so we don't have to walk between the shed and the barn to do our work. Besides, that will free up room in the barn for the equipment, the truck, and James's car. There's room on the land to make the shed bigger without disturbing the flower beds. What do you think?"

Coral was silent for a few moments. *I don't want Kamika to spend the money she has saved on this idea. But that's what being a business partner is all about. We both need to contribute to help the business grow and be successful.*

"How about this? I think the shed should be doubled in size. That would add about three hundred square feet. And you're right, keeping the supplies in the shed would save us time and energy in walking between the shed and the barn. It's a very good idea, and we really need the space. But we'll have to get some estimates first." Coral said.

Kamika nodded. "I asked Mama and Papa about it. They said that it was an important business decision that the partners should discuss. I'm glad we agree on this. It will make our work go much faster." Kamika hesitated.

Coral asked, "Something else on your mind?"

"I want to design a new brochure for Lily Hills. We have much more to offer now that we have a bigger variety of flowers here. And I heard that there is going to be a new festival in Ashland this summer. Actors will be performing the plays of William Shakespeare out in the parks and the public square and also on the stage in the theater. In those days, women wore flower crowns when they went to festivals and dances. We could make flower crowns to sell." Kamika was breathless with excitement over the new turn their business could take.

"Let's focus on expanding the shed right now. We'll have to draw it out and get permits in town to build it. We need to go one step at a time. Where will all the supplies be stored? How many drawers and shelves do we need? How big should the work tables be?" Coral asked.

Kamika stopped bubbling over, reached into her backpack and started writing on a notepad.

"I guess I don't know very much about the process for enlarging the shed. I just have a picture in my mind about how it should be. Do we really have enough money to do this now?" Kamika felt her stomach drop.

"Business has been good for us, but we won't know until we get quotes from some contractors who can do the work. I'll talk to Suzy Jenkins about the crew she hired a couple of years ago to build her work shed. She told me they did a good job. If they're still around, we can get the plans written out, then we'll know where we are." Coral paused to consider the other information Kamika had presented.

"How did you hear about the festival in Ashland?" Coral asked.

"One of the teachers at our school, Mr. Egerton, is working with the performance group to prepare the sets, props, and costumes to be accurate. Kenji told me he is a very good teacher. Kenji said he told the class about what it was like in England when Shakespeare was writing his plays," Kamika explained.

"I see," Coral replied. *Let's set some deadlines for her to see if she can handle the pressure.* "I would like to see a draft of the brochure you're thinking of in...two weeks. Do you think you can squeeze that in between your homework assignments? Homework comes first."

"That's what Mama says. Kenji can help. He took a drawing and drafting class for his science and engineering classes. But Kenji is very busy with his schoolwork, too. I might need more time. How about four weeks?"

Coral nodded and thought, *The shed expansion might be a good project for Amos to manage. He has some friends in the construction business that he can contact for an estimate of the costs and timing.* "I think I'll ask Amos to help us. We can work on the layout for the shed, where to keep the supplies and storage for the bulbs and equipment we need in there. You have the extra time to develop the new brochure. Ask your parents to call and tell me if they agree with our plans." Coral sighed, smiled at Kamika and gave her a quick wink, as she thought, *Kamika is becoming the spark that our business needs.*

Yoshio and Hiromi were finished with their nightly tea and ready to talk about the issues facing their family. "How is Amos doing?" Yoshio asked.

"He is getting stronger. I think he knows that he cannot do the outside work anymore. But if I know Coral, she will find other ways to keep him involved," she explained.

"Now that I head up the Research and Development section, I've been asked to go to India to gather information about their planting and harvesting techniques. Dealing with monsoons has forced them to develop new systems for ensuring a productive harvest. We need to develop our own systems for what to do in extreme weather conditions." Yoshio paused and put his hands on his knees. Hiromi knew this was how he behaved when dealing with a sensitive subject. She waited patiently for him to continue.

"I accepted this opportunity and have gotten approval to take James with me on the trip. If he can come, we will be there for about three weeks. I am worried about leaving Coral without him as they prepare for the Easter shipments. Also, I didn't want to put any additional stress on Amos. If James is away, he might feel that he has to get back to the fields, and that would be very bad for him." Yoshio paused. "This is a fantastic opportunity for James, something that might never come his way again. The trip to India will leave in ten days. But I don't think that James would even consider leaving Coral and Kamika alone with the work ahead of them. Do you have any suggestions, Hiromi?"

Hiromi sighed. "After all this time, you still do not understand how the farming community works. Coral can hire a young man to help with the work while James is gone during the busy season. Coral and Kamika are going to need more help anyway if their plans for growing the business and expanding the shed take place while the Easter harvest comes due."

Hiromi continued, "In fact, one of the women at the Saturday market, Mrs. Jenkins, might be able to help. Her middle son, David, has worked on their land for many years. She and I have become friendlier due to our common interests. She is a clever woman and always knows what is going on. Maybe she would be willing to loan David to Lily Hills part-time, as long as the pay was good, and they could get along well."

"I think that we should have some options in place before I tell James about the trip to India. But we need to discuss it with Coral—and Kamika. Will you invite Coral over for dinner tomorrow or the day after? We don't have much time before I need to leave," Yoshio said.

"This will be an interesting discussion," Hiromi responded.

During their dinner, Coral sat quietly as Yoshio brought up the trip and the options they had discussed to minimize the impact on Amos and the flower business.

However, Kamika was *very* vocal about it. "You can't take James away now! We need him more than ever. He knows the whole system we use so well that it's like Amos is still working with us. How can you even think about this?" She was outraged.

Coral looked at her and said, "Cut that out! You're being disrespectful to your parents—and to me. Every business faces situations where changes must be made. As my partner, you need to listen and keep your mind open, the way that I listened when you had suggestions for making changes."

Kamika looked down to hide her embarrassment. She gulped, took a breath, and said, "Mama, Papa, Grammy Coral, please forgive me for being so selfish. I am sorry that I didn't listen."

Yoshio said, "Thank you, Coral. Kamika, you are still very young. You must learn to control your passionate nature. It is one of your best qualities, but it can get in the way of making good business decisions. We included you in this conversation because you are Coral's partner." He directed his next question to both of them. "Now, what do you think of the suggestions we made?"

Kamika waited for Coral to respond first.

Coral said, "I don't want James to miss the opportunity that you are offering him, Yoshio. I think it will help him to see his path in life. He's pretty confused right now. Also, I think I met Suzy Jenkins's boy a few years ago. He's got plenty of the kind of experience we would need. I think we should talk to them both about the possibility of him working for us over the spring and summer," Coral answered.

Yoshio nodded, then looked at Kamika. "Have you taken some time to think about this situation?"

"Yes, Papa," Kamika replied. "My feelings are getting mixed up with what I want and what would be best for the business, so I will be guided by Grammy Coral in this. I'm still learning how to be a good partner."

"The next step is for us to talk with Suzy Jenkins. Kamika, I would like you to ask Amos to think about the questions we should ask Suzy about her son's qualifications. I'll take a look at our projected sales and determine a reasonable wage. We should also think about what our next steps should be if her son is not able to help us," Coral said.

Two days later, on Saturday, the list of questions was ready for Coral's interview with Suzy Jenkins. She decided to talk with Suzy at the Farmers' Market. Coral took Kamika with her, on the condition that Kamika would only *listen* while they discussed Coral's proposal.

Mrs. Jenkins had long, corn-colored hair that she wore in braids wrapped around her head. Her green eyes were widely spaced, and freckles dotted her nose and cheeks. Suzy explained what her son David had done during the past three years on the farm, including operating and maintaining the tractor and rototiller, planting and harvesting vegetables, controlling pests, and maintaining the compost heap. "You know, David's goin' to college now, takin' some classes in business. What's the pay and the hours for helpin' you at Lily Hills, Coral?" Suzy asked.

"I'm thinking $50 a week for regular farm jobs. With him going to college, I guess we'll have to work around his class schedule if he wants to come work with us. Of course, he would be trained by Amos. Do you remember him, Suzy? He's got a brown and gray beard now, but he's still hard to work with, so you know what a challenge that could be!" Coral replied.

"Yes, I sure do. I'll talk to David and see if he's intrested in the job. He'd sure be happy 'bout the money." Suzy waved goodbye as Kamika and Coral walked toward the truck.

"I think that went just fine," Coral told Kamika on the drive back to the farm. "How do you feel about it?"

"I'm kind of nervous about working with someone new. But based on what Suzy told us, David meets the qualifications that Amos set up," Kamika said. "I'll try to give him a fair shot. I mean, I'll keep an open mind about him."

"That's better. It sounds like Suzy raised him up right, and now he's in college, too.

That's a plus for us, Kamika. He's taking courses in business. Think of the things he can share to help our business run better!" Coral was getting more enthusiastic the more she thought about David working at Lily Hills.

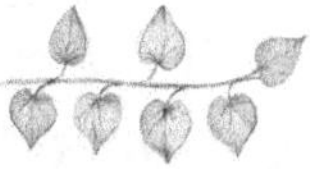

Two days later, Suzy convinced David to go to Lily Hills to meet with Coral, Amos, Kamika, and James. Kamika and Amos were skeptical about the tall, well-muscled young man with short blond hair with brown streaks who showed up at the farm on Monday afternoon. Coral and James were much more optimistic, knowing that David was eighteen years old and could operate all the equipment in the barn, including the new stump cutter.

Coral told David about working closely with Amos Matthews. She directed him around the house to the area north of the barn. David found Amos outside the construction area of the shed.

"Hello, Amos. My name is David Jenkins." He stretched out his right hand, giving Amos a smile as they shook hands. "Mrs. Russell said that I should talk to you about possibly working at the farm. What is happening here?" David asked.

Amos saw from the expression on David's face that he was genuinely curious. "This here shed is where the flower arranging business happens. Coral and Miss Kamika decided that it was too small. They have lots of new flower customers in line and so need more space to process orders. Coral showed me the plans for storage, supplies, work areas—all that. She put me in charge of working with the construction crew to make sure evything is done right," he explained.

"You know everything about this farm, don't you, Mr. Matthews?" David said.

"Just call me Amos. I bin here a long time. I watched Coral raise her boys and girls. Me and my boy, James, sorta became part of the family. You thinkin' bout working here?"

"Mrs. Russell said that I should talk to you first. I'm sure that we do things differently on our farm than you do here. Would you be willing to teach me how to do a good job for her? I know you have a lot of work with the shed construction, but maybe you could spare a couple of hours after dinner for a while?" David asked.

Amos looked him up and down. "I like that you are respectful to Coral. She deserves that. There's a lot to learn. I'm pretty busy with the shed construction crew, but Coral will tell you what needs to be done. If you have questions, don't be afeared to ask."

Two days later, David began working at the flower farm, evenings and weekends when he wasn't at class or studying. He won Kamika over when he showed her a more effective way to wire harnesses for flower wreaths, saving at least thirty minutes per wreath. David created a jig, a pre-constructed pattern, for the wreaths in different sizes, that was screwed into a square piece of hardboard. It was light and easy to move around. Coral was also impressed.

"Just in time for the Easter arrangements! Thank you, David. Come on, Kamika. We have to prepare some bouquets for a wedding next weekend. David, here's a list of the flowers we need and a map of the beds. Try to pick flowers that are not fully opened yet. Then they will be at their peak in time for the wedding," Coral told them.

Decisions Are Made

James had so many thoughts, ideas, and feelings whirling around inside that he didn't know what to do next. India! He rushed to the library to do some research. He vaguely remembered some of the world history he had been taught: the sociology of the caste system, the English occupation, the Taj Mahal, and the revolution in 1947. He wanted to learn as much as he could before the trip.

"You shouldn't rely on books by American or English authors. They are bound to be biased and will not give you an accurate picture of the country, its rich culture, and the people," Yoshio told him.

"What do you mean, Mr. Satsuma?" James asked.

"It's hard for us to remember that recorded history in America is relatively new. Other countries in the world have recorded history for thousands of years. That information is rarely exchanged. India was colonized by Great Britain so they could obtain cotton and fabric dyes for the textile industry portion of their economy. They had little regard for the heart of the country. Like other colonizing countries, they wanted access to natural resources in other places to support the 'mother country.'" He paused, watching the expressions as they chased themselves across James's face. "Just keep an open mind. I think you will find this trip fascinating. I am looking forward to it." Yoshio told him.

Before Yoshio and James left for their trip to India, Hiromi was watching for an opportunity to talk with Amos. "Hi, Amos, I haven't had a chance to talk with you about the trip James is taking with my husband to India. How do you feel about it?"

Amos was silent as he tried to put his feelings into words. Finally he said, "I don't rightly know how I feel. I know that Yoshio will take good care of the boy. India sounds like a strange place from what Jimmy has told me about it."

"India is certainly much different than the western United States," Hiromi said. "But what I think you should understand is that this experience will change your son. Many cultures have a rite of passage for young boys and sometimes girls, when they have an experience that prepares them for being adults. I know that James will always be your child. But even though he will only be gone for three weeks, when he returns, he will be a young *man*. He will have seen the world. Is this making any sense to you, Amos?"

"I remember the day when my pa handed me the keys to his truck. I was so surprised. I was 'bout Jimmy's age, too. My pa started treating me different 'cause I had grown up. Guess I should be callin' him James now, like the rest of you do," Amos said with a sad smile.

Hiromi said, "Now that Coral has David Jenkins to help out with the harvest, James will have more choices about his future. He may choose to work with Yoshio at his firm. He may decide to travel and see more of the world. Or he may decide to attend college. I am facing the same thing with Kenji. He is growing up so fast." Hiromi's eyes closed, and her mouth drew down when she thought about this.

Amos noticed and took her hand. "You shouldn't worry about that boy. He's got a real thinkin' man's brain. But he became a real friend to Jimmy, right when he needed it."

Hiromi sighed. "Thank you, Amos. I am glad we had this chance to talk. We both have fine sons." She wiped a tear from her eye and went to help Coral set up for dinner.

Three weeks later, the travelers returned from India. James slept for a full day. When he woke up, he wanted to talk with Coral about the trip. He found her in the shed with Kamika and asked if she could talk with him for a little while.

"Sure, James. Walk with me. I need to check on the new flowers in the bed up on the hill."

James wasn't sure where to start. "India was so different. My head was spinning trying to understand what was happening."

"Can you give me an example?" Coral asked as they climbed the hill.

"Women are not allowed to own businesses. And the men were shocked and embarrassed when I offered to help cook dinner at a home where we were staying. It made me feel...awkward. I felt like I couldn't ask questions. I didn't know who I could talk to. When I asked Yoshio, he said he couldn't help much, but he was not surprised by the strict roles men, women, and even children have in Indian society."

When Coral and James reached the beds, they found the beautiful light blue irises blooming and healthy. Coral said, "It just shows how 'equal under the laws of the land' applies in America. As America grew, the laws were changed to keep up with the times. During World War II, women were critical to the workforce. And when they began to get into politics, they pushed for changes to equalize opportunities for minorities and women. Change is slower in other places." She bent over to cut some flowers, then placed them in the basket she carried.

"Let me do that for you, Mrs. Russell." Coral turned to see David's head pop up on the other side of the hill. He took the basket and clippers from Coral. "Hi, James. If you have time later on, I would love to hear about your trip to India."

"Uh...sure, David. I've got a lot of catching up to do. Maybe tomorrow?" James replied.

"Fine with me. Let me finish here and get these flowers down to Kamika. Mrs. Russell, watch out for a slippery part of the path on the next hill." David knelt to continue cutting the flowers.

"Looks like David is fitting in well here," James observed, after he and Coral had walked out of earshot.

Coral noticed the chagrin in his voice. "We were lucky that he was available to fill in when we needed him. Does that make you feel unhappy?"

James hesitated before answering. He knew he had to face what he was feeling and deal with it like a man. "It makes me feel like I'm no longer needed here. And that makes me very unhappy."

Coral stopped walking. She faced James squarely with a crooked little smile on her face. "James, you are *family*—not a hired hand. Family is always needed, no matter what needs to be done, no matter where you are. When David is here, we might not need you to tend the land, but we need you to keep our family whole."

Tears sprang into James's eyes. He couldn't help himself as he grabbed Coral in a tight hug. His voice wavered as he said, "You have been more than a mother to me. Thank you for everything you've done for Pa and me. When I think of home, I will always see this farm and hills covered with flowers."

The flower shipments that year were extremely successful. Lily Hills actually ran out of flowers for the final orders and filled them in with other native Oregon foliage. Coral and Kamika emptied the compost bins over the rows now empty of flowers. David used the cultivator to turn the soil, preparing the beds for planting in the fall. James and Amos took the promised trip to the falls at St. Justin's Gap, where they spent two days fishing and enjoying the cool air and sparkling water from the falls.

One day, as summer was winding down, James heard the phone ringing as he was passing through the living room. "Lily Hills. How may I help you?" he answered.

"James, is that you? It's Benita. How was your trip to India? I thought I would get a letter from you, but I guess you were too busy to write," she teased.

"Benita! How wonderful to hear from you. I thought about writing to you at least ten times during the trip, but there was always another place to go and see. The trip was amazing and confusing all at the same time. How are you?" he asked.

"I am fine and have some good news. But I want to tell Mama first. Is she there?"

"She's here helping Kamika and David clean up the new shed building. I can run and get her, or do you want her to call you back later?"

"Please go get her. I can wait."

James put the phone down on the coffee table and ran to the shed to get Coral. He had stopped calling her Mrs. Russell and adopted Kamika's moniker, calling her Grammy Coral now. "Grammy Coral, Benita is on the phone. She wants to talk to you right away."

"Oh no! What's wrong?"

"Oh, I'm sorry. She is fine. Just go in and talk to her. I'll help Kamika and David with the cleanup." James turned to Kamika and asked, "Where do you want these extra vases stored?"

Kamika walked James over to one of the new sections of the shed and pointed out the shelves they were using for the vases. They had extra protection on the front of the shelving to keep the vases from falling.

Coral left quickly. She rushed to the living room and grabbed the phone, flinging herself into her favorite chair. "Hi, Benita. Your old mom is here. What's happening?"

"First of all, who is David? James mentioned him when we were talking."

"He's Suzy Jenkins's second son. We asked her if he could come work with us for a while when James and Yoshio went off to India. He has been a godsend! I don't know what he said to Amos, but they became partners in making sure everything was done right so that the shipments could be sent off without a hitch," Coral explained.

"That's great, Mama. During Kenji and Yoshio's trip to the Mount Wilson Observatory, I met Bianca's brother, Gerardo Torres. We have been dating for a while and became engaged last night! I couldn't wait to tell you about it." Her announcement was met with silence. "Mama, are you there? Please say something!"

Coral took a moment to catch her breath. The announcement was sudden, but she knew that a smart, good-looking woman like Benita was sure to attract the attention of men. She just wasn't prepared for it to happen so soon. "I'm happy for you, honey. Have you told Polly?" she asked.

"I haven't told her about the engagement yet, but she knows I've been dating Gerardo. We want to start submitting job applications to places where we can be together and not have to travel so much. It will probably take about a year to get everything worked out, so we think the wedding will be next September."

"Tell me about Gerardo. I know he works at the observatory, but what's he like?" Coral asked.

"Oh Mama, he is so intelligent. He could probably work at NASA because he has degrees in engineering *and* astronomy. But the best thing about him is the way he makes me laugh. He has a wonderful way of viewing the world. And family is very important to him. We spend time with Bianca and their parents, going to movies or museums, even the county fair. I think you will really like him, Mama," Benita explained.

"Looks like you've got a good one, baby. Why don't you send up some pictures? I think it's wise for you to take time to plan your future together before you get married. I only wish your dad and brothers could be here to celebrate with you," Coral said wistfully.

Benita felt the tears start, but she didn't want to dwell on sadness in this moment. "I wish that, too. Can you put James back on the phone? I have a couple of questions I want to ask him."

"Sure...be well, baby. I'll talk to you again soon." Coral said goodbye and went to get James from the shed. She met him as he walked into the kitchen, reaching for the lemonade pitcher in the fridge.

"Benita wants to talk to you. Grab your drink and go on into the living room," Coral directed.

James took a quick drink to satisfy his thirst and picked up the phone. "I'm here, Benita."

"James, I just read about a new agriculture program that is starting at Oregon State University in Corvallis. I thought that you might be interested in going to school there. Yoshio and I could write recommendation letters for you. What do you think?" she asked.

James had not thought about going to college and assumed that he would go to work at Yoshio's firm when his internship was over. But after his experience in India, he realized that it would be a good idea to learn more about other aspects of land management. He just didn't know if they could afford it. "You know, that's a good idea. But isn't it very expensive to go to college? I don't have very much money, and I don't want to ask Pa for some either."

Benita said. "That's a good point, James. You might qualify for a scholarship. If you call or write to the school, they'll send you the application materials and financial information. I think that Mama would be happy to support you in this if you'll share some of your college knowledge with her and Kamika."

James realized that she was right. He could be very helpful to both Yoshio's company and Coral's business. "I'll talk it over with Pa and Grammy Coral. School starts in September, right?"

"You don't need to rush into it. Why not review all the information first? Then it will be your choice to apply now or later." Benita advised.

"I can do that. Thanks for thinking of me. I'll write to you about my trip. There is a lot to tell." James hung up the phone and went to talk to his dad.

Near the end of 1963, President John F. Kennedy was assassinated while riding down a street in Texas. The country was in shock. The last president to be assassinated was William McKinley in 1901, before the two World Wars. So much had changed during those years, and violence was a big part of it. Vice President Lyndon Johnson was sworn in as president to cover the remainder of the term. He was elected as president in 1964, determined to enact legislation to promote civil rights and access to voting.

Coral was excited to listen to the radio, where broadcasters talked about the marches during the Freedom Summer. The marches were staged to draw attention to the vastly unfair practices of business and land-owners, school systems, and public transportation. Congress was forced to acknowledge the sweeping prejudicial practices and passed legislation to correct the problems. President Lyndon Johnson signed the Civil Rights Act, outlawing racial segregation and discrimination in public accommodations and employment. The Satsumas, Coral, Amos, and James had a celebration tea, grateful that their friendship had only grown stronger over time. And when Dr. Martin Luther King, Jr. won the Nobel Peace Prize, Amos loudly proclaimed, "Well, I never!"

Kenji would graduate from high school at the end of the semester in December. He had been ahead of his classmates due to his mid-year transfer when the family moved to Oregon from California. He was still deeply committed to the exploration of objects in space and understanding the expanding universe. He and Gerardo had become pen pals, and Gerardo had written that the University of California in Los Angeles had a very good undergraduate program in astrophysics. Kenji wrote to UCLA requesting their course catalog, an application, and acceptance requirements. When he thought about which colleges to apply to, he wanted to have options. He knew that his choices would make a big difference in his career and his life— especially when the Gulf of Tonkin incident in August spurred military involvement by the United States in the war between North and South Vietnam.

When Kenji needed answers, he usually started with his father. "Excuse me, Papa. I don't understand why our country is involved in the war in Vietnam. Do you know what is happening there and why?"

Yoshio shook his head. His eyes filled with sorrow and worry. "Kenji, Vietnam is half a world away. The people of the world continue to fight about freedom, power, control of resources, and money. Information that comes to us is often unreliable because it's influenced by people with their own interests and agendas." Yoshio paused, seeing the confusion on Kenji's face.

"If you want to understand, you must find different sources of information to see the bigger picture. Understanding often takes time and many different viewpoints. Do you think I always have the answers to everything? Remember what James told you about our visit to India, how different it was from what he had read about the country! I cannot answer your questions without my own bias and experiences coloring the information. You must start thinking for yourself," Yoshio stated.

Kenji was stunned by his father's response. He felt as though the stable earth beneath his feet was heaving up and down, with no safe place to land. He couldn't form his thoughts into words. As his hands balled into fists, there was no place to release his anger. "I think I need to take a walk outside," Kenji said between clenched teeth, then headed out the front door.

Yoshio's eyebrows climbed up his forehead. He knew that his son was a young man of deep emotions, but that level of anger was unexpected. He sighed. "Oh, Kenji," he whispered. "It's hard for me to shield and protect you now. You are almost an adult and must learn to face whatever comes."

Kamika celebrated her fifteenth birthday that year. She was perfectly content in her role as junior partner in Lily Hills and working to become a savvy business owner. She thought about taking undergraduate courses in accounting and business management at the local junior college after she graduated from high school, but she wanted to accomplish so much before then. She imagined new floral designs, and she planned to showcase their work in more public forums.

Now that they had more storage space in the shed and a more efficient workflow, Kamika knew that Lily Hills could ramp up their business by showing their new floral designs to existing customers and the general community.

Advertising! Kamika thought one day while working on the brochure draft she promised Coral. *Papa has worked with so much marketing material at Carstairs, I bet he has some good ideas I can work with.*

Yoshio had been very busy through the spring and summer, but Kamika was hoping to catch him one evening after her homework was completed. She knew it was important to talk over her ideas with Coral, but her father had more experience. She thought, *Marketing is where the business of Lily Hills needs to grow now.*

Kamika knew the best time to approach her father would be during tea time.

"Mama, can I make Papa's tea tonight and take it to him after dinner? I want to ask him some questions about Lily Hills."

Hiromi turned to see Kamika's expression. "I see. Have you completed your homework?"

Kamika nodded. "I spent extra time in the library after school to get my English assignment done. I'm all caught up now."

"Please be respectful of his time. He has been working hard and may need to relax tonight. Ask him if he would like to answer some questions before you bombard him. You know how you are." Hiromi tweaked Kamika's nose and laughed.

"Yes, Mama. I will ask him first," Kamika promised.

After the dinner dishes had been washed and put away, Kamika prepared the jasmine tea her father drank to relax and unwind from the day. He was reading a magazine in the living room when she deposited the tea tray on the table. He looked up, his eyes widening to see Kamika there instead of Hiromi.

"So...you are bringing my tea and a multitude of questions. Yes?" Yoshio asked her.

"Only if you want to talk with me now. I can wait until later if you just want to relax tonight," Kamika said.

Yoshio took a sip of his tea, as Kamika clasped her hands, trying to be patient. "Well, let's see what you are getting into now! Just know, you may not like my answers," he said with a slight nod.

"Now that we have a new shed and new flowers at Lily Hills, I think we should be getting more orders. But how do we get them? You know about advertising. How much does it cost? Should we use magazines or newspapers?"

Yoshio held up his hand to stop her. "Slow down, Kamika. Before you ask me any more questions, I want you to think about what will happen when you get a lot more orders for flower arrangements. Yes, you have the shed to work in, but who will answer all of those calls? Who will prepare and ship all of the extra orders? You are still in school and will have more difficult subjects to learn this year and next. Take your time and think about this for a minute." He picked up his teacup again and sipped the fragrant brew.

"I know I'm right about this, Papa. Why are you trying to slow me down? I'm excited about our progress, and I know that our business can be more successful than ever!" Kamika stood up and started pacing in front of the tea table.

"You need to consider how your ideas to increase business will affect your partner as well. Successful marketing will increase her workload significantly. You were only four when she had a stroke. Do you remember all the pressures she had weighing on her?"

Kamika stopped pacing and stood ramrod straight. Her eyes grew wide and started flicking back and forth. Then she placed her hand over her heart. "Coral..." she whispered. "How could I forget about how this could impact Grammy Coral, Papa? Lily Hills is her life, her home! It's not about the money for me. I'm just so proud of our beautiful flower arrangements, the wreaths, the wedding bouquets, even the funeral flowers. I want everyone to know about them. " Kamika explained,

She continued, "But I don't think of Grammy Coral getting older and not being able to take on more work. Maybe we should make changes a little bit at a time," Kamika said, disappointment showing in her frown.

"First you must talk to your partner. How do you think Coral managed Lily Hills almost by herself for so many years?" Yoshio asked Kamika.

"She had to have a plan," Kamika said softly. "She could see the big picture, the end goal, and all the steps between. How come I don't think that way?"

"Your understanding will grow when you and Coral update the plan together. Ask her about what the plan looks like now. Maybe a small amount of exposure will provide a light to show the way to a reasonable process for expansion. Several events in Oregon feature flower shows, like the State Fair in Eugene. But you can start with a smaller event first," Yoshio explained, then he pointed to Kamika. "However, your primary task is to learn as much as you can in school and do well there. Your partner is wise and experienced. Talk to her."

"You know I'm not patient, Papa. Changes happen, but they are too slow. I wasn't thinking about how these changes might affect Grammy Coral—and also Amos and David. They are all so important to me, and I don't want them to get hurt." Kamika sighed.

"Those are good thoughts. Now it is time for you to sleep." Yoshio said as he picked up the tea tray and headed into the kitchen.

"Goodnight, Papa," Kamika said, as she tried to stop her thoughts from whirling around and prepare to sleep.

"So, how was your conference with our little businesswoman?" Hiromi joked with Yoshio as she stepped in to wash and dry the teapot.

"She is quite ambitious. I hope that I showed her to think about the consequences of her actions *before* she actually does something. But at least she asked first this time!" Yoshio shook his head. "Why are teenagers so difficult?"

"Because they are ours," Hiromi replied.

The Fall Flower Show

James decided to continue his education
and applied to Oregon State University. He
would be attending classes and living in
the men's dormitory in early September.
Amos was proud of him, but he knew that
Coral would need more support during the
late fall and winter than he could provide.
Shortly before James left, Amos asked
Coral to talk with him at the kitchen table.
He brought the coffeepot, cream, and sugar
over, along with a plate of cookies that
James had made for them.

"Now, Coral, I bin thinkin' that with
Jimmy goin' off to college, we need to
keep David working with us for a few days
a week. We haven't really talked about how
long David would work fer us, but I think he
should continue as long as he can. I can't
run that heavy equipment anymore. And I
got another project I want to start on."

Coral had been thinking the same thing
about keeping David on at the farm, but
Amos's project was news to her. "What kind
of project do you want to start working

on? We haven't talked about anything new," Coral replied.

"I still gotta work out the details. Don't worry. I'll talk to you about it later. You got enough on your plate. What about asking David to continue working during the winter?" he asked again.

"Suzy says that David is still taking classes at the community college two days a week this semester, but that he can work for us for a few hours on his days off." Coral sighed. "Seems like everyone is going off to college now. Kenji will be going after Christmas. Then Kamika. It'll just be you and me rattling around this old farm."

Amos laughed. "You haven't talked to Kamika lately, have you? She's gonna either be the best or the *worst* partner you ever had. Her papa is tryin' to get her to slow down a little before she plows over you with all her new ideas. She'll keep you busy for years to come, just wait and see."

Coral smiled and sipped her coffee. Yes, it was time to catch up with Kamika and see what plans she was developing for their business. She called Hiromi to see if Kamika could stop on her way home from school, then she called Suzy Jenkins to see when David would be available.

Early the next morning, just as Coral was getting bacon frying in a pan, David came over. "I forgot about the good smells that are always coming out of your kitchen," he said as he opened the back door.

"Come on in. You had breakfast yet?" Coral asked, then saw David shake his head. "Well, hand me that canister on the counter. I'll show you how to make biscuits. Then we can do business over breakfast."

David smiled and brought over the canister. He also grabbed a large bowl and the butter and milk.

"I see you know your way around the kitchen," Coral added. They worked in comfortable silence until the biscuits, eggs, and bacon were ready.

As they sat down to eat, Amos came in and joined them. "I hear yer takin' some classes at the college," Amos said. "What're you intrested in now?"

David finished chewing a big mouthful of eggs and drank some milk before he could answer Amos. "I've always been interested in music. We're always singing songs while we work at our place, both inside and outside. I'd like to play an instrument. I'm taking a class that teaches you how to read music and provides a piano and some other instruments to practice on. It's really fun to learn and play music with other students in the class. The other class I'm taking is bookkeeping. Mom always keeps our household financials in her head, but I know that we need to keep better track of our money," David explained and went back to his breakfast.

"Well, I never!" Amos exclaimed. "You takin' music lessons."

"Amos, don't tease him," said Coral. "College is a good place to try new things. David is young, and he has opportunities that weren't available for us at his age." Coral wanted to encourage higher education for all the young people around her. "David, do you have some time when you could come by and run the equipment? I'd like to set up a barrier and grade some of the land so that the snow melt and rain won't flood the beds in spring."

"That's a good idea, Mrs. Russell. I'll do some research at the library. But I think Mr. Satsuma could make some good suggestions. He really knows a lot about agriculture," David replied. "I can work on Monday and Wednesday afternoons. Depending on what's happening at our place, maybe some of Friday. Will that work for you?"

"Sounds good to me. If you're not busy now, the equipment needs to be checked for wear. Amos can show you the service that's needed and where to find the tools and manuals. You men get going. I'll clean up the kitchen." Coral shooed them out and took the dishes to the sink.

Later that day, when Kamika showed up at the flower farm, Coral was cleaning out some of the beds to make room for the new bulbs. They needed to go through a cold-weather sleep period before they would grow in the warm spring weather.

"I'm here, Grammy Coral. Can I help you with that?" Kamika asked.

"I'm almost done, but you can take the cuttings down to the compost bin. Amos put some newspaper in there this morning. The cuttings will help them break down."

Kamika took the five-gallon bucket of leaves, stems, and roots down the hill to the compost bin. Compost was a much better additive to the soil than commercial fertilizers. Kamika had learned that the hard way a few years before when she sprayed liquid fertilizers on the peonies. The flowers and leaves shriveled when it grew warmer. The liquid mixture was too strong, and the fertilizer on the leaves concentrated the sunlight until they burned.

Coral stood up and went to the shed to wash her hands and put the tools away. Kamika brought in the bucket and washed her hands as well. "Mama said that you wanted me to stop by. Is there something on your mind?"

"Amos told me that you are full of ideas for our business. How about sharing some of them with me? I *am* your partner," Coral teased.

Kamika blushed. "I talked some of my ideas for advertising over with Papa. He pointed out the consequences of successful advertising before the production area was ready to handle the demand. So I cut back a little."

"Go on," Coral sat down in the rocking chair and motioned to Kamika to sit on the bench.

"I've started to redesign our brochure to showcase the variety of flowers we have now. The new arrangements are much more eye-catching, too. Papa suggested that we could participate in a flower show. If we try one of the smaller ones first, we can see the effect it has on our business. What do you think?" Kamika said.

"Hmmm. Actually, there is usually one right before Thanksgiving. I think it's in Grants Pass. That's a small town on the Oregon/California border. It's south of Ashland, so we might need to stay overnight somewhere, especially if the weather is rough. That might cost a bundle. Plus we have to pay a fee to set up a table for our products. I wonder what the entry fees are now. I think we have enough money in the budget for a short trip like that," Coral said, thinking about the details. "We could make some Thanksgiving and Christmas wreaths, and the brochures would show our other products. It would be a big job to set up the tables, canopy, and displays and then to pack it all back up again. Maybe we should get some additional help?" Coral's head tilted to the left as she looked carefully at Kamika's expression.

"Oh Grammy Coral! You're the best," Kamika exclaimed. "How much help do you think we need? I think Mama would come with us."

"We might need someone like David. He's strong and knows a lot about our products. I don't want to chance your mama getting hurt lifting heavy tables." Coral said.

"Maybe both of them could come? Mama is so talented at displays. You know what I mean," Kamika offered.

"Here's what we'll do. You talk to your mama about doing this, and I'll talk to David. In the meantime, finish updating the brochure so I can check it before they go to the printer." Coral was thinking about everything they would need.

Kamika was excited and nervous. *My first road trip! I wonder what it will be like. I hope Mama will come. With Mama and Grammy Coral along, everything should be just fine.* But Kamika knew there was a lot of planning still to come. She hoped that the weather wouldn't be nasty. No one would want to go to a flower show in bad weather. Kamika thought about gathering pinecones and other supplies for the wreaths. Holly berries would be ready in another few weeks, and

she would use gold and silver ribbons
to add sparkle. She went to the shed,
grabbed a sketch pad from the worktable,
and started to draw some designs for the
wreaths.

Coral chuckled to herself. With Yoshio's
help, Kamika was doing a better job at
thinking things through. Her creative mind
made working with her delightful as well as
challenging. *A flower show. I haven't been to
one since before Jesse passed away. I need to
call the flower show organizer in Grants Pass.
We might need a permit. Amos will be a good
organizer for the trip. He can keep an eye on
the weather and make reservations for us at
one of the inns near Grants Pass.*

"Don't stay in there too long. I don't
want you walking home in the dark." Coral
said goodbye to Kamika and went into the
house to make some calls.

As the sun began setting earlier in the
day, October breezes cooled the land,
preparing the flowers for their winter
slumber. The leaves on the trees began to
sport their fall colors, golden and flame
orange, blending with the sundown in the
early evening. The first weeks of November
were much cooler than October had been.
Rain began falling at irregular times,
catching the Lily Hills crew out in the fields
or scouting for flexible pumpkin vines for
the wreaths.

Everyone pitched in to prepare for the flower show. Coral prepared the application for the show and sent in their fees two weeks before the due date. Kamika started fabricating the Thanksgiving and Christmas wreaths with help from David. He found the most amazing tiny silver bells, grape vines, red/white/green striped ribbon, and best of all, snowdrop flowers for the wreaths. Yoshio used his flash attachment, lighting screens, and backdrops to take pictures for the new brochure. Amos found the Weasku Inn in Grants Pass and made reservations for the group. The women would all stay together in a large suite, and David would have a smaller room down the hall. He made reservations for two nights because the weather this time of year could be dangerous with wind, dropping temperatures, and ice on the roads.

Hiromi was a necessary addition to the group because her station wagon was needed to carry the wreaths, boxes, brochures, and suitcases. Coral's truck was filled with the heavier items needed to display the products. The weekend before Thanksgiving, James came home from college to help them pack the wreaths and load the truck. He stayed to spend the week at Lily Hills with his father and to help prepare Thanksgiving dinner.

On Monday, after both vehicles were finally loaded, Coral, David, Kamika, and

Hiromi headed out for Grants Pass. The weather was cool and sunny, perfect for the drive and flower show. When they reached Grants Pass, both vehicles drove to the regional park where the show was being held. Some of the display areas had already been set up. There was a stage for musicians and for the show coordinators to make announcements. Coral looked at the map to see where their table was assigned. They found it in a partially shaded area next to the park office building. The outside lights would illuminate their display when darkness fell early in the evening the next day.

"Mrs. Russell, do you want to set up some of the tables now? Or do you think we should hold off on everything until tomorrow?" David asked.

Coral thought about David's questions. "Let's go to the park office and talk to them about security. They'll know best because they're here every day."

Kamika and Hiromi wandered over to the stage and sat down on the rustic steps. "You were so impatient to get here yesterday, and now you are so quiet. What are you thinking about?" Hiromi asked.

"I've been thinking about Kenji. I'm going to miss him very much when he goes to college. With the flower show and schoolwork, I haven't made time to be with him. We used to talk about the stars and planets almost every day when I was a little girl. When he got the telescope, we found new things to look at all the time." A slow tear trickled down Kamika's cheek.

Hiromi sighed. "I will miss him, too. I love talking with him about the things he is learning. He asks the most amazing questions. But we will call him and write letters. He will always be present in our lives, whether he is physically here or not."

Kamika smiled as she wiped the wetness from her face. "I know you're right, Mama. But it feels like he's all grown up now, and I can't catch up to him."

"I feel that way about both of you. You were my little children, and now you are young adults. Where did the time go?" Hiromi shook her head.

As Hiromi and Kamika started walking back toward their display site, Coral and David were coming out of the park office with a tall, dark-haired woman. Coral said, "Natalie says that it might get windy tonight, so she suggests that we wait until tomorrow to set things up."

Natalie nodded. "It's safe to leave your tables here, but I wouldn't want them to get damaged," she said. "It's supposed to be sunny tomorrow for most of the day. But you know how fast the weather changes at this time of year."

Coral and David both nodded. They thanked her and walked back to the parking lot.

"I have the map Amos made for us to drive to the Weasku Inn. See, it's along the Rogue River Highway," David said, unfolding the map and holding it open for Hiromi and Coral.

The Rogue River was wider and livelier than Kamika expected. Fishermen stood on either bank, casting their lines into the foaming water. Bushes and blackberry brambles climbed up the sides to the tall white oak and Jeffrey pines lining the roadway.

As they drove along beside the river, Coral asked, "Would you please tell me more about your family, David? Your mama doesn't talk much about that when we see her on Saturdays at the Farmers' Market."

"Most of my family lives in Minnesota. Our ancestors came from Ireland, some from Britain, and a few from Germany. That's why most of us have blond hair and blue eyes. Lots of the family are fishermen, dairy farmers, and woodsmen. Mum and Dad came to Oregon to try something new. It's warmer here most of the year, so we could grow vegetables and have fruit trees. Umm, I have two brothers and a younger sister. That's why I always wear clothes that don't quite fit me. Hand-me-downs are the rule in our family, except for Lila. Most of her clothes are new." David explained. "I'm sorry we don't talk much. There's always so much to do. But you can ask me questions any time."

"Thank you. I probably see you more than your family does right now, and I want you to know that I appreciate having you helping us at the farm. You're a fast learner and get along with everybody—even Amos! And he's a grumpy sort most of the time," Coral said.

"Aw, he's not so bad. Look, Coral," David said, pointing to a bend in the river. "It sure is pretty down here. I've never seen the Rogue River. It looks like a good place to go rafting—unless it gets real windy."

"Let's pull over when we get to that hardware store." Coral pointed toward an oversized A-frame building along the right side of the road. "I want to ask Hiromi and Kamika if they have rainboots and slickers. I always bring mine. We'll need them if the weather changes."

After they had all parked in front of the store, Hiromi got out of her station wagon to talk with Coral. "Is something wrong?" she asked.

"We all need rainboots and slickers. I should have asked you about them before we left. Did you pack them for the trip?" Coral replied.

"Kamika needs a new raincoat. She's outgrown the one from last year. I'll send her in to get one."

Kamika was surprised by the variety of merchandise in the store. They had everything from animal feed to wheelbarrows. She found a rain slicker and took it to the counter as David was checking out. "Did you need a new raincoat, too?" she asked.

David laughed. "With two brothers? I got one of theirs that almost fits me," he explained. "Coral wanted some extra canvas for the sides of our display in case it gets windy."

Kamika realized that she hadn't thanked David for his contributions and decided this was her chance to speak up. "You did a great job with the wreath materials and wiring setups. I think they look fantastic and will sell very well at the show. Have you been to other flower shows?"

"This is my first one," David said. "I don't know what to expect, but I'm looking forward to seeing what other people have created. We only have a little way to go to get to the inn."

"See you there!" Kamika said as she walked out to the station wagon.

The Weasku Inn had a giant river-rock fireplace in the main lobby. After their overnight bags were stored in their rooms, the travelers sat around the flames, drinking hot chocolate and tea. A tray of freshly baked cookies was placed on a table between the chairs. Lights from Grants Pass could be seen twinkling through the trees around the inn. Coral watched Kamika as her head started to droop.

"I think your daughter has had enough excitement for one day," she whispered to Hiromi.

"This is quite an adventure—for me as well as Kamika," Hiromi whispered back.

David stood up and gently tapped Kamika on her shoulder. "Excuse me, but I'm heading up to my room. I can't keep my eyes open much longer. See you all in the morning!"

"Good night, David," Coral said. "We'll be right behind you."

A Disastrous Decision

Tuesday dawned with bright sunshine and a gentle wind. David and Coral were up early to get the display area laid out at the park. Hiromi and Kamika had a quick breakfast, packed up some food for David and Coral, got a large thermos of coffee and another of tea to last through the day. They were about an hour behind the others when they finally drove away.

"Will I have time to walk around and see the other flower displays?" Kamika asked.

"We will all need to get up and walk around for a little while during the day. We can take our breaks separately to make sure that enough help is available to restock the display or move things around," Hiromi said.

Kamika and Hiromi put on their coats and boots when they arrived, then began unloading the station wagon. David had the display area all set up, including tripods for the larger wreaths, which he hammered into the ground so they wouldn't blow over in the wind. Coral attached the Lily Hills sign to the front of the tables. Five trips to the station wagon were needed to move all of the wreaths out to the tables.

An hour later, the flower show was officially open. Crowds of people came in from the parking lot to look around and buy the fantastic arrangements. Coral gave away little decorated pinecones for families with small children, who returned their beaming smiles as payment. Everyone from Lily Hills was very busy for most of the morning, handing out the new brochures and talking with interested customers. It was lunchtime before anyone had a break.

"Whew!" David said as he finally sat down to eat a sandwich and have some coffee. "I think I should ask for a raise," he joked with Coral.

Coral laughed and said, "You'll get extra pay for this day. I know we couldn't have pulled this off without you."

Hiromi handed Coral the lunch basket to make sure she ate something before beginning another round of sales. Hiromi had packed rice and vegetable bowls with pork and teriyaki sauce for the trip. She took out her chopsticks and dug into one.

David asked to try one—if she had a spoon. "I'm not skilled enough with chopsticks yet. And I don't want to drop the food all over our display area."

Hiromi lifted an eyebrow and handed him a spoon. Kamika was off looking at the other flower displays. She particularly liked the large sunflowers that had been dipped in resin to preserve them at their peak color and texture. She spent some time talking to the sunflower merchants, who used many techniques that were new to her. Kamika handed them one of the Lily Hills brochures and invited them over to see their display. The older man followed her and introduced himself to Coral.

"Good afternoon," he said. "My name is Mark Lindstrom. This young lady invited me over to see your flowers. I realize that you can't show all of the arrangements in your brochure, but these wreaths are just beautiful. I'd like to buy the big one on the display stand for my family."

"Nice to meet you, Mr. Lindstrom. My name is Coral Russell, and the young lady is my partner, Kamika Satsuma."

"She is?" he exclaimed. "Well, she certainly knows a lot about flowers. How did you two become partners?"

"It's a long story. The Satsumas are my neighbors, and Kamika was the first person to inadvertently introduce herself to me." Coral winked at Kamika, who blushed and smiled.

Meanwhile, David and Hiromi walked around the show, commenting on the unique containers and displays. Hiromi suddenly exclaimed, "Look, David! A bonsai tree!" She pointed to a small tree in a glazed blue ceramic flat pot with short sides gently sloping upward. It looked like a miniature of the tall pine trees along the Rogue River.

"I've never heard of them. Is it a special variety?" David asked.

"Growing them is an art in Japan. It's a tradition that actually started in China between the seventh and ninth centuries. They are often grafted from larger trees, then clipped and sculpted into interesting shapes. They are deliberately kept small and compact. Each one is unique, based on the artist's inspiration," she explained.

As they walked toward the display tables, David saw a small Japanese man who reminded him of Yoshio. Hiromi came over and bowed to the man and the woman beside him, then began speaking to them in Japanese. David waited until they were finished, then asked, "How long does it take to grow a bonsai tree?"

The Japanese man smiled and said, "Some of the ones here are eighty years old. My father started growing them when he was young, and I inherited them after he passed away."

The woman said, "We live in Portland, in the far northern part of Oregon. The trees grow very well there. The cool air and moisture are just right for bonsai."

David asked Hiromi, "Can I buy one for Mr. Satsuma?"

Hiromi gently caressed his cheek. "A bonsai is a very special gift. They often remain in families for many generations. Why do you want to give one to my husband?"

David blushed at her touch. "He's been so kind to me, always willing to help when I have a question about the plants or machinery. And he encourages me to be creative. I would really like to get one for him. Which one do you think he would like best?"

Hiromi said, "My father told me that the gift says more about the giver than the receiver. This is a gift from your heart, so you should select the one that speaks to you."

David selected one with the main trunk spiraling upward and two side branches. The leaves were shaded from light to dark green as they grew outward. The tree was in a shallow clay pot with sculpted feet at each corner. "I would like to buy this one, please."

The Japanese man bowed to him and said, "That tree is one of my favorites. May it bring luck, health, and happiness to your friend."

The bonsai tree was placed in a sturdy wooden box with a close-fitting top to prevent damage while it was being moved. Hiromi and David started back to the Lily Hills tables just as the wind started to pick up.

Their first flower show was a great success.

Around 5:00, Coral noticed dark clouds moving ever closer to the park. "I think we'd better start packing up," she said as David and Hiromi arrived back at the tables. "I'd rather leave a little early to get ahead of the bad weather. Or we could stay for another night at the inn. Amos booked two nights in case the weather turned bad."

Hiromi nodded. "Kamika, place the brochures in the lunch basket. Then unlock the car and put the basket in the backseat. It looks like we sold most of the wreaths."

David said, "I'll take the tables and tripods back to the truck. The canvas should come down last. Then we can use it to cover everything in the bed." He used the claw end of a hammer to pry the poles out of the ground, then started folding up the tables. All of the other vendors were packing up their displays as well.

Kamika waved to Mark Lindstrom as she passed by. "It was nice meeting you. Maybe we'll see you at the next show," she shouted to be heard over the wind. Mark waved back and pointed to the brochure, where the Lily Hills phone number was printed on the front.

It started to rain before they were fully packed, but they got everything into the vehicles and followed the crowd out of the parking lot toward the highway.

David drove the truck slowly, knowing that the road would soon be slick with mud and dangerous if they drove too fast. Hiromi also drove slowly, but the winds were pushing the lighter station wagon around on the road. It took all of Hiromi's concentration to keep the vehicle from sliding.

By the time they reached the highway, conditions were growing worse. The temperature was dropping, which would cause additional problems on the highway. Coral told David to pull over before they reached the on-ramp. Hiromi pulled off the road behind him. Coral walked back to the station wagon and opened the door, motioning for Kamika to release her seatbelt and slide over toward her mother.

"We could turn around and go back to the inn for another night or head home. It's your choice. The truck won't have problems on the highway. But your station wagon will." She looked sternly at Hiromi and put her hand over Kamika's mouth so that she would not interfere with the decision.

Hiromi thought she could handle the drive. "I think we should go home. I will drive slowly. Just keep an eye on us behind you."

Coral sighed. "Okay. Let's get going before the weather gets worse."

They entered the highway and started the journey north. The weather became an unpredictable enemy, making the drive more dangerous with every mile. The wind was driving the rain sideways, and David could barely see the station wagon behind them. The temperature was dropping, and David and Coral knew that there would be black ice on the road soon.

Black ice is the most dangerous driving condition, especially after dark, when it cannot be detected on the highway. If a vehicle hits a patch of ice, there is no way to control it. Even the truck, with its much heavier load, could not be controlled on black ice. Fortunately, there were only a few cars and trucks travelling on the highway.

About twenty-five minutes later, Hiromi hit a patch of black ice, and the station wagon began to slide toward the edge of the highway. Another car tried to pass them and hit the back bumper, sending them into a spin. Hiromi was thrown against the driver's side door. She screamed as her shoulder hit the window and dislocated. The car kept spinning and eventually stopped when it hit the gravel in a gully on the side of the highway.

Kamika did not know what to do. "Mama, Mama?" she asked on the edge of panic.

Hiromi was taking deep breaths to control the pain and focus on their situation. "Little Flower, I think my shoulder is broken. I need you to go into my travel bag and get a sweater. We can use it to stabilize my arm."

Kamika's hands started shaking; her whole body was trembling. "Mama, I'm afraid! I don't know how to help you. I don't know what to do."

Hiromi reached over with her right hand to touch Kamika. "I am afraid, too. It is okay to feel afraid, but you must not let the fear keep you from doing what needs to be done. We will go one step at a time. Can you do that?"

Kamika worked hard to still her trembling hands. She knew that she needed to help her mother first. Then, they would do the next thing, and the next, to make the situation better. She was not alone; they would figure it out together.

"I'm okay now. I'll get your sweater out of the bag."

Hiromi leaned forward, and Kamika gently put the sweater behind her.

"Now, take one of the sweater arms and pull it beneath my left arm. We will make a sling. Now pull the other arm around the side of my neck."

Kamika followed her mother's instructions, binding her arm close to her body so that it would not move.

"What next?" Kamika asked.

"We need to change places. I will sit over there, and you will sit where I am. You will need to help me move over because I can't push myself with my left arm. Put your arm around my waist and pull me toward you."

Kamika carefully moved her mother from behind the steering wheel. She squeezed down in front of the passenger's seat to make sure her mother was fully seated, then pulled the seat belt across her lap.

"This next part is where you need to take charge and listen to me very carefully. You will need to get us back onto the highway. Driving the station wagon is not hard. You are big enough to control the steering wheel and reach the gas pedal and the brake. Sit down, and we will rehearse the movements you will make."

Kamika was still shaking as she sat behind the steering wheel.

"Take deep breaths now. Turn the key in the ignition to start the car." Hiromi encouraged her and instructed her to gently step on the gas to move them forward.

The rain was still coming down hard, and it was difficult to see. But the station wagon was not damaged, and Kamika was able to pull it back onto the highway after traveling forward through the gully.

"Now, I want you to practice flashing the headlights. If we get close to David and Coral, it will tell them that we need help," Hiromi said.

It was hard for Kamika to drive and flash the headlights at the same time. She kept trying until she was able to carefully control her movements and keep the car steady. At this point, Hiromi was getting dizzy from the pain in her shoulder. She thought she might faint or black out. "Little Flower," she spoke softly to Kamika. "I may not be awake for much longer. You are doing fine. Shake my leg hard if something else goes wrong, and we will handle it together. I will stay awake as long as I can."

"Yes, Mama," Kamika said. She realized that her mother was in great pain and was trying to stay calm and help her as much as she could. *I can do this. I will drive and keep flashing the headlights, even if I have to drive all the way home.*

Coral and David were worried. Although they couldn't see much behind them, the headlights from the station wagon should have been visible when the rain slowed slightly. "David, have you seen the headlights from the station wagon? I know it is hard to see in the rain and darkness. I think we should pull off the highway and see if they catch up to us."

"I was thinking the same thing myself. I haven't seen the headlights from any cars for about fifteen minutes. I hope they're alright," David said. He pulled over. Visibility was just as bad through the side window, but he could see the headlights of the cars on the other side of the highway as they got closer to their location. Coral opened the coffee thermos and poured cups for them both as they waited.

Kamika drove very slowly for what seemed like an eternity. When Hiromi finally fell asleep, she tried to speed up and almost immediately lost control of the car. Kamika took her foot off the gas and gently tapped the brakes to slow down. She exhaled when the car didn't swerve, driving steadily and slowly from that point on. Flashing the headlights seemed to attract the attention of other cars. But no one stopped or pulled over to help them.

After ten minutes, Coral put on her rain slicker, rain boots, and hat, took a flashlight, and got out of the truck. She stood just behind the bed. Her rain slicker was bright yellow, a necessary precaution in Oregon's rainy weather on a large farm. She spotted flashing headlights just as she was about to go back into the truck. David spotted them as well, pulled on his rain slicker, and stood beside Coral with another flashlight. He began to flash the light back to let Hiromi and Kamika know they had been spotted.

Kamika thought she was seeing things when a flashing light began to appear in the distance. *Please, let it be someone who can help us,* she prayed. When she finally saw that there were people standing by the side of the highway, she pulled off immediately and jumped out to talk to them.

Coral stood her ground until Kamika grabbed her in a bear hug. Kamika pulled back and quickly said, "We started sliding on the road and another car hit us. We ended up in a gully on the side of the road. Mama is hurt. She talked me through driving the car so we could get help. I think she passed out from the pain. It is her left shoulder; we tied it up, but please be careful."

"Oh, child! What a horrible thing to happen! Don't you worry. We'll check on her now." She turned to David. "Kamika says Hiromi is hurt. Go check on her while I put Kamika in the truck." She took Kamika to the passenger's side. "Just stay here for a few minutes. I want you to check this map to see where the nearest hospital is. Here, use my flashlight." Coral pointed to a marking on the map. "Look for this mark. It's the symbol for a hospital. I'll be right back as soon as we have a plan."

David entered the station wagon on the driver's side, noting that the seat was vacant. Hiromi was breathing slowly. Using his flashlight, he checked her over. Her face was very pale, but he couldn't see blood on her body anywhere.

Then Coral opened the passenger's side door of the station wagon. "What's up?" she asked.

David replied, "Mrs. Satsuma is not bleeding. There's an improvised sling around her left arm. My guess is that her shoulder is dislocated or broken. She's breathing normally, but she's very pale."

"I want you to drive the station wagon," Coral told him. "Kamika is looking for the nearest hospital on the map. When she finds it, I'll drive the truck, and you can follow us. Do you have any questions?"

"What do I do if Mrs. Satsuma wakes up?" he asked.

Coral said, "Just talk to her calmly. Let her know you are with her, and Kamika is with me. Tell her we're going to the nearest hospital. Hiromi should rest as much as she can until we get there. She managed to tell Kamika how to get a sling on and instructed her to drive and signal for help. That's quite a feat for someone with that kind of injury. I don't think she'll panic if she wakes."

Coral went back to the truck and took the other flashlight from Kamika. She bent over to look at the map. Kamika said, "I think I found one over here. We haven't passed Roseburg yet, have we? There's a hospital there. Or else we will have to go all the way to Eugene."

"It's hard to see signs with all this rain. But I think you're right. We should be just south of Roseburg, maybe another forty minutes of slow driving." Coral flashed the light back at David to let him know she was ready to leave. Coral pulled onto the highway and instructed Kamika to watch behind her to make sure that David was in sight.

Kamika was shaking with reaction to all that had happened, but she told herself, *This is not the time to fall apart. I don't want to distract Coral while she's driving in this terrible weather. What if she needs me to do something for her? I must stay calm and be ready.* Kamika decided to concentrate on watching for signs and checking behind her for the station wagon.

David did his best to keep the truck in sight. At least the wind had died down a little. The rain was still coming down hard, but it wasn't as dangerous to drive a little faster. He still needed to watch for black ice. The station wagon was likely to drift if it hit a patch in the dark.

Hiromi started to wake up, groaning as she tried to move. David spoke to her softly. "Hi Hiromi. It's me, David. Kamika caught up with us after we pulled off the road to wait for you. She's in the truck with Coral. We're taking you to a hospital so that you can be checked by a doctor and given proper care. You should try to rest and stay still to avoid moving your arm."

"Are Coral and Kamika okay?" Hiromi asked.

"They're fine. You should be very proud of your daughter. She did a great job of driving and signaling to us. She kept her head on straight and made sure that you were safe." David took a breath and briefly looked over at Hiromi, who had a slight smile on her face. He thought he saw a tear on her cheek, but it was hard to tell. It might have been rain from when Coral opened the door to check her injuries.

A short while later, Kamika pointed to the right and said, "Look, there's a sign for Roseburg! I wish I had a better map. I can't tell where we should get off the highway."

"Don't worry, honey. There will be a hospital sign on the road at the exit we should take. Is David still behind us?"

"Yes, they are right behind us," Kamika answered.

"Good. Watch for the hospital sign. It should be coming up soon." Coral relaxed her shoulders. They were almost there.

Sadness and Happiness

Sure enough, the hospital sign was posted at the next exit. Coral pulled off the highway with David following her. The rain was starting to ease up, but it could start pouring down again at any moment. Coral drove a little faster. There was better lighting on the street, and the hospital was easily visible up ahead. David kept pace with the truck as she pulled into the emergency entrance.

Coral entered the admitting area in her rain slicker and boots, water streaming around her on the floor. "We have an injured woman in the station wagon outside. We think her left shoulder may be dislocated or her left arm broken. We didn't find any open wounds when we checked her over. But she has been in and out of consciousness during the drive here." Coral gave the nurse Hiromi's information and asked where there was a telephone she could use to call Hiromi's husband.

Kamika went to the station wagon to see her mother. Hiromi opened her eyes and reached her right hand up to Kamika's cheek. "Little Flower, you did everything right, even though you were afraid. I am very proud of you." Kamika put her head into her mother's lap and cried. Hiromi patted her head. She couldn't blame her daughter for letting the pent-up emotions out now. Then there was a nurse and another person standing next to the passenger's door with a wheelchair. "Guess it's time we went in," Hiromi said.

David gently pulled Kamika out of the way. "Coral has checked your mother in and gone to call your father. Let's go in and sit down in the waiting area," he said. Kamika brushed the tears off her face, took David's hand and walked in with him.

It was a very long night. Kamika fell asleep in a chair in the waiting room while David and Coral talked softly beside her. Yoshio showed up with Kenji at 2:00 a.m. He walked quietly over to Coral to see what was happening with Hiromi.

Coral explained, "The doctor took some X-rays, and her clavicle, I think that's what he called it, is cracked. Her arm is okay, but she shouldn't move it very much. It will take a while for the bone to heal. There isn't a whole lot they can do but bind it up and give her pain medicine."

"Oh, my poor angel! She is the strong backbone of our family. Thank you for taking care of her and Kamika. I want to hear all about it, but first I want to speak to the doctor." Yoshio headed to the admitting desk.

Kenji went to David and asked, "Is there someplace where we can get a cup of coffee or tea? I'd like to hear about what happened from you."

David nodded, and they walked down a long hallway, looking for signs to the cafeteria. The arrows directed them toward another part of the hospital.

The doctor told Yoshio that he wanted to keep Hiromi overnight. He explained the healing process, telling him to encourage her to move her fingers, hand, and wrist. He said that if she felt any numbness in her hand or fingers, Yoshio should take her to see a doctor right away because nerve damage sometimes happens in this type of injury. Yoshio asked if he could see her. The doctor nodded, pointing to the emergency room patient area.

When David and Kenji returned, Coral was asleep on a couch with Kamika curled up beside her. Yoshio was reading a magazine, watching over them both.

"How is Mama?" Kenji whispered to his father.

"The doctor thinks she will be fine. The recovery time will be about three months, so we will need to help out as much as we can around the house. I hate to say this, but

I think you will have to postpone going to college for a little while."

Kenji looked at his father and saw dark rings around his eyes. "Papa, this is *Mama* that is hurt. Of course we will take care of her. It wouldn't hurt anything if I postponed going to college until next September. And I wouldn't be surprised if Coral practically moves in with us! I don't know how you feel, but this accident really shook me up. From what David told me, Kamika was the hero of this trip."

Yoshio nodded, letting a great sigh escape as he looked down at his hands. "Our Little Flower—she is growing up so fast. Your mother is the foundation this family is built on. I was also shaken when Coral called last night. She has not needed hospital care since Kamika was born. It is always frightening when someone you love is hurt." He looked up at Kenji and David. "We will take care of her the way that she has taken care of us. Now you should both get some sleep if you can. We will leave for home at first light."

When Hiromi woke up the next morning, she asked the nurse to invite Coral, David, and Kamika to come to her hospital room for a brief chat. When they arrived, Hiromi's face grew red. She cleared her throat before speaking to them. "I owe all of you an apology. I let my desire to return to my home and husband interfere with my judgment. Coral, you were clearly worried about the weather. But I ignored your wisdom—to my detriment and trouble for the rest of you. David, thank you for caring for me when my daughter needed the comfort of Grammy Coral." She paused, taking a deep breath. "Kamika, even parents make mistakes. But we must face those mistakes and learn from them. When we make judgments based on our hopes or fears, mistakes are more likely to happen. I should have taken more time to get the facts about the dangers we were facing *before* making a decision. You suffered the most from my selfishness. I am so sorry, Little Flower. I am so proud of you, and I hope that you can forgive me." Hiromi's eyes were filling with tears.

Kamika walked slowly to her side. She bent down to kiss her mother's cheek. "Mama...I feel like I grew up in those hours between the accident and now. I'm glad that I recognize this turning point in my life. It's a good thing. I realize that I can handle adult responsibilities...with a little help from my friends and family."

Kenji was surprised when his mother insisted that he take at least one course at the community college starting in January before going off to UCLA. He had been accepted there but would start in the fall. There were many classes available to him locally, and he might be able to coordinate his schedule with David. They could travel together, sharing the college experience. Hiromi was worried about Kenji going to school at UCLA. But he made friends easily and was a good student. And she knew that he would keep in touch.

During the spring, Kenji decided to take a calculus class. It was the basis of the physics background he would need for a career in astronomy.

One morning, Kamika was gathering laundry from the bedrooms and stopped to talk with Kenji when he passed by the washing machine. "I'm glad you'll be here for the flower season and summer. I'll really miss you when you go to California."

I'll miss you, too. We haven't really been doing things together for a while now. At least we'll be here for Mama while she heals up. Besides, I like going to school with David. We share information about our classes during the drive to the college. You know, he is really smart. He could do anything he wanted," Kenji said.

Kamika said, "I know David is smart. He has had some of the best ideas about our flower business. What I like most about him is the way he treats people. He is always respectful and supportive. He makes me feel like I can accomplish anything! When we get to talking too much, Coral reins us in so we stay focused on the business. But as I have worked with him and gotten to know him, I feel that he is a very wonderful person to have as a friend."

Kenji smiled at her. Kamika rarely praised other people that way. He suspected that she felt very deeply about David, but wouldn't realize how she felt until later on. It was his turn to shop for groceries, so he grabbed the keys to the station wagon. "Want to go shopping with me, Little Flower?" he asked.

"I'm on laundry duty today. And I don't want Mama to be alone in the house. Doc McGuire said she's healing up well, but I'll be swamped with flower orders in another month and won't be able to spend as much time with her. Thanks for asking though." She waved goodbye and went to collect the rest of the dirty clothes, towels, sheets and pillowcases from around the house.

At Lily Hills, remodeling of the farmland was taking place. Yoshio had set up a grading plan with David for dealing with the accumulation of snow melt and rainfall away from the main flower beds. This plan would save the high production areas from damage, ensuring that income from the spring harvest was stable. Coral noted that one of the flower beds would need to be taken out in order to grade the runoff area. She gave David the approval to start the grading in February, after the last snowfall.

Coral also had an idea to discuss with Kamika and Amos, so she invited them to dinner on Wednesday night. Kamika waited until her father got home to be with Hiromi before she went to Coral's house. She followed her nose to the luscious smell of beef stew into the kitchen where Coral and Amos were seated at the table.

"How is your Ma doin'?" asked Amos.

"She is much better. The rest has really helped her. We didn't realize how much she was handling for us. Thank you for asking, Amos. I'll let her know you say 'Hi,'" Kamika replied.

"Sit down and eat, honey. We can talk after dinner." Coral directed her to a chair and ladled out the beef stew from a blue-and-white serving bowl. Amos handed her a dinner roll from the basket on the table. They shared news from the farm and school while they ate. After they had finished, Kamika gathered the dinner plates and flatware, putting them in the sink.

"Let's talk before we have dessert and do the dishes," Coral said.

"So what's up? I haven't got a clue here. I've been so busy with Mama's recovery, schoolwork, and chores. Thank goodness this is our slow period," Kamika said.

Coral replied, "Well, we lost one of the main beds on the west side of the highest hill when David completed the grading. I've been thinking about how we could replace those flowers without putting additional stress on the other beds. The portable sand barrels in the shed gave me the idea. What if we built some raised bed platforms that can be moved around to provide the right amount of sunshine, water, and drainage needs based on the type of flower we plant in them? Then we can rotate and grow different flowers for the seasons."

Amos was nodding his head.

Kamika was thinking hard about the different areas around the farm where the portable beds could be located. But she couldn't picture how to make them portable.

"How would we move them around? The sand barrels are on wheels and a hard surface inside the shed. We can't use wheels for the portable beds around the farm. They'll just get stuck." Kamika noted.

Amos's face lit up. "I know how to do it. We just need to use rotatin' tracks, like on the backhoe. Put on a small motor and BAM! It'll be easy to move them."

"Can we do that?" Kamika asked.

"I think so," Coral replied. "We just need to think out the materials that will withstand the weather, hold up under moving around, and allow drainage. It might be more expensive than I thought at first. Hmmm...Sounds like a good project for James and Amos to work on together," she said as she winked at Kamika.

"What about it, Amos? Do you think that James would be able to help? He's pretty busy at school in Corvallis, isn't he?" Kamika hadn't kept up with James's school schedule, but she knew he was a wizard when it came to farm machines.

"Our reglar call time is on Saturday mornings. I'll ask him about joinin' in. David might be able to help, if'n he has time," Amos said.

"Wonderful," Coral sighed with relief. "If they get started now, we might be able to harvest the flowers from the portable beds by mid-summer. Then we could grow flowers that could be dried and used in wreaths later on in the year." But Coral especially wanted to grow some special flowers for Benita's wedding in September. Coral, Amos, and James developed the first two portable flower beds by early April. Kamika was delighted to share the cost when she learned the flowers were for Benita's wedding. Coral planted blue cornflowers, pink peonies, and white bellflowers for the special day. David helped to position the beds so that they would receive at least five hours of sunlight and only light breezes until the stems were stronger.

One afternoon, David went to the kitchen for a glass of lemonade, finding Coral deep in thought. "Good afternoon, Mrs. Russell. What are you thinking about so hard?" David asked.

"Goodness, David. You should be calling me Coral by now. You're practically one of the family!"

"Thank you, ma'am. I surely will. Are you working on Miss Benita's wedding?"

"Yes. The only problem I have is with the music. We have lots of records, but they are old and a bit scratched. I was hoping for live music, but the only person I know of is the church organist, Mrs. Gentry. We don't have a piano or an organ, so that doesn't really work. Got any ideas?"

David looked at Coral and took a few sips of his lemonade. "You know, I can play the guitar. I'm getting pretty good. And some other music students at the college might be available," he suggested.

"Why, David! That would be lovely. What songs can you play? Do any of your friends at school sing? You can practice in the shed after we're done with the spring harvest."

"We can all read music, so you should just pick out songs you want. We can work on them with our teacher to get ready. As long as you feed us and save a few pieces of the wedding cake, I think it would be fun!" David winked at Coral.

Coral sighed, then stood up and kissed him on the cheek. "What would we do without you, David? Now you'll be part of a day Benita will never forget."

David had an idea for a few songs that were sung as duets, so he decided to ask Kamika if she wanted to do a few songs with him. He knew that she had a very nice singing voice because she often sang softly when she was arranging flowers or out walking along the beds. She told him that she had a music class in school this year and was learning to read music and playing different instruments to learn rhythms and tones. David had been thinking about Kamika a lot more lately. He would look at the sunset on the way home from school and see her face between the light and the edge of the mountains.

Kenji and Yoshio were involved in other aspects of Benita's wedding. They prepared an area for taking pictures, setting up a white tent, with a background of the night sky with sparkling stars. Yoshio set up screens to soften and reflect the light. Kenji and James built a water fountain to sit on top of a small table. There were stools, pillows, and chairs so that the entire family could gather around for pictures. Gerardo had a very large family, including five brothers and sisters, his parents, grandparents, and a five-year-old niece, who would be the flower girl.

One evening after David finished loading the truck for deliveries, he found Hiromi in the kitchen with Coral. They were planning the wedding dinner and making a schedule for getting everything ready. He sat down next to Hiromi, clearing his throat to get their attention.

"Ahem...Excuse me. Could I break in to ask a few questions?"

Coral looked at his dirty face and hands. "You better go wash up first, young man. We'll be ready to talk when you get back."

David walked out to the shed to wash and dry his hands.

Coral told Hiromi that David had volunteered to provide music for the wedding.

"Does he play an instrument?" Hiromi asked.

"He plays the guitar. I gave him a list of songs, and I still need to call Gerardo's sister to ask for some songs her family would like as well. He's coming back," Coral noted, turning around to face him.

"I'm sorry, Coral," David said. "I know better than to come to the kitchen with dirt from the farm."

Coral twinkled at him. "Let's get down to it. We're very busy here!"

David laughed. "I can see that. Well, my question is really for Hiromi." David turned to her. "I'd like to ask Kamika to sing some songs at the wedding with me. Do you think she would do it?"

"Hmm. My girl never backs away from a challenge. If you seem doubtful that she can do it, she will probably jump at the chance to prove you wrong!"

David gasped. "Well…I didn't expect that! But I think you're right. You know your daughter better than anyone. Can I come over tomorrow night after school with my guitar to see if she will take the bait?"

Hiromi and Coral both laughed at the thought of David hooking Kamika. "Sure, David. Drop by with some music. I can take out my pipe and play a little with you to draw her in. Then it will be up to you."

"Wish me luck, ladies. I'll see you tomorrow. And thank you." He bowed to them, opened the back door, and walked out to drive the truck into town.

Kamika was intrigued by the challenge David presented when he asked her to sing with him at Benita and Gerardo's wedding. She knew that many hours of practice would have to be fit in between the Lily Hills production schedule. But she found she was eager to work with David on this new project.

Kenji helped David and Kamika write a special wedding song, with details about how Benita and Gerardo met. Kamika and Kenji both remembered meeting Benita when Coral had her stroke. The words came easily to Kamika when she worked with David. Somehow, his guitar found the perfect melody to bring the words to life. Kenji was the first to hear them sing it. "I hope you remember this song, because I want you to write and sing something just as special for my wedding someday." Kenji sighed. "I think Gerardo and Benita will be very happy when they hear it."

The wedding day dawned clear and cool. Benita and Gerardo were glowing, snuggling in each other's arms next to the fireplace. Somehow, the wedding planners had found rooms for everyone. James returned from school and shared his room with Gerardo's brothers. Bianca, her sisters, and niece stayed with the Satsumas in Kamika's room while Kamika slept with Coral at the flower farm. Kenji moved in with David and his roommates temporarily, getting a taste of college life away from home.

Suzy Jenkins, David's mom, stayed up all night with the musicians to help them rehearse for the wedding and reception party. She wasn't familiar with many of the songs they played, but thought they sounded "purty good."

But it was the flower girl, little five-year-old Maria, who charmed the entire group. Her radiant smile, generous hugs, and kisses quickly made her welcome by all. Amos was particularly taken with her, practicing with her as she dropped flower petals carefully along the path for the bride.

Coral, Hiromi, David, and Kamika were at the church shortly after morning services concluded. The decorations seemed to fly out of their hands, down the aisles, onto the doors. Blue, pink, and white flowers bloomed around the altar. Light shining through the stained glass windows seemed to convey blessings from the heavens.

After everyone had completed their labor of love, Kamika drew David aside. "Isn't it beautiful? Everything turned out perfect," she said. Her voice was trembling slightly, and David immediately picked up on her nervousness.

"You know, Kamika, I've never performed in front of people before. I think I'm getting nervous. How do you feel?"

Kamika hesitated to answer him. *Should I be truthful? Or should I show confidence to help him get over his fears and maybe take his mind off them?* "What I admire about you, David, is the way you get lost in the music. I can see it in your face and hands. The music becomes part of you, and when it comes out, you are sharing both the music and yourself with those who listen."

Seeing David's face light up, Kamika continued, "But I'm scared, too. I've been trying to feel the music the way that you do. It's kind of like how I feel when I'm arranging flowers for someone. I see the people in my mind. Then my hands select the flowers and arrange them to produce a smile or a look of comfort on their faces." Kamika blushed slightly, aware that she had been sharing some very personal feelings with him. "I will do my best to follow your lead. I want the music to be special for Benita and Gerardo, but mostly for Coral. She has lost so much, and this day marks the continuation of her family into the future."

David took hold of Kamika's hands and looked deeply into her eyes. "Kamika, you never cease to surprise me. I knew you would rise to this challenge, just as your mother told me you would. Don't you realize how much you have supported everyone around you for so many years? I feel honored to have your friendship and respect."

Kamika's eyes shone with unshed tears. "David, you've given me strength and support when I needed it most. And I know I don't say it often enough: Thank you." She looked around and noticed that the guests were starting to arrive at the church. She pointed to the doors opening near the back of the church.

David said, "I guess we'd better change into our performance gear. Are you ready?"

Kamika nodded. "Let's go."

As Maria walked down the aisle, sprinkling flower petals, David and Kamika started to play and sing.

David: That sunny day we met, I was captured by your eyes.

Kamika: The sunny day we met, you showed me starry skies.

David: And now the flower you planted in my heart has led me to believe that we never will part.

Kamika: Your smile, your laughter, the strength of your hands has led us to share these wedding bands.

Both: Whatever the future holds, come rain or shine, my love is yours, and your love is mine.

Whatever the future holds, come rain or shine, my love is yours, and your love is mine.

Kamika watched tears pour down Coral's face, but she was smiling as Benita stepped to Gerardo's side and faced the minister.

The Family Grows

Two years later, Benita and Gerardo welcomed twin boys into the family, naming them Jesse and Antonio. Kenji was attending UCLA and working with Gerardo on various projects at the Jet Propulsion Laboratory in Pasadena. Benita begged Kenji for help raising their rambunctious sons, asking Kenji to *please* share his training to instill discipline and respect with her and Gerardo.

It seemed to Kenji as though Benita and Gerardo had little influence over the twins' behavior as they grew. Constantly into one thing or another, they reminded Kenji of Kamika when she was a little girl.

Polly somehow found the time to visit from the Oceanographic Institute in San Diego. Even though her visits with Benita, Gerardo, and the twins were not frequent, like Kenji, she was also good at getting Jesse and Antonio to sit still.

The young parents were delighted when licensed preschools became available in the greater Los Angeles area. These preschools often accepted children as young as eighteen months when both parents were employed. The boys were quickly enrolled in one near UCLA, where Kenji could look in on them at least once a week.

Hiromi, Yoshio, and Kamika travelled to California twice a year, usually at the start of summer and then after Thanksgiving, to catch up with Kenji's academic achievements. And through Kenji, the Satsumas were introduced to the twins, becoming part of their extended family.

Coral often went to California when Polly was visiting Benita and her family. They were both there to celebrate at the twins' third birthday party. At the party, Polly announced that the Intergovernmental Oceanographic Commission of UNESCO (IOC) was sending her and her research partner, Dr. Amanda Wright, to South America to study the Amazon River basin and its effect on the currents as it flowed east toward the Atlantic Ocean.

"What an amazing opportunity!" Benita exclaimed. "How long will you be staying in South America?"

"At least two years," Polly said. "We are the first women in oceanographic science to take part in this program. Thank goodness Dr. Wright speaks fluent Portuguese and Spanish. She's been teaching me, but I'd love to practice my Spanish with Gerardo and Bianca."

"I think that can be arranged, *mija*," Gerardo said, grinning from ear to ear. "But you will probably learn better from the boys. They are fluent speakers and love to talk, especially with adults. Don't ask me why…I don't have a clue. Personally, I think it's because of Kenji. When they were very little, Kenji would correct their English, and they would make him talk to them in Spanish."

Coral couldn't help but laugh. "Oh my! The little scamps! That doesn't surprise me. But Polly, that's a long time to be away. And South America is very far from Oregon."

Polly nodded. "I know, Mama. I will call as often as I can, but we'll be travelling a lot. The Amazon River is huge, running from west to east across the northern part of the continent. There is so much to see and learn. I'm very excited to get started."

Benita watched as Coral's face took on an introspective look. She nodded to Gerardo, their secret signal that she needed time away from the twins.

Gerardo grabbed the twins and several balls, dragging them across the street to the park. "Let's go!" he cried. "Polly, could you get the bag with the juice boxes? We will all need them before this game is over."

Coral got up to go with them, but Benita held her back. "We need to talk, Mama. I know that wrinkle between your brows.

You're worried about something. What's bothering you?"

"Well, here it is. Kenji, James, and David are all eligible to be drafted into the war in Vietnam." She shook her head, closing her eyes to hide her distress. "If Gerardo weren't working for the government, he might be drafted, too!"

"Oh, Mama! No wonder you're so worried. Without David and James, how will you run the farm and business? There must be something we can do. Isn't there?" Benita asked.

Coral took a deep breath. "I'm not worried about the farm. I'm worried about the boys. I don't think I could handle it if one of them were killed. It broke my heart when we lost your brothers."

Tears came quickly to Benita's eyes. "This is just awful. What about exemptions?"

Coral took a breath before responding. "There are deferments for full-time students and young men working under contract to the government on war-related production. The definition of full-time, according to the exemption, is six to eight hours per day in classes or activities related to class credits for at least four days out of seven. David, Kenji, and James all have part-time jobs to help pay for part of their college education. They would have to quit their jobs to take additional classes and complete the assignments. The deferment also requires that they perform well in their classes."

"Have you talked to Yoshio and Amos about this?" Benita asked.

"Not yet. I'll need to talk with Suzy Jenkins, too. I don't think she can afford to pay for David to attend college as a full-time student." Coral took a handkerchief out of her sleeve to wipe her eyes and blow her nose. "Thank you. I feel better now. Let's go see what the boys are up to."

"Grammy!" The boys screamed as they saw Coral emerge from the house. They started to run across the street, but Polly caught them before they could cross.

"You know that you must cross the street with an adult," she explained. "Wait for us there, Mama."

Coral sat in the porch swing that had just enough room for a twin on each side of her. Benita brought out a pitcher of lemonade for the crew.

"Read a story for us?" Jesse asked.

"*Por favor*, Grammy?" Antonio echoed.

"Would you like to hear about the time your Mama and Aunt Polly snuck off to go fishing?" Coral tempted the boys.

"Oh, Mama! Not that!" Polly gasped.

"Yes, yes, yes!" said the twins.

"I'd like to hear it, too," said Gerardo with a twinkle in his eye.

"Well, when Polly was seven and your mama was only five, they used to watch their older brothers go fishing. They decided to take the fishing gear from the shed and hike out to the creek one morning, just as the sun was coming up..."

Benita sat down next to Gerardo and rested her head on his shoulder. "We need to take the boys up to Oregon so that they can see what it's like to live on a farm. Then Mama's stories about what happened when we grew up there will stay with them always."

Gerardo kissed Benita's cheek and said, "I couldn't agree more."

Coral returned to Oregon with a heavy heart. During the flight, she had decided that if no other way could be found, Lily Hills would provide the funds for the three young men to become full-time college students.

But when Coral arrived home, Amos was in trouble. She found him in the shed, passed out on the floor. His face was gray. She knelt next to him and put her fingers on his neck to check for a pulse. His heart was beating erratically. She took a deep breath and yelled for David and Kamika. She knew that if someone didn't come in soon, she would have to leave Amos to call for an ambulance. Coral started talking to him.

"Hey there, Amos. It's me, Coral. I'm home, but I see that you're not doing too well. We're gonna take care of you. You hang in there, you old codger!"

Amos opened his eyes. It took a while for him to focus on Coral's face. He smiled a little, tried to say something, but no sounds came out.

"Hush now. You just rest." Coral looked around, but no one had responded to her calls. "I'm gonna call for the doc. You better promise me that you will rest easy till I get back here."

Coral saw Amos nod. She stood up slowly because she got light-headed sometimes when she stood up too fast. As she started toward the house, David drove up in the truck. He waved at Coral, then lurched to a stop after he saw the look on her face. He jumped out and ran over to her.

"What's happening? Are you all right? You look terrible." He grabbed her shoulders to steady her.

"It's not me. It's Amos. He collapsed on the floor of the shed. We need to get him to the hospital. He's still alive, but very weak. He couldn't talk," Coral gasped out.

"I'll go get him. You drive the truck. I'll put Amos in the bed and stay with him in case he needs resuscitation. I took a weekend course in college and learned the steps to take."

"Go...I'll drive."

Coral got her purse and a jacket from the house. She started to pray as she walked. "Lord, I know you've got a lot on your plate. But we surely could use a little help here. Hold Amos in your hand until we can get him to the hospital. He's a crusty, old fussbudget. But he deserves all of our support. He's worked hard his whole life. Shine your grace on Amos and let him live to enjoy the peace of seeing his child and friends grow into the wonderful people you mean them to be. Amen."

Coral drove them to the hospital in record time. David was shocked to see her driving so fast. But he realized that Amos had been part of her life for nearly forty years. She cared for him deeply, the way that she loved all the people she drew into her extended family.

During the drive, David kept Amos warm, wrapping him in a blanket and leaning him against his own body in the bed of the truck. He waited with him until the emergency room staff came out to the truck with a gurney. When David picked Amos up, he was as light as a feather. David gently placed him down on the gurney and followed them into the emergency entrance.

Coral ran into the emergency admission desk to check Amos in. She felt cold; it was much cooler in Oregon than it had been in California. The sky was bright with the setting sun, and stars were beginning to show in the east. She stood in the waiting room, hoping to speak with Doc McGuire.

One of the nurses came toward Coral, saying that Dr. Blakemore was with Amos because Doc McGuire was not on duty that evening. The nurse told Coral that the doctor had put Amos in an oxygen tent to help his breathing, and they gave him a shot of nitroglycerine to help his heart to beat more normally. Amos would likely be in the hospital for several days. David came over to join Coral. She said, "Thank you," as the nurse returned to the emergency room.

David said, "I'll call James. I have the phone numbers for his apartment and work. Is there anyone else you want me to call?"

Coral looked up at him. "No, I'll stay here and wait for Dr. Blakemore. We can contact Kamika and the Satsumas tomorrow when we know more about Amos's condition. It's a good thing you came when you did. I don't know if I could've handled getting him here without you. I was going to call for an ambulance."

"Coral, it seems like you always know what to do in a crisis. I've seen that so many times over the last eight years. It's hard to realize I've been with you for that long! I'll go call now and bring you back some tea." David nodded, then ran down the hall to the phone.

James arrived at the hospital around 10:00 that evening. He went to Coral and pulled her into a big hug. They stood holding onto each other for several minutes. Both wiped their eyes when they broke apart.

"Thank you for taking care of Pa. I got here as soon as I could." He leaned over and smiled at David. "I owe you one," he winked.

Coral pulled James down to sit in the chair between her and David. "Dr. Blakemore says that Amos's heart started to beat too fast and he couldn't breathe, so he passed out. They're going to keep him here for a few days to take more tests and figure out what medicines he needs. How long can you stay?" she asked him.

"I wish I could stay longer, but you know, I need to be taking courses in college, or I'll be eligible for the draft. But I won't leave until he is released to return to the farm." James told her.

"Good," Coral said. "David and I will go back to the farm. We'll check back tomorrow. If anything happens, please call me there right away."

"Coral," James said. "Pa is going to make it. I'm going to talk to the doctor and see if I can go in and sit with him in case he wakes up. I know it's stupid to say this, but try not to worry."

David helped Coral to stand up, and they headed out to the truck. David drove back to Lily Hills, knowing how badly Coral was feeling by the look on her face. It wasn't likely that either of them would sleep.

Although Coral was worried about Amos, she knew the real cause for her concern was the fear of what might happen to her. She was struggling with her responsibilities to the flower business, Polly heading off to South America, Benita and her grandchildren, David, James and Kenji, and now Amos. The stroke she had so many years ago occurred at just such a time as this: There were too many stressors that she could not control. Money was not the problem this time. It was her emotional attachments that kept pulling her in different directions. Why couldn't she just let go, leaving other people to live their lives as they saw fit? She made herself a cup of tea and went to her favorite chair in the living room to try to make her heart listen to her head.

Kamika knew something was wrong as soon as she woke up. It was still dark, but she vividly remembered knowing that Coral was in trouble when she was just a little girl. It was the same feeling, pulsing madly in her head. She went to find her mother, knowing she would be in the kitchen.

"Mama, something is wrong with Coral. Don't ask me how I know. I just need to go over there right now. Can I please use the station wagon?" She pleaded.

Hiromi looked into her daughter's eyes. She, too, remembered Kamika's insistence that something was wrong when Coral had her stroke. "If something is wrong with Coral, we both need to go there to be with her. You might try calling first, just in case she needs a doctor. I will tell your father we are leaving. Go get dressed. I will meet you by the car."

Kamika quickly dialed the number to the farm. *Come on, Coral. Pick up the phone and tell me you are all right.* The phone kept ringing with no answer. *Don't panic. Maybe she is out in the shed. We should install another phone out there! Or maybe she is sleeping soundly after her trip to California.* After the phone rang ten times, she ran to her bedroom to get dressed. Her mother had the car running when Kamika opened the front door.

"Let's go, Mama. There was no answer when I called." Kamika's voice was shaking.

Hiromi drove much faster than she ever had, and they got to the farm just as the sun rose above the trees behind the house. It was too quiet as they got out of the car. They split up, Hiromi knocking on the front door while Kamika went around to the back.

"Coral? Coral? It's Kamika," she cried. "Where are you?"

Coral had finally fallen asleep in the chair. She seemed to hear Kamika calling her from very far away, but she was muddle-headed and groggy. She struggled to open her eyes; they felt like they were glued shut. Then she remembered: Amos was in the hospital. James was there with him. That jolted her awake.

Kamika had opened the back door and was running toward her. "Coral, talk to me. Are you okay? What's happening?" Kamika knelt by Coral's chair and held her hands.

"Kamika, oh child! Amos had a heart attack yesterday. David and I took him to the hospital. We called James, and he came down from Corvallis to be with his dad. I need to call the hospital to see how he is doing," Coral explained.

Kamika shook her head. "No. That's not it. Something is happening to *you*. Don't try to distract me with Amos's condition. If he's in the hospital, he's getting the care he needs. But you are not. You need to talk to me. I'm not going anywhere until you open up."

Meanwhile, Hiromi went around to the back door and walked in through the kitchen. Coral was awake with Kamika by her side. "I think we all need some coffee. Thank goodness you are awake, Coral. We were worried when no one answered the phone. You two stay there. I know that look on my daughter's face. You are in for a long discussion this time!" She returned to the kitchen.

"Let's sit on the couch. I'm not a little girl anymore, and my knees are getting sore from crouching down," Kamika said.

Coral groaned and took Kamika's hand to help her out of the chair. "Kamika, give me a few minutes to gather my thoughts. This is a conversation that I've been putting off. But I really am concerned about Amos. Could you please call the hospital and find out how he is this morning? I'll have some coffee, then we can talk."

Kamika nodded and picked up the phone on the oak side table to call the hospital. The phone started to ring just as she was about to pick up the receiver. "Lily Hills. This is Kamika. Can I help you?"

"Hi, Kamika. It's James. I was calling to talk to Coral about my dad. Is she awake?"

Kamika motioned for Coral to stay put on the couch. "Hello, James. She's awake, but a little groggy this morning. I was just about to call the hospital. How is Amos? We're all worried about him."

"He's been moved to the Intensive Care Unit. He's still in an oxygen tent and receiving medication for his heart. We talked for a little while when he woke up, but the doctor wouldn't let me stay with him for very long. He looks better than he did last night. He has more color in his face. The doctor said he would be there for at least three more days," James told her.

"Thank you for calling to let Coral know what's happening with Amos. I'll tell her about his condition. How are you? You must be knocked out after driving down here and being up all night," Kamika said.

"You're right about that. I'm going to check into the hotel down the street and get some sleep. Then I'll come back to the hospital this afternoon. The doctor said they would call me there if his condition changes. But he seems to be improving. It's hard to realize your father is getting old. But I guess we all have to face it sooner or later." James sighed and hung up the phone.

Kamika went into the kitchen to talk with her mother. "Amos had a heart attack last night. That was James calling to let us know he is doing better. Is the coffee ready?" Coral asked for a cup to help her gather her thoughts.

Hiromi nodded and handed Kamika the serving tray. She had laid out large mugs, sugar, and milk while the coffee was brewing.

"Go ahead. I think I'll go back home and make breakfast for your father. You and Coral need some time alone. I can drive into town later this morning to check on Amos. Take care of Coral. She looks like the ground under her feet has suddenly disappeared," Hiromi said, once again demonstrating her penetrating observation skills.

Kamika kissed her mother on the cheek, lifted the serving tray, and went in to talk with Coral.

Coral quickly poured a mug for herself, taking several gulps while it was still hot. She had gone to the bathroom, washing her hands and face before returning to the living room. "Tell me about Amos first," she ordered.

Kamika quickly gave Coral the details James had told her about Amos's condition, adding, "Mama will go see how he is after she and Papa have breakfast." Kamika felt that should be enough to satisfy Coral for now. The conversation about Coral's current struggles was more important to Kamika.

"Thank you. Your mama is always a great help when things are going south here." Coral said.

"Coral, I am your friend, your partner, and your adopted granddaughter. Speak freely. Why are things going south? I'll try to hold my tongue and listen. Whatever is troubling you, we'll work it out together," Kamika assured her.

"The first problem is that damned Vietnam War. Do you realize that your brother, David, and James could all be drafted and shipped overseas?" Coral asked.

Kamika gasped. Could Kenji be drafted? Her stomach rebelled. It was a good thing it was empty. She clasped her hands together to still their trembling. "I need to pay more attention to what's going on in the world. This is terrible! Is there some way we can help?"

Coral sighed. "Yes, there is. There's a deferment for young men who are full-time college students. I'm gonna ask Suzy Jenkins and your parents to come over here to talk about it. James is already in school full-time, but he will have to let the college know he'll be staying here for a few days while Amos recovers from his heart attack." Coral looked deeply into Kamika's eyes. "I've saved up enough money to keep them all in full-time college programs. There are other deferments, but they are much more involved and require lots of paperwork and time. This is the best option." Coral smiled at Kamika. "Thanks for not overreacting today. I don't think I can take it."

"Mama and Papa won't have any trouble covering Kenji's expenses to go into a full-time college program at UCLA. And I would be happy to help with David and James if more money is needed." Kamika returned Coral's solemn expression. "So, what else is going on with you? You have a solution for the first problem. What are the others about?" Kamika asked.

"Little Flower, this health episode with Amos reminded me of how fragile we are. There is so much happening in my life that I'm finding it hard to keep up. I don't have the energy I had when I found you soaking wet under that tree on my farm. I'm spread too thin. How am I to choose between the farm, our flower business, my children, my grandchildren, you and your family, and Amos and James? It's just too much. Did you know that Polly is going to South America to study the Amazon River? She'll be gone for two years. And Jesse and Antonio just fill my heart with joy! But they're far away, and I miss them so much." A few tears gathered in Coral's eyes. "How am I going to handle all of this? I am getting old, honey. It's time for me to slow down."

"That's what James said about his dad when I talked with him," Kamika whispered to herself. She reached for a tissue to blot Coral's tears. "Grammy Coral, what do you truly want for yourself? You can't be in two or more places at once, even if you want to be. Let's think about this...what will happen if you slow down? Take one thing at a time."

"I'd like to start letting go of the flower business. Maybe we could scale down for a while, especially with Amos being sick and David needing to attend college full-time.

You're already my partner, and this decision will affect you the most. I was wondering if I could sell my portion of the business to someone else. How would you feel about that?" asked Coral.

Kamika was silent for a full minute, trying to understand Coral's feelings. "I think that scaling down now is a great idea. You can slowly teach me more about handling the finances, insurance, and other aspects of the business. Moving some responsibilities to me, at least for a while, will be good for both of us. "

"I don't want all of the stress of running the business to be on your shoulders alone. You could make it work, but it would be better if you had a partner, someone you trusted who would work as hard as you do. I'd like to eventually sell my portion of the flower business to David. I think the two of you would be a great success. David could probably get a loan from the bank to buy me out after he's done with college and the war is over. The two of you work together even better than Amos, Jesse, and I did. You have the creative spark, and David has the practical applications to make those ideas of yours work," Coral explained.

Kamika nodded. "Thank you for telling me how you feel. I guess I should have seen this coming. Right now, there are people in our lives who need our support and care.

Selling flowers should take a back seat to them. And I want you to enjoy this time in your life. Jesse and Antonio love being with you, and you should be with them."

"Kamika, take some time and think about this. We need to ask David how he feels as well. He has been part of the business for eight years, as he reminded me the other day. But he may have other plans for his life. And Amos...that's another puzzle that we will have to figure out. The farm has been his home, but as long as he is here, he will feel compelled to work."

"Well, making sure Kenji, David, and James stay in college is certainly the first priority we should work on together. Then we can think more about how you can let go of Lily Hills."

I wonder what David will say, Kamika asked herself.

Together Sharing Love

The next day, Coral met with James. "I know Amos will be in the hospital for a little while yet. Thanks for coming over to talk with me."

"Pa is looking better, and Doctor Blakemore is putting him on the new medication for his heart. But that's only part of it, isn't it?" James said.

"It's almost time for your college graduation, but if you're not in school, you will likely be drafted into the war in Vietnam." Coral watched James's face as he realized what that meant. "I would like to pay for post-graduate education for you, so that you can remain in the United States. Care for your father is also a priority. I can supplement the cost of care for him at a nursing facility until we can determine a better place for him to be."

James was smiling, though his eyes teared up quickly. "Your generosity is overwhelming. But with both you and Pa to raise me, how could I not be prepared for this moment?" He shook his head and grasped her hands in his. "I've applied for a position with the Oregon Department of Agriculture in Portland. If they hire me, I'll be exempt from the draft. I have great recommendation letters from three of my professors at Oregon State College. But I also plan to take additional classes in land management. Oregon has prioritized protection of farmland from urbanization."

"Listen to you! Talkin' like a big city lawyer! How wonderful that college has given you more opportunities. But what about your father? If he stays here, it's going to be hard to keep him from working on the farm. And that would be very bad for him." Coral would not let this additional worry go without further discussion.

James thought about what would be best for his father. Coral couldn't take care of him, and with his future uncertain, a place with competent medical care would be essential. "I think we may have to take your offer for help with the medical costs for Pa and move him into a senior care or nursing care facility, at least for a while, until he is medically stable and stronger."

"I think that's probably the best place for him. But he's liable to be very ornery about it. Maybe Doc McGuire can recommend a place. If I don't need to pay for your college courses, I can pay for Amos to stay in a good care facility. Will you look into that for us?"

"I surely will," James said as he reached over to hug Coral.

She put her head down on James's strong shoulder. *Another weight lifted off my heart.* "Let me know what you find out. I'll be going to the hospital to see him later today.

A week later, as David worked around the farm, he couldn't shake off the feeling that something big was happening. Coral was not her usual bubbly self. Of course, she was concerned about Amos, but he was recovering well in a skilled nursing facility just north of town. After Coral talked with his mother about the draft for the Vietnam War, she agreed to accept money to pay for more classes. David was taking classes to provide the basics for any career opportunities: science, economics, and psychology. He was so busy that the atmosphere around Lily Hills finally penetrated his overcrowded consciousness.

David had often seen Kamika walking around with a worried wrinkle between her brows. David knew that look. She often got it when things were not going the way she had planned. It meant that she was thinking hard, trying to come up with solutions or a new plan. Why wasn't Kamika talking to him about it? She usually did, and the fact that she hadn't meant either that this problem was very personal or that she no longer trusted him. Again, why? He searched his memory for clues, anything that would point him in the right direction.

When David couldn't figure it out, he decided to confront Kamika until she talked it out with him. He approached her while she was sitting at her desk in the shed. She was turning the pages of their latest flower catalog, but not really looking at them.

"Kamika," David said, pulling up a chair to sit beside her desk. "If I have done something wrong, I really need you to tell me about it. Both you and Coral have been so closed off. What is happening? Just talk to me. I promise to listen without judgment."

Kamika sighed. "I'm sorry, David. I've been so wrapped up in my own thoughts that I wasn't paying attention to how this is affecting you. I should have talked to you earlier, but there didn't seem to be a good time. Coral talked to me after she got back from her latest trip to California. She said there is so much going on in her life that she feels like she is being torn apart. After Amos had his heart attack, and she realized that you, James, and Kenji have to be protected from the draft, she realized that things couldn't stay the way they are. It's hard for Coral—and Amos, too—who have worked hard for a very long time to slow down now. Their health is suffering, but they don't want to let us down, especially Coral. Are you getting the picture?"

David closed his eyes. He could imagine the struggle that Coral was facing. His mother had gone through the same thing three years ago. Luckily, his aunt, uncle, and their two boys wanted to relocate from Minnesota and asked to move in with his family. David moved into an apartment with some of his school friends, so his extended family would have enough room. He didn't know anything about Coral's extended family, but with Benita building a life in California and Polly in South America, he knew that Coral didn't have many choices. When he opened his eyes, Kamika's face was a portrait of solemnity. "Go on," David told her.

"Coral wants to retire from the flower business. She suggested that I could buy her out if I wanted to. She also thought that you might be interested in becoming a partner—" Kamika hesitated before going on. "I thought that my family might be able to help when I presented them with this opportunity. But they said that I was an adult now and needed to make my own decision about the business and my future." Kamika shook her head. "It's hard being a responsible adult. I wanted to beg for their help, but I knew they were right. I love Coral, but I can't make this decision based on what's good for her. She could easily sell the business to someone else. It's very successful. The land is productive. The business is financially sound. She wanted me, and you, to have the first chance at this opportunity. I've been thinking so hard about it, I guess I haven't really been paying attention to anything else."

Kamika paused, trying to feel her way into the next question. "David, how do you feel about the flower business? Do you see yourself as a businessman? Or would you like to pursue a different career? I have been taking your support for granted for too long. I'd like to know what you think and feel."

David said, "No wonder everyone has been so quiet! When things happen around here, they don't hold back, do they?" Kamika shook her head, and David continued, "I understand how you feel. I feel like Coral is the Nana I never had. I remember when you used to call her Grammy Coral. We've grown up with her wisdom, guidance, and love of life. It's hard to think of the future without her constant presence in it." David stopped talking and looked at Kamika.

After a moment, David spoke quietly. "The flower business is special to me, but it's mainly because of you. Doing anything with you makes me feel so alive, so joyful. Whether we are singing, making flowers, cooking, or talking to our customers, it just feels right. I should have told you how I felt about you a couple of years ago, when I realized that I missed you when you went to California with your parents to visit Kenji."

He paused. Kamika was sitting quietly in her chair. Her eyes were sparkling, but David couldn't tell how she felt about what he had said. "And now I have added another layer of complication to your decision-making process."

"Kenji was right when he told me that I cared for you more than I knew," Kamika whispered. She reached forward to hold David's hand. "I can't see a future without you, so I guess we need to make this decision together. What do you want to do now?"

David stood up, pulling her with him. Kamika melted into his strong chest, then tilted her head up for a loving kiss. "That was worth waiting for," David said. "First, I have to stay in college as a full-time student to keep my deferment from the draft." Kamika nodded.

David paused, then his words rushed out. "I can work toward becoming a partner, but I need to know how much that will cost. Recommendation letters will help with a loan application later. Robert Browning could look at it as another investment in the success of the businesses here." He took a breath. "I think we should go talk to Coral."

Kamika nodded. "I think this will make her very happy."

Christmastime snuck up quietly around Coral, her family, the Satsumas, and their friends. James was hired by the Oregon Department of Agriculture, and his deferment was changed to "government support." Kenji took on a full-time course load at UCLA. With Gerardo's support, he would begin an internship in the spring at the Jet Propulsion Laboratory, working on space-based communication systems that supported the military during the war in Vietnam.

Kamika and David quietly planned to have everyone come to the farm, so they could be together to share all the news. Polly was able to get a week's leave from the Amazon project and decided to bring Dr. Amanda Whitmore with her.

When Benita and her family arrived, Gerardo took Kenji, James, and the twins out to play in the snow. It wasn't often that there was a white Christmas in Southern Oregon, so sledding was the first order of business. Polly, Amanda, and Benita closeted themselves in the girls' old bedroom, talking quietly and unpacking. Coral's heart was full, watching them settle into the house routine.

Dinner was a lively meal, with lots of conversation about different dishes, cultural traditions, and demands for recipes. Jesse and Antonio sang "Feliz Navidad" in celebration of the coming holiday. The thunderous applause encouraged them to sing a variety of other songs for their audience, including *"Konnichiwa"* (taught to them by their Uncle Kenji), "Mary Had a Little Lamb," and "Twinkle, Twinkle, Little Star," which brought tears to Kamika's and Coral's eyes.

Two days before Christmas, the twins decided that their family must move to the farm. They jumped into bed with their parents that morning and would not let them up until they promised to ask Coral about it.

Benita reminded Gerardo that they had talked about visiting the farm more often during Coral's last visit. "You know," Gerardo said, "I would have to take a leave of absence from JPL and NASA. My deferment from the Vietnam War might be rejected."

Benita paled. "No, we can't let that happen! There must be something we can do. You're a critical member of several projects, not to mention Kenji's mentor on satellite communications. Come on! Use that engineering brain of yours and figure it out!"

Gerardo started thinking out loud about their options. "We have enough money saved up. We could live on the farm for about a year. I might be able to act as a consultant during that period. I would have to travel to the NASA site in Florida, probably once a month, to maintain my connection to the military projects. Or I could stay in Los Angeles, and you could move up here with the children."

Benita shook her head. "No, that kind of separation wouldn't be good for any of us. Let's investigate the consultant option. Mama would be so happy to have us. How do you think your family would feel about us moving here for a little while?"

"Take their grandchildren away for one year? They'll be furious—for a few days at least. But it's not like they don't have other grandchildren to keep them busy. I think they'll understand. They have a lot of respect for Coral and want her to be happy, just like we do," Gerardo noted.

"Let's talk to Mama about it today." Benita got out of bed to get the children dressed.

The families were all bubbling with excitement when they got to the farm on Christmas Eve. James was in the kitchen, making breakfast for the crowd. He still loved to cook. He picked up Amos from the care facility and brought him to the farm, so that they could celebrate with Coral and all their friends. Amos was stronger now. The senior care facility staff encouraged him to interact with others who were undergoing treatment there. But Amos was slow warming up to new people. The staff challenged him to walking races as he became stronger. Amos walked slowly around Coral's kitchen, getting the silverware, milk, and breakfast foods on the table while James cooked.

Amos had never seen the twins. That morning, the twins ran into the kitchen calling for Grammy Coral. When they saw Amos, they stopped short, stumbled, and fell at his feet, causing him to fall back into a chair at the table.

"Holy cow! Who let a tornado in here?" Amos offered the twins a hand to help them get up.

Benita and Gerardo came in behind them. Benita bent down to give Amos a big hug, then introduced her children to him. "These are my children, Jesse and Antonio. Boys, this is Amos. He worked with Grammy Coral for many years on the farm."

"Hello, Abuelo Amos," Jesse said.

Antonio shook his hand and bowed. "It's an honor to meet you, Mr. Amos."

Amos could not hold back any longer and laughed until tears formed in his eyes. "It sure is nice to have young 'uns around here again. Yer boys are mighty fine. Now we better git some food for 'em." He went over to the stove and prepared plates of pancakes and eggs for the boys. The twins looked up at their mother with questions in their eyes.

"Go on and eat!" she told them. "Your papa and I have business with Grammy Coral right now."

Coral had gone out to the shed for some quiet time before breakfast. She was surprised when Gerardo came in with Benita. "Good morning! Have you had some breakfast yet?" Coral asked.

"No," Benita answered. "We left the twins in the kitchen with Amos and James. Amos made plates for them, and they are wolfing down pancakes as we speak."

Gerardo cleared his throat. "Ahem. We've been thinking and have a proposition for you."

Coral stopped looking at the wreaths on the assembly table and turned to see Gerardo's face.

Gerardo continued. "We know how much the boys love being with you. And we've been thinking it would be a good thing for them to spend some time here on the farm. This morning, they cornered us in the bedroom and demanded that we ask you if all of us could move to the farm."

Coral's mouth dropped open. "How would that affect your government-job deferment?" she asked anxiously.

"Mama, Gerardo thinks we could move to Oregon for a year and he could act as a consultant for his NASA and JPL projects. He would have to travel once or twice a month to attend meetings. But we want to be here. If you don't have room for us on the farm, we'll find another place. The twins want to spend more time with you. They were quite insistent. And we want them to understand what it means to have a farm, a place where people connect with the land and work together to build a future. There's no better place for them to learn that lesson than here. What do you think?" Benita asked.

"Are you kidding? Having you live here would be a dream come true. It will be tight quarters, but I think we can make it work. You and Gerardo can update your old bedroom, Benita. And the twins can have their uncles' old bedroom. As long as you're sure about the deferment, Gerardo. I don't want you to jeopardize your life or career," Coral stated.

"I will make sure of my status before we move to Oregon. We have saved some money, and we can rent our place to one of my cousins. We have lots of options. But we don't want to put any extra stress on you," Gerardo replied.

"Kamika and David have decided to buy me out of the flower business." Coral watched as surprise lit their faces. "Please keep this information quiet. They will be announcing it to the family and friends later. I'm so happy about their decision. I will act as an advisor for a little while as they gain confidence to run the flower business. But now I can spend time with the boys around the farm. They can do some planting, go fishing with Yoshio, learn music from David, and so much more. We'll put them to work, but I think they will love it." Coral sighed and pulled Benita and Gerardo into a big embrace.

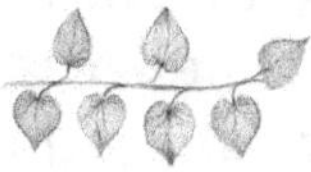

Christmas Day was cold, with scattered clouds and bursts of wind driving everyone indoors. The living room fireplace was lit early with a big stack of wood piled up for the rest of the day. The Christmas tree had been lovingly decorated the day before, with everyone participating in hanging ornaments, popcorn strings, and ribbons. There were so many presents that most of them were moved into the bedrooms. Only Coral's gifts were placed under the tree.

James, Kenji, and Kamika were in charge of preparing Christmas dinner. They made most of the dishes in the Satsuma family kitchen. Then they piled them into the station wagon and drove over to the farm to set up.

Before dinner was served, everyone gathered in the living room. Coral stood next to the fireplace, gently tapping her glass of eggnog to draw the group's attention. "It is so wonderful to have you all here. I want to invite each of you to stand at the fireplace and share what is happening in your life with the rest of us. Benita and Gerardo will start."

Benita winked at Polly. "I do have some news to share with you all. I am three and a half months pregnant with a little girl!"

"Yay!" the twins yelled at the same moment, running over to hug their mother. Gasps spread out around the room.

Hiromi also went to hug Benita. "Congratulations! We are so happy for you. Perhaps you should sit down now, yes?" Hiromi helped her to the rocking chair near the fireplace.

Then Gerardo started to speak. "We have also decided, with Coral's permission, to move to the farm for the next twelve to eighteen months." Jesse and Antonio clapped with delight. Gerardo looked at them sternly. "Living on a farm is not easy. There will be work for both of you every day. You'll be learning from your Grammy, Kamika, and David, who will teach you about growing and selling flowers. But your most important job will be to take care of each other and to help your mama with the new baby. Can you do that?"

Jesse stood up, pulling Antonio with him. "We will, Papa. We will be farmers, helpers, and good brothers—won't we, Grammy?"

Coral nodded to the boys. "We'll see. You're still little. But you must prove to us that you can keep your promises. Now sit down and let your Aunt Polly talk to us."

Polly and Amanda walked to the fireplace. Polly started, *"Feliz Navidad, mi familia!* We've been in South America, travelling on one of the most amazing riverways in the world, the Amazon. There are turtles, giant otters, flowering plants, frogs, and snakes that live in the river itself. We saw so many different kinds of fish! As you can imagine, the river and jungle are home to many people as well as animals and plants. We travelled through Ecuador and Peru. The people there are fighting hard to maintain the river basin that provides food, water, and shelter for them. Amanda and I took pictures and made records of everything we found on our journey. After dinner, you're welcome to look at some of the pictures and drawings we brought to share with you."

Amanda took up the narrative. "Polly has been a wonderful partner to have on this expedition. People everywhere seem to be very comfortable talking to us. They shared their homes, told us stories about their culture, and helped us to be safe on our journey. I'm very proud of the work I accomplished with Polly's help. Our friendship has grown into one of the most important things in my life. Thank you for inviting me here to share Christmas with you." She blushed and took Polly's hand. Polly kissed her on the cheek, and then they walked back to the couch to sit down.

There was no mistaking the love between them. Polly had brought Amanda home to meet her family. Benita knew they had been together even before the Amazon expedition. But she had kept their secret until they were ready to make their relationship known.

Amos looked completely confused. Coral looked over at Benita and raised her eyebrows. Benita only smiled and nodded. Coral was happy for Polly, but wondered if they needed to keep the relationship secret to keep their jobs. *It seems like prejudice is still around. What a shame! Love is love.*

Coral nodded to Kamika and David. It was their turn to talk to the group. Kamika stood nervously in front of the fireplace. "Ever since I blackmailed Coral into accepting me as a partner in her business when I was just six years old, she has been teaching and helping me to fill my world with flowers. When she was short-handed, David was hired to help with the manual labor and soon became an important contributor to the business. He brought new techniques for us to try and was always ready to lend a hand." Kamika paused.

David took up their story. "Now it's Coral's wish to retire from the flower business. Kamika and I have offered to buy Lily Hills, with Coral acting as advisor for six months. Since she'll be busy with her grandchildren, we'll do our best to handle the business without too many intrusions, but I still have a lot to learn, and I'm looking forward to it!"

Kamika winked at Benita. "I expect there will be other willing hands nearby, so we'll handle things together, just like we always do. Now...I don't know about the rest of you, but I am starving! Dinner smells so good. It's a wonder you're all still sitting here! Let's go eat."

After dinner, they all crowded back into the living room, opening presents and sharing stories of the past year with each other. Coral listened to the happy buzz travel around the room. Something was missing, and she finally realized what it was. Once again, she tapped on a glass, this time one filled with a hot toddy, to get everyone's attention. "*Almost* everyone has shared their news. But we haven't heard from two important members of our family: James and Kenji. James, why don't you go first?"

James stood up and went to the front of the fireplace. "Whoa," he jumped forward. "It's too hot to stand there. Think I'll move over to where Pa is sitting." He stood behind Amos, placing his hands on his shoulders. "Mostly, I have been busy in the Cascade mountains for the past six months, working for the Oregon Department of Agriculture. There's a lot to learn about mountain environments, as Polly and Amanda can tell you from their travels. Growing up on a farm, working the hills with gentle streams, is nothing like being in the mountains. Nature is wilder there—the animals, the trees, the way that water collects and moves. It's a different world. But I did have time to do some thinking. I found a wonderful community of people from the Paiute Tribe who are caretakers of the land, just like Coral and my pa. They live in a small town at the base of the Three Sisters Mountains near the larger city of Bend. They would like Pa to visit them to see if he would like to move into their community."

Amos gasped, "What's this? Movin' me around from place to place? Without a 'never you mind!'"

James moved to kneel in front of him. "Pa, I'll be working in Central Oregon for the next couple of years. I have to present information to the government in the capital city of Salem. If you like it there, this community will be close to where I will be working. I want to be able to see you more often than I do now. I think you'll find that you have a lot in common with them. Of course, if you don't like it, you can live wherever you want. But it was very hard for me to be so far away from you. And that hit me like a thunderbolt when you were in the hospital after your heart attack. Please, think about it."

Amos sniffled and rubbed his nose against his sleeve. "Jimmy, I didn't know you felt that way. I thought you was off makin' a life fer yerself. 'Course I'd like to be closer to you. When can you take me up there to visit?"

Benita and Polly started laughing. "Isn't that just like Amos? Ornery one minute, and gentle the next," Polly said.

Coral smiled over at them. "I don't know what we would have done without him here when you were little. Thank you, James. And now, maybe Kenji would like to share what he has been doing with us?"

Hiromi pushed Kenji off the couch. "Go on. Take us on an adventure to the stars. That is where you've been for the last couple of years, is it not?"

Kenji walked over to Coral and kissed her on the cheek. "It was right here in this living room where Coral gave me my first telescope for Christmas more than fifteen years ago. She joined me out in the fields at night to look at the planets. And I'll never forget how excited she was when we saw our first meteor shower. I guess my head's been up in the air ever since then. Now I'm working with engineers to develop rockets that land on the moon. I've used telescopes in California and Hawaii to see galaxies that are millions of light years away from us." Kenji took a breath and squatted down next to Jesse and Antonio.

"My friends at UCLA and I can study the sun using special filters. We can see solar flares. They're massive explosions of electromagnetic forces," he said, spreading his arms wide in front of the twins. "Those solar flares even affect our radio communication. The universe is so big, I could study it for ten lifetimes, and there would still be much more to learn. I couldn't be happier. Thank you, Coral, for helping me to go down this path. And thank you to my parents, my sister, and my friends here, who always encouraged me to keep looking at the stars."

Everyone was quiet, thinking about what Kenji had said and looking out the window at the sky, sprinkled with twinkling lights on that cold winter night. They spoke in whispers and listened to the crackling of the fire.

Then they all heard Antonio begin to snore at Gerardo's feet. "We'd better get these little ones to bed," he said, lifting the child into his arms. "It's very late for them, and it's been busier than usual today." Benita pushed Jesse ahead of her into her brother's old bedroom. As they lay the twins under the covers to sleep, they whispered to each other, "Merry Christmas."

Complications

Two years later, Coral sat on the front porch enjoying the early spring sunshine. Kamika was out in the fields, selectively distributing a new fertilizer that James had developed especially for flowering plants.

Coral explained to Kamika and David, "Because we keep growing the same type of flowers here each year, the nutrients they take from the ground don't have time to be replaced. Our compost pile provides some additional food for them, but we don't have enough compost for the total acreage of flowers. The important thing to remember about using chemical additives is to use the weakest concentration first in a small area to see how the plants respond. If you start now, mix up some different concentrations of the fertilizer, and try them in small areas around the farm. You can check the results and move on from there."

"I remember my first experience with fertilizer was a disaster! It was way too strong and burned the leaves." Kamika replied.

Kamika asked her father to provide a soil analysis for them. Samples from around the farm showed that the slopes nearest to the streams had the lowest amounts of nitrogen and phosphorus. Yoshio explained that those compounds often washed into the streams each year after the winter rain and snow melted. Kamika and David discovered new challenges for the flower business every year. David teamed up with James to engineer a distribution system for fertilizers. Kamika preferred something that could deliver it directly into the ground. She didn't want to spray the chemicals, fearing it could be dangerous for people and animals.

David returned from the city with hoses, clamps, and nozzles that they could use for fertilizer. He entered through the kitchen, leaving the general mail on the table. Then he walked out to the porch, handing a letter from California to Coral. "Looks like it's from Benita. I'm going to check in with Kamika. But we'll be back to hear about Benita, Gerardo, and your three grandchildren."

Benita and Gerardo had named their little girl Cara. She had a heart-shaped face, just like her Aunt Polly, surrounded by wavy red-brown hair. She was cared for almost equally by all of the adults surrounding her. But somehow, she always ended up in Coral's arms at the end of the day. Jesse and Antonio, now Tony, built a

little wagon with wooden planks on the side
so they could pull Cara along with them
as they did their chores at Lily Hills. A pair
of binoculars in the shed allowed Coral to
watch the children. She knew that Gerardo
and Benita had been generous to keep
the family in Oregon for the full eighteen
months. Gerardo's parents in California
missed them, too.

Coral was quite surprised by the
contents of Benita's letter.

*I'm teaching part-time in some of the
inner-city schools in Los Angeles. It's terrible
there. The schools are run down. There are
no supplies or books. The children always
look tired and hungry. If I were teaching full-
time, the first thing I would do is have them
start a garden for vegetables, then show them
how to cook a decent meal for themselves!
I never get to talk with their parents, so I
don't know what's going on at home. I just
can't understand any of it. Some of the other
teachers have told me about the drug and
alcohol problems occurring in these families.
Doesn't anyone care what is happening to
them? It just makes me want to run home to
my children and shower them with love and
FOOD! I know there's no easy answer for this.
The worst part is the politics. The politicians
promise they will work hard to make life better
for the people in their communities. But if you
look hard, they're only making life better for
themselves.*

Enough of that! We got bicycles for the twins for Christmas. They used them to go up and down the hills of Pasadena right away. Going downhill was the real challenge. When Jesse tried to slow down, he flipped over the handlebars and split his chin open—six stitches. Tony sprained his ankle jumping off the bike to avoid hitting a tree. Cara went to the hospital and saw them being treated for their injuries. She asked the doctors questions in Spanish and English, with occasional words of Japanese. The nurses couldn't help laughing. They tried to translate, but it was Tony or Jesse who finally made sense of her questions. She cried when the boys were all patched up. There were bandages in so many places! Maybe she'll become a doctor.

Gerardo's sister, Bianca, got married in January. She and her husband moved to Veracruz in Mexico, along the eastern seacoast. They're both teachers and got good jobs there, teaching English and science (of all things)!

Kenji was offered a job at the Jet Propulsion Laboratory after he graduated. Gerardo is off in Florida, working at the Space Center on the Space Shuttle program. He estimates it will launch in about six years. He calls us every couple of days to talk with the boys about what is happening there. Cara babbles at him in her multi-lingual speech as well; it seems he understands her perfectly.

Please tell me all about what is happening on the farm. How are Kamika and David doing with Lily Hills? Are Hiromi and Yoshio coming to visit Kenji anytime soon? How is Amos adjusting to life with the Indian tribe? And how are you feeling? The boys and Cara ask about you almost every day. I think they miss the farm, too. I know I do. It was so wonderful when we were all together.

I haven't heard from Polly for a while. They were going to the southeastern part of South America next to study the fish populations. She told me that commercial net fishing is killing dolphins, and the pollution from the boats is screwing up the migration patterns of some of the larger animals, like whales. Unexpected side effects from the advancement of technology keep popping up every day. Hopefully, studies from people like Polly and Amanda can help to balance environmental needs with those of growing populations.

We're looking forward to the next time you come down to visit. I'll send some pictures soon. Take care of yourself and give my love to everyone.

Your very grateful daughter,
Benita

Coral shed a few tears, then reached into her sleeve for the handkerchief she frequently kept there. After she blew her nose, she felt a dull pain in her heart, thinking about how hard it was for poor people to get ahead. *Thank goodness Jesse and I moved to Oregon when we did. We had a chance to build a life here where we could prosper.*

After dinner, Kamika, David, Hiromi, and Yoshio gathered in Coral's kitchen to hear the letter from Benita. They were quiet after hearing what Benita observed at her job and what Polly had said about changes in the ocean. They never really thought about those things, isolated as they were in the farming community of Central Oregon.

Hiromi looked at Yoshio. "Maybe you should run for public office in Oregon."

"No amount of money could induce me to look for that kind of job," he said.

Yoshio paused, then looked into Hiromi's eyes. "Remember the McCarthy scare? People can be turned against each other when fear takes over. There is still too much bias between male and female and cultural and ethnic populations to build a political system that can help everyone. America has built the framework for a good government system. But we are a long way from making it a reality."

David nodded. "It's people like Benita and Gerardo who'll start the movement to really implement the principles of our Constitution. They'll do it for their children."

Kamika sighed. "It's interesting that the world of business is less restricted than other areas of our lives. In business, new ideas are encouraged, and methods to do things in better ways flourish. Women can own businesses and control their direction and growth. But public systems seem to be uselessly tied to the past. They don't change fast enough."

Coral looked at them all, sitting around her table as they had so many times. "In business, it becomes obvious very quickly when you are failing. Then you must make changes: Some will work; some won't. So you just try again. In public systems, it's not so obvious when things are failing. People might see that unemployment is very high, but they might not connect it to poor education, lack of nutritious food, or cultural or language differences that create barriers to success."

"Just think how easy it would have been for Lily Hills to fail after my stroke," Coral continued, "If it had not been for a caring Japanese family that lived down the road, where would I be today? When you live in a big city, it's hard to care about everyone around you. There are just too many people. How do you choose where to direct your efforts? Sometimes there is barely enough to provide for a roof over your head, food on the table for the family, and clothing and shoes for everyone to wear," Coral told them.

"How clearly you see everything, Grammy Coral," Kamika said.

"Well, when you're as old as I am, you'll see things clearly, too," she teased Kamika.

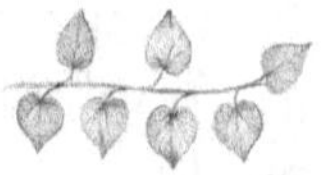

A year later, the Vietnam War ended. The soldiers who returned were barely able to find their way back to live in a greatly changed America. Coral felt a huge weight lifted from her shoulders because she knew that Kenji, David, James, and Gerardo were safe. The young men could now step into their lives with additional knowledge that would serve them well against future challenges. She made herself some tea in the kitchen, remembering the discussion that had taken place the evening after she received the long letter from Benita. She realized that she needed to set up plans so the things she wanted to happen for her family would come to pass. She decided to call Robert Browning at the bank in the morning.

Robert Browning's secretary set up an appointment for Coral to see him that afternoon. He hadn't heard from her for at least six years. He was invited to her daughter Benita's wedding but couldn't attend because he had the flu. He sent his regrets and a gift. He was curious about why Coral wanted to see him now. She arrived promptly at 2:00, greeting him with a warm smile.

"Mr. Browning! You're looking like a young buck. How is your family?" asked Coral.

"A young buck? Would you like to borrow my glasses?" he laughed with her. "The family is doing well. Thank you for asking. You have a few more gray hairs since I saw you last. I hear that grandchildren can do that to you," he chided her.

"As if you don't know! I hear you have a grandchild or two of your own," she replied.

Robert laughed. "There is no trying to fool you, is there? Well, what brings you in to see me today?"

"There are three things, really. First, I want to update the information about the money in my accounts. Second, I want to set up my will and a trust for my grandchildren. I'm hoping that I can do it through the bank, or that you can recommend a lawyer that you trust to help me. And third, I want to get a safe deposit box here for some of my special things."

"I would be delighted to help you with all of those requests. Let's check your accounts first." There was a brief pause as Robert checked the bank records. Computers had been installed in banks during the late 1950s. Now that it was 1975, information was kept up-to-date and available to all bank employees and accessible to their customers.

"You have $526,849 in your personal account. The Lily Hills account has $2,445,198 in it. The funds there were substantially increased when Kamika

Satsuma and David Jenkins purchased your share of the business. You know, they set up their own account here for Lily Hills operating expenses, opened a line of credit, and set up a savings account as well. They haven't used their credit line, which is a tribute to their business acumen. I can print out the balances for you now if you wish," he explained.

Almost three million dollars! Coral nodded her head, glad that her estimates corresponded with the bank's records. But she had plans for how to use it now. "Please print out the balances for me. I'll need that information for the lawyer. Do you have a recommendation for one?"

"Actually, I have several that I refer to our bank customers. Here are cards for the two that I think are the best. You can call them and choose for yourself. I think you might like working with Bernard Kielan. He hired Mercedes Dorrel, the first Black woman to be admitted to the Oregon State Bar, and they have built an incredible practice together. She specializes in contracts, wills, and trusts. Mr. Kielan travelled to the Southern states in 1970 to provide legal services to people that have been denied their civil rights under the new laws."

"Really? That's amazing. What a journey that woman must have had. I would enjoy hearing her story. Let's move on to the safe deposit box," Coral said.

Robert took her into the room where the safe deposit boxes were stored. He explained that she would have access to her box during normal bank business hours. The boxes were not meant to store large items, so she would need to make other arrangements if she wanted to do that. She would be issued two keys. One could be kept at the bank, in case she lost the key issued to her. Or she could give the second key to someone else. That person would not have access to the safe deposit box unless Coral was with him or her. She could also provide instructions for disposition of the safe deposit box contents in her will.

"Do you have any questions about what I have said?" Robert asked her.

"I think I understand everything, but it would help to have the information in writing," she told him.

"Of course. Here is a pamphlet explaining how to use the safe deposit boxes at our bank. And you're welcome to call me with any other questions that come up. You need to fill out this card, and we will assign a box number for you. Then I'll make a copy for you to keep at home. Anything else?" he asked.

"Whatever happened to Don Jackson? I haven't seen him around town for a long time," Coral said.

Robert wondered whether there were still hard feelings between them. "After Don was fired, he and his wife moved up to Portland. Turns out that Don's girls are amazing athletes. They received athletic scholarships to Portland State University. I think one scholarship is for volleyball, and the other is for tennis. He found a job at an accounting firm and is doing well there."

"That's good. Isn't it amazing how women can succeed no matter the hardships they encounter from men? I believe that equality through education, as it's now enforced by the federal government, will create a real perceptual shift in the future. Please excuse me, but, I need to be on my way."

As Coral drove home, she was pleased with the way things were falling into place for her. Driving was becoming more difficult because her eyesight was getting worse. She was overdue for a checkup with Doc McGuire. Time was no longer on her side. She vowed to call Mercedes Dorrel first thing in the morning.

"Good morning, Little Flower. What is happening with you today?" Hiromi asked as Kamika entered the kitchen. Kamika often stopped by her house on her way to Lily Hills to catch up on her parents' activities.

"Hi, Mama," she said, reaching for the teapot. "Coral has been very busy the past week. She hasn't said anything to me about why, and I hope that nothing is wrong. David told me that she went to the bank one day and to the hospital later in the week. Do you know what's going on with her?"

Hiromi sat down at the table and motioned for Kamika to join her. "How old do you think Coral is now?"

"Hmmm...she is probably about seventy, but I can't be sure. Why do you ask? If you really want to know, I can call Benita," Kamika told her.

"No, Kamika. I don't want you to call Benita. Coral is over eighty years old now. What kinds of things do you think you will be doing when you reach that age? And please take some time to think about it seriously. I want you to think about Coral's life," Hiromi said sternly.

Instead of thinking about Coral, Kamika thought about Amos. Amos was *old*. After moving in with the Indian tribes, his health and strength were visibly improved. James moved him to Central Oregon, where he worked so that they could be together more often. Amos needed other people around who would care for him until...She gasped.

"But Coral's not old like Amos, Mama. She isn't dying, is she? Please tell me she isn't dying!" Kamika begged Hiromi.

"Kamika, it does not matter whether you think she is old or not. What matters is how she feels. If you think your end will be coming, you start to prepare so that the people you love will be cared for after you are gone. Your father and I made wills several years ago. As you and Kenji grow and our family changes, your father and I will change our wills to include the others."

Kamika was quiet. *No one I've known has died, but no one lives forever. I remember when Kenji told me about James's mother and sister dying in the fire. Thoughts of death have been far away. The closest we came was during the Vietnam War, when James, David, and Kenji were eligible for the draft. That was a scary time. It's worse when young people have to face death. But now, thinking about Amos and Coral, it's just as bad. I don't want them to pass away...but they will.*

"I think I understand now, Mama. Is there something David and I should be doing to help Coral?"

"If I know Coral, she will ask if she needs your help with anything. Just check in with her every couple of days to ask what is going on. Stay involved with her life. Talk to her about how you and David are doing and what is happening with the business. She just needs to know that she is not alone."

"We will, Mama. She got new glasses so she can continue to drive. But she doesn't really leave the house and farm much now," Kamika said. "I think I'll bring her some ice cream as a special treat. See you later."

Tying Up Loose Ends

I wonder how Amos is doing, Coral thought. *It's been six months since I talked with James about him. I'd better give him a call. I'd really like to visit him out at Rimrock Ranch.*

James answered the telephone on the third ring. "Hello, this is James Matthews. How can I help you today?" he replied cheerfully.

"Well, hello there, young man. Got time to speak with your old Grammy Coral?"

"Coral! It's so good to hear your voice! How are you feeling? I understand that you're looking chic in your new glasses," James teased her.

"Who told you? Never mind. I've got more important things to discuss with you." Coral said.

"No problems at the farm, I hope."

"Naw. I was just thinking about your father. I...miss him. He's my oldest friend, and I still look around for him after I make coffee in the morning. Do you think we can visit him if we get permission from those Native tribes he's living with?" she asked.

"He's staying with the Paiutes right now. They're a branch of the Cherokee tribe. There are actually three native tribes living there. And Pa has spent time learning from all of them. I'll call in and ask about arrangements for a visit. Can you spend a couple of days there? Pa would love to show you around his new home and introduce you to his friends there."

"Does that mean I'll be sleeping in a teepee? I don't think my old bones could handle that," Coral teased James.

James laughed. "No, you won't be sleeping in a teepee. We'll drive a camper in to visit the site, and you can stay overnight in it while I bunk with Pa. How does that sound to you?"

"Sounds like a camping vacation. Call me back with the details, so I can pack the right clothes and my hiking boots. When do you think we can go?" asked Coral.

"I'll need to see when I can take some time off. Pa says they celebrate the Treaty of 1855 in June. That established the tribal lands and charged them with caring for the animals, plants, and each other in peace. The tribes invite the community to take part in the festivities with them, and there's a rodeo, pow-wow, singing, and dancing. When is a good time for you?"

"Oh, James! The sooner, the better. We're not getting any younger. See what your boss says and let's go!"

"Yes, ma'am! You just start packing. It should be pretty warm, but Pa will want to go to the Deschutes River to fish, so bring your waders. I'll call back when everything is ready to go."

"Thank you, James. I'll be waiting for your call." Coral sniffed as she hung up.

True to his word, James arrived on Wednesday in a 1975 Winnebago Minnie Winnie motor home that he rented for their trip. It took five hours to drive from Cottage Grove to the Warm Springs Reservation. Coral sat in the copilot seat as James drove, whistling a happy tune. She loved to see the changing scenery. The reservation was north and east of Lily Hills. Coral could smell the juniper forest when they got closer. The wind also carried the smells of the grassland at the bottom of the valley. When they pulled up to the check-in area and stopped, Amos walked out of the building with two of the tribal elders.

Coral was surprised to see him standing so straight and tall. Kamika had told her that Amos was getting stronger by following the tribe's wellness traditions and diet. *He looks ten years younger! I'm so happy this place is good for him,* Coral thought.

Amos walked over to Coral first and wrapped his arms around her. "Coral...I'm so glad to see y'all. Look at this place. It's jest amazin'," he spread his arms wide to encompass the land.

"Hey, Pa. You're looking spry. Been out walking the trails?" James asked.

"You bet, son. Chief Wallulatum and Chief Heath go walkin' with me every day. Then we go into the steam tent fer a bit and then get a good wash down. Doc McGuire told me it's good fer my circleation."

"Amos, why don't you show me around a little, then take me to a quiet, shady place where we can talk and remember," Coral sighed and clasped his hand.

"Pa, you and Grammy Coral go along. I need to talk with the elders about where to park the camper," James told them.

Amos pointed to the Three Sisters volcanic peaks in the nearby Cascade Mountain range. He told her the three Native tribes that lived there called them Faith, Hope, and Charity. As they walked along the edge of the forest, Amos said there were salmon and steelhead in the rushing water of the creek. The sun was just starting to paint the sky the deep golden color that signaled an end to the summer day.

Coral was very quiet as they walked along. When Amos turned toward her, he saw a few tears shining on her cheeks.

"Let's sit over here on this fallen tree, and you can tell me what those tears is all about," Amos said, gently settling Coral where he could watch the area around them.

Coral brushed the tears from her face. "I'm glad that this place is responding to the care of these people. It's beautiful here. And now you can take in the energy that Lily Hills drained from you for so many years."

"That's not so, Coral," Amos cried. "It was my home. You and your kin was my family. We took care of each other. I jest got so knocked down by that newmonia, I couldn't keep up anymore."

"I know, Amos. I just miss having you with us. But are you happy here?"

"You know, at first, I stayed with the Wasco tribe. Their ways was so strange to me. But they took me fishin' every time I was ornery, and so we became friends. The elders listened to my heart and chest. Then they talked with Doc McGuire about changin' the things I 'et. So many herbs and grasses! Good thing they were perty tasty. They walked with me a little each day, showin' me the mule deer, the elk, and the golden eagles. The Warm Springs tribe is the animal caretakers. They know about everythin' that lives here. I started to see the little critters. I feel the cool wind comin' down the pass. The land here is special." Amos stopped and put his finger to his lips.

He pointed to a deer and her fawn coming out of the forest to the creek for a drink.

When the deer turned back into the forest, Coral stood up. "I think we should start going back. I know James wants to spend time with you, too." As they walked back along the ridge, the cry of a hawk echoed through the trees. The hawk broke cover and sped across the valley, a blur of brown with white tips on its feathers.

"You were right. This is an amazing place," Coral told Amos. "We're planning to stay for another couple of days. And I want you to show me everything."

They went fishing the next day through the afternoon. When they returned, the men and women of the tribes were lighting bonfires as night fell. They recited the terms of the Treaty of 1855 in solemn voices. The drums and flutes somehow harmonized with the crackling fire. The small children danced until the sky grew dark and filled with bright stars. As the fire burned down, they said their goodnights and drifted away to their homes. Coral listened to the sounds of the night and fell into the deep, restful sleep of a child after a long, happy day.

Coral carried memories of the visit in her heart on the drive back to Lily Hills.

She felt lighter knowing that Amos was well. That was another concern checked off her list, but there was still so much to do. Mercedes Dorrel was coming to visit and review the paperwork for her estate. Robert Browning had told Mercedes that Coral was an amazing woman, a business owner for many years, running the farm, raising four children, and now with three grandchildren.

Coral didn't know what to expect but wanted Mercedes to see the farm and flowers that were so much a part of her life. Mercedes arrived on a bright summer day in July. The skies were crystal clear and so blue that Coral felt they could reach infinity. The air was scented with the many varieties of flowers that grew on the farm now. Growing up and down the hills in bright colors of pink, white, blue, and red, they were especially breathtaking in the sunshine.

Mercedes stepped out of her car and onto the path, taking in the scope of the business the farm represented, then walked up between the row of stones to the front door.

The door opened before she could knock. Coral had been watching as she drove up the road. "Come on in! I baked some muffins for us to have with our coffee. Would you like to talk in the living room or at the kitchen table?" asked Coral.

"Hello, Mrs. Russell. It's a pleasure to meet you. The kitchen table would probably be better so that we can review documents. Does that suit you?"

"Please call me Coral. The kitchen is a good place to chat and get work done. What should I call you?"

"I prefer Mercedes. As a lawyer, I want to understand the people I work with. Every client is important, and I want our relationship to be friendly as well as professional. Those muffins smell wonderful!" Mercedes exclaimed.

Mercedes spent most of the visit listening to Coral talk about her extended family. She was surprised to hear about the Satsumas, the Japanese family who had entered her life thirty years ago. They were as important to Coral as her biological children. She felt the same way about Amos and James Matthews.

It took two full days for them to hammer out the details of Coral's endowments, the trusts for her grandchildren, and the disposition of her personal property and land. Coral had very specific instructions for Mercedes regarding when her children would receive copies of the will and trust documents. She also had instructions regarding her safe deposit box at the bank.

Mercedes told Coral she would be back in about a week with the final documents for her to sign. She suggested that they meet at the bank, where there would be a notary, and Robert Browning could act as a witness. When all of the paperwork was completed, Mercedes would keep the original documents at her office in Salem.

Coral searched through her keepsakes from a life filled with adventure, love, loss, and surprises. She wanted to find meaningful gifts for the people who had brought so much joy into her life. She went to the bank several times to put those gifts into her safe deposit box.

Finally, the day came when Mercedes called to tell Coral that all the documents were ready to sign. *This is it. Lord, I want to thank you for the wonderful family you have given me and for taking care of us through all the hard times. Thank you for giving me the strength to be there when they needed me. I'm looking forward to seeing Jesse and the boys when you bring me home.*

Coral met Mercedes at the bank the next morning. It only took about an hour to get all the documents signed and notarized. She thanked Mercedes and Robert for their help, handing each of them a handkerchief with their initials embroidered in the corner. Coral was tired but happy that she had accomplished what she set out to do. As Robert escorted her out to her truck in the parking lot, Coral finally broke down. She turned to thank him but started to cry. He pulled her into an embrace and slowly rocked her back and forth.

"Mrs. Russell, Coral. Let's sit down on the bench over here." Robert supported her as they walked to a high-backed bench under a shady elm tree. "You never cease to amaze me. It must have been hard for you to go through all of this by yourself. Please let me help you now if I can."

Coral looked into Robert's concerned face. He was such a good man. He really understood how she felt. But she was so tired that she wasn't sure if she could drive back to the farm.

"Do you think I could use your phone to call the farm? I need someone to drive me home," asked Coral.

"Nonsense! It would be my honor to drive you back myself. My secretary will follow us and bring me back here. Besides, I want to make sure you're resting comfortably when you get home," Robert told her.

After Coral returned to the farm, she asked Robert to leave her on the porch in her rocking chair, where she could watch the sun setting over the flowering hills she loved so much.

The Past, the Present,
and the Future

Coral passed away, gracefully in her sleep, three weeks later.

Per instructions given to Mercedes Dorrel, her will and trust documents were mailed to Benita and Gerardo in California. Polly's copy of her will was also mailed to Benita for safekeeping because she had no permanent address while in South America. James received a copy of her will with a letter telling him to kiss Amos for her. Kamika received a letter a week after Coral's death, with a key and instructions for the safe deposit box at the Farmers and Merchants Bank in town.

News of Coral's death spread quickly through the area. Condolence letters and cards poured into Lily Hills every day.

Doc McGuire had examined Coral and signed the death certificate. He, Kamika and David wept silently at her bedside that morning. Doc recovered first and called Benita in California to tell her the news.

Benita thanked him and then asked for Kamika.

Kamika dried her eyes, reaching for the phone receiver. "Oh Benita! I am so sorry. I just..."

"I know, Little Flower. The world seems a little grayer without her already. But she sent me specific instructions regarding the funeral arrangements, and it seems that you and David play an important role in them."

"Of course, Benita. Anything you need," Kamika replied.

"I'll call the mortuary to pick up her body. It seems that Mama already made the arrangements with them and picked out a simple casket. We'll fly into Eugene either Thursday night or Friday morning."

"How many of you will be coming? I'll try to arrange transportation for everyone." Kamika said.

"It will just be our immediate family— Gerardo, me, and the kids. But if Kenji wants to fly up with us, we'll book an extra seat for him. Will you call him for me?" Benita requested.

"I'll call Mama and Papa first. I think Mama will want to talk to him. Call me again when your travel plans are set. My heart is aching, but I'll try to do my best for you...and for Coral."

Gerardo spent the entire day on Monday calling UNESCO to track down

Polly. He located her in the port town of Bahia Bianca in Argentina. She said she could book a flight from Buenos Aires the next day. She would land in Miami, then take another flight to California. She told Gerardo she would be in Eugene by the end of the week.

"Give Benita and the children a big hug and kiss for me," Polly told him while crying and blowing her nose. "I'll be there as quickly as I can."

Mercedes travelled down to Lily Hills to talk with David and Kamika about Coral's will and trust. Kamika wondered what Mercedes would say to them, offering her a seat on the couch.

David brought in some coffee and placed it on the table in front of the sofa. He was the first to speak. "Coral told us how much she admired you. You had a lot in common, achieving success against great odds," David said.

"And I admired her. But I am envious of those of you who worked with her, lived with her, and grew with her. It's you she loved, during her life and beyond." Mercedes took a breath and drank some coffee. "Now, I must tell you both about a provision in her will. Coral wanted me to talk to you about it, rather than send you a copy of her will."

Kamika couldn't imagine what Mercedes was going to say. "I did receive a letter telling me about the safe deposit box. I know that I need to retrieve it and distribute the contents during her funeral."

"That's right," Mercedes told her. "But this is about the farm and the business. Of course, the flower business now belongs to you and David. In her will, Coral left the farm to both of you on the condition that you marry and start your life together here. I know that this decision is really yours to make. And there's no time condition in the will. If you decide not to marry, but continue as business partners, the farm will be offered to her daughters first. If they decide not to take ownership, the farm will be sold, and you will need to contract with the new owner to use the farmland to continue your business."

David and Kamika were both silent on hearing this news. Mercedes sat quietly drinking her coffee, waiting for them to come to grips with Coral's wishes. David took Kamika's hands in his.

"What do you think we should do about this?" he whispered.

"David, I love you. You know that. I don't want you to feel like we must get married now. We should decide on our future when we are ready," Kamika said.

"Well," he responded, "I've had this engagement ring burning a hole in my pocket for about six months. Maybe it's time to take it out and see if it will fit you?"

Kamika's mouth dropped open. David gently lifted her lower jaw, taking her left hand in his. He took the ring and placed it on her finger. "Look at that. It's a perfect fit."

Kamika looked into David's eyes, then at the beautiful ring. "Oh David. I'm so stupid sometimes!"

David laughed and wrapped her in his arms.

Mercedes was smiling broadly. "Coral seems to have known your hearts better than you two. Congratulations!"

David and Kamika invited Mercedes to attend the funeral on Saturday. Mercedes promised she would be there.

The day of Coral's funeral dawned bright and clear, with a rose-colored sky climbing up the hills on the east side of the farm. Amos and James walked in through the back door to the kitchen at 5:00 a.m., trying not to wake the rest of the family. But Benita was awake, with two-and-a-half-year-old Cara in her lap.

"Hello there. I don't think you know this little girl. Cara, this is James and his father, Amos." Cara smiled at them, waving hello. Then she offered Amos her stuffed rabbit to play with.

"Well, I'll be darned. Thank you, little lady. I don't think I ever seen a finer bunny rabbit." Amos looked at Benita with tears in his eyes. "Yer beginnin' to look like her, ya know. Yer mama was a beautiful woman. It was my privlege to know her."

James reached over to hug Benita. After a few moments, Cara started to giggle as Amos made the stuffed rabbit dance on his lap.

"I'm going to take over chef duties today," James insisted. "What shall we have in honor of your mama?"

Polly walked in and answered for Benita. "Eggs, bacon, and biscuits with gravy. Right, Amos?" Amos nodded. "I'll work on the bacon, James, while you get the biscuits started."

The kitchen became chaotic when the twins, Gerardo and Kenji, came in. Gerardo kissed Benita and Cara, then quickly took charge. "Come on, boys, we've got work to do this morning. You go out to the shed and help Kamika prepare the flowers. Kenji and I have to set up the chairs and the arch. Benita will call us when it's time for breakfast. Now, *vamonos, mi ninos.*"

Hiromi wore her white kimono, and Kamika had prepared a flower headband for her hair. Yoshio set up a table with picture albums from their time with Coral. He sighed when he realized that the pictures covered more than twenty years spent with her in their lives. Hiromi acted as the hostess for the funeral; it was really more of a memorial with a burial included.

Guests began to arrive shortly after lunch. It seemed like half the town was arriving. David directed guests to areas where they could park their cars. Suzy Jenkins walked around to the back of the farm and corralled Amos and James to come sit with her. Robert Browning and his wife walked up the road to the house. Benita greeted them, showing them to the table where Yoshio had left the photographs. Robert teared up when he saw the birthday picture taken at the Satsuma household when Kamika was only five.

"Seeing this picture brings back so many memories," Robert said to Yoshio. "What a difference Coral made in my life. In just a few short months, she taught me how to be part of a family."

"I know what you mean, Robert. She had a special way of working with people that brought out the good in them," Yoshio agreed.

After all of the guests, family, and friends had been seated, Kamika took her place under the arch, which had been decorated with beautiful flowers from the farm.

"We are here today to honor a uniquely wonderful woman, Coral Russell," said Kamika. "She meant different things to each of us. To me, she was a substitute grandmother and my business partner. Coral charged me with distributing the contents of her safe deposit box before we bury her. She asked to be buried on the highest hill on the farm, next to her husband, Jesse. There they can watch the sunrises and sunsets together, as they did when they lived on the farm."

Everyone looked toward the casket, sitting atop the picnic table used so often for informal gatherings.

Kamika used her key to open the safe deposit box. Attached to each item was a note, written by Coral to the recipient.

The first gift was for Kenji. Kamika read, "Kenji Satsuma opened my eyes to the heavens. I didn't realize how much I was looking down to tend my flowers. This bronze star was given to me after my oldest son was killed in World War II. I want Kenji to have it. He had the courage to do something new. He worked hard to learn, and yet there was always more. And he was like me, always wanting to share what he knew with others. And so, here's a shining star for a shining star."

Kenji came forward and whispered to Kamika, "Should I really accept this? Don't you think Polly or Benita would want it?"

Kamika shook her head. "Coral put a lot of thought into this day. This is what she wanted you to have. Other gifts have been given to her daughters. Be gracious and say something about what she meant to you." She dabbed her handkerchief at the tears forming in her eyes.

Kenji straightened his shoulders and looked at the people seated before him. "Coral was like a second mother to me. She worked with joy and love in everything she did. She encouraged everyone around her to explore options for making their lives the best they could be. I'm glad she knew how much I loved and respected her." He sat down next to his father, burying his face against Yoshio's shoulder.

Next, Kamika lifted a heart-shaped locket from the box, bending down to read the note. "This locket contains a picture of me and Jesse when we were married. I leave it for you, little Cara, so that you will remember your grandparents and the farm they had in Oregon." Benita stood up with Cara and came to Kamika to get the locket.

"I remember this picture and the locket. Mama wore it when we were little. It's perfect for Cara." Benita opened it for Cara to see. Cara took it in her little hand and said, "Gammy."

"Mama also left trust funds for her twin grandsons, Jesse and Antonio, and for Cara that will be used for higher education or to develop the business of their dreams as they become young adults. They will always remember the time they spent here,

learning to love the land from Mama."
Benita said.

She continued, "Gerardo's job takes him to Florida and Cape Canaveral, so many different places. The farm property, as well as the flower business, are being left to Kamika and David. And I know that they will welcome us here whenever we can come to visit."

The people attending the funeral smiled at the newly engaged couple, and there was a round of applause for them. Benita kissed Cara on her forehead and returned to sit with her family.

Next, Kamika held up a crystal butterfly. The sun lit the crystal with shades of green, blue, and gold. "This butterfly is for Hiromi and Yoshio, my Japanese neighbors who became my lifelong friends. Thank you for teaching me about your culture. In Japan, the butterfly represents the soul of both the living and the dead. It symbolizes joy and longevity. That is my wish for you. May this butterfly remind you of the flower farm, and when the sun hits it, may it fill your home with color and joy."

Hiromi walked to her daughter, gently taking the crystal butterfly in her hands. A few tears leaked from the corners of her eyes. "She was a great woman. Coral inspired us to reach out and to share both hardship and times of wonder. We will miss her."

The next item was for Polly. Kamika lifted out a white lace bridal veil. "My dearest Polly, I wish you and Amanda a lifetime of happiness together. Perhaps there will be a day when you can wear my bridal veil to marry her. Please tell her, 'Welcome to the family' for me." Along with the veil was an envelope. Polly opened it and stared at a check for $250,000.

The last item was a small box tied with a red ribbon. Kamika said, "This last gift is for James and Amos. When Amos's wife, Rochelle, brought her little daughter to me for her first haircut, I asked her if she knew about an old custom from the South where I grew up. I told her that when a daughter has her first haircut, a lock of it is woven into a braid with a lock of her mother's hair. This box contains that braid. I should have given it to you long ago. May you remember the loving wife and daughter, mother and sister you shared when you touch this braid." James walked slowly to Kamika and held his hand out for the box. He undid the red ribbon and lifted out a braid of shining gold-and-brown hair.

James held the braid to his cheek and sighed. "Coral became the rock for me and Pa after we lost Ma and little Bonnie. Her gift of $150,000 for Pa will help him through the rest of his life with the Confederated Tribes of Warm Springs. She left the same amount for me so that I could buy my first house. Coral taught me what love is, and I am forever blessed because of it."

James wiped the tears from his eyes, then brought the braid over to where Amos was sitting next to Suzy Jenkins. Amos cried a few tears, held the braid in his hands, and said, "God bless you, Coral, for saving this for us."

The last item of the day was presided over by David. All of the guests, family, and friends gathered together on the road to the farm between the two hills with shining white stones. The hill on the left had a large "L" on it. The hill on the right had a large "H." David looked at the crowd while Kenji handed more shiny white stones to the family. "The L and the H stand for Lily Hills. Today, we add an upper row of stones to the capital L that will turn it into a C. Would the family please place the stones on the hillside?" Everyone scrambled up to put the white stones in. When they returned to the bottom of the hill, David explained.

"We now change the name of our farm to 'Coral's Heart,' in remembrance of the woman who brought us together today. If you would honor her, we ask you to pay forward the love, the wisdom, the laughter, and the never-ending joy in learning new things that Coral gave to us."

Kamika stood at David's side as they watched the sun set. It had been a long day. They had carried out their tasks as Coral would have wished. The twins ran over to them, grabbing their hands and dragging them to the house. It was time for dinner. The family and their friends were spread out around the living room, kitchen and front porch, talking, telling stories, and laughing as the loving spirit of Coral watched over them.

Acknowledgments

We live in a world of other writers, readers, editors, designers, and publishers who help us hone our craft to produce works of wonder. My special thanks to the Long Beach (California) Coffee Club Writers Group, who listened and laughed and corrected my mistakes with me until Lily Hills was born. Not to mention my publisher, Bright Communications, who gave me much more than I expected. Jennifer Bright is now a trusted friend, supporting me and other writers, linking us to each other and experts who can introduce our writing to the world. They say, "It takes a village." I believe it.

About the Author

Patti Mobile grew up with many generations of family around her—cousins, parents, aunts, uncles, siblings, grandparents, great grandparents. These people surround all of us, and as we grow up, we become intertwined with the generations of family of our friends, our teachers and mentors, our neighbors...well, you get the picture.

Patti's undergraduate education focused on Developmental Psychology, starting with children. As much as she learned from books, tests, research papers, and teach-ers, she learned more from talking to chil-dren. She heard from them the influences of family members, good and bad. She experienced the pain and joy of every day with them and their families. They shared success and failure, they tried new things, and most of all, they inspired hope.

So Patti offers you *Lily Hills* and the question: What is a family? You can define it any way that feels right to you. Notice how your family changes as you grow and how new people come into your life and become family.

For her debut novel, *XL-ENCE: The Human Development Project,* Patti received the Global Book Awards Bronze medal in the Science Fiction/Genetic Engineering category.